THE DARENTI PARADOX
COLONIAL EXPLORER CORPS BOOK 4

JULIA HUNI

IPH MEDIA

The Darenti Paradox Copyright © 2022
by Julia Huni. All Rights Reserved.

All rights reserved. No part of this book may be reproduced in any form or by any electronic or mechanical means including information storage and retrieval systems, without permission in writing from the author. The only exception is by a reviewer, who may quote short excerpts in a review.

Editing by Paula Lester of
Polaris Writing and Editing

Cover Design © J. L. Wilson Designs
https://jlwilsondesigns.com

This book is a work of fiction. Names, characters, places, and incidents either are products of the author's imagination or are used fictitiously. Any resemblance to actual persons, living or dead, events, or locales is entirely coincidental.

Julia Huni
Visit my website at http://www.juliahuni.com

IPH Media

*For my friend
Myrna
who is always seeking
new adventures*

CHAPTER ONE

THE CLOUD-COVERED planet rotated beneath us, its thick atmosphere blocking all visual inspection. From the science station, I flicked through my screens, reading off my results for the bridge crew. I sucked in a deep breath, hoping to hide the excited tremor in my voice. This data was being dissected by the planetary science crew housed deep within the ship—my job was to give the captain the highlights.

"Atmosphere suitable for humans. No toxins detected. Life scan shows a wide variety of flora and fauna, as expected for a jungle planet. Probes have returned with air, soil, and vegetation samples."

"Your assessment, Lieutenant Kassis?" The captain's words were formal. This entire exercise was for the official recording—and the hovering media drones.

"Based on this data, and the analysis of the science team, the planet is safe for exploration. I recommend we proceed with the mission." I waved a hand through the green icon in my interface as I recited my line. On any normal Phase 1 mission, the head science officer's sign-off would be crucial. But I wasn't a science officer, and this was not a normal mission.

"Thank you." She flicked her own interface, and her voice carried throughout the ship. "Attention, crew of the *ECS Verity*. Based on preliminary data, the mission to Darenti Four is approved. Away teams, report to your stations." She turned to the man at her side. "Major Percival, you have the conn."

"Aye, Captain." Percival moved to the captain's chair. "The officer of the deck has the conn. Navigation, status."

As Percival worked through the customary status checks, I followed Captain Kim to the float tube. Dozens of media drones streamed in behind us. We dropped to the shuttle bay and marched to the first ship—a Commonwealth Navy vessel. Normally, the CEC would use their own ships, but this visit was a big deal, and the Navy wanted to be part of it.

A full team of explorers snapped to attention when the captain arrived.

I slipped away and took my place in the rank behind the away-team commander and beside Lieutenant Joss Torres. My sair-glider, Liam, leaped from his shoulder to mine. The small blue and white striped animal had been with me since I found him on the ship to Earth. He'd gotten me through some tough times. I rubbed my cheek against his soft body, then stood at attention.

Captain Kim cleared her throat. The sound echoed through the vast shuttle bay, amplified by the still-active ship-wide comm channel. "This is a historic occasion—the return to Darenti Four. The Colonial Explorer Corps high command has hand-picked this team for this mission. Each of you was selected for your specific expertise to ensure this mission is performed to perfection."

She waved at the drones circling overhead. "Our actions will be beamed almost live to every human being in the galaxy. I am counting on you to do us proud."

Joss leaned a little closer and spoke under his breath. "Makes you wonder why she picked us."

I smothered a snort and straightened my spine. "Speak for yourself, Torres. I'm a delight."

The mission commander glanced my way but said nothing. The captain spoke for another five minutes, each carefully crafted phrase carrying a reminder that we would be under media scrutiny at every second. When she finally finished, the drones flew a lap around the shuttle bay as we turned and marched into the small craft.

I dropped into a seat beside Joss and fastened my five-point harness.

Liam crawled down my arm and into the special pocket in my jacket. I closed it and patted him through the fabric. Meanwhile, a drone slid across the row, filming each of us as we secured our restraints. Joss winked and mugged for the camera, and I tried not to roll my eyes.

"You're off to a good start. Being all respectable and whatnot."

Joss's grin widened. "If they wanted respectable, they shouldn't have added me to the roster."

"They didn't really have a choice. You're the galaxy's golden boy." I tightened the last strap and sighed. "Or at least one of them."

"Look who's talking. The daughter of the Hero." He smacked my arm. "Face it. We're here because of our dads, and there's nothing we can do about that. But if the cams are going to be on us full-time, I aim to make things interesting. I know how reality shows work."

I shook my head. "I've watched enough *Ancient TēVē* to know there was nothing real about them. At least I hope not."

"You'd have to ask my dad."

Joss's father, Zane Torres, had starred in a very popular VidTube series as a teen on Earth. Five hundred years later, episodes of his show were still trendy among Ancient Earth aficionados in the Colonial Commonwealth. Their popularity had increased exponentially when my father, Nathanier Kassis—already known in the Commonwealth as the Hero of Darenti Four—discovered the star had spent the intervening centuries in deep sleep. Zane Torres became Earth's representative to the Commonwealth, and my father was promoted to admiral and commandant of the CEC Academy.

Joss and I had both garnered a lot of attention during our years at the academy and our first assignments on active duty. But over the past five years, the media attention had faded. Until now.

A familiar voice came through the ship's speakers. "Secure the hatches!"

While the crew chief closed the door, I craned my neck to try to peer into the cockpit. "That sounded like Derek Lee. What are the odds that the Navy would send *him*?" Lee had attended the CEC academy with us but transferred to the Navy before commissioning.

Joss waved his hand in a swirling motion. "Hurray, the gang's all here."

I grinned at his flat tone. "Still not a big Derek Lee fan? 'Nibs' saved our bacon."

"Yeah, *after* he threw us to the wolves. He was cleaning up his own mistakes. That's not exactly noteworthy."

"You can't blame that whole situation on him. Most of it was Marika's fault." My fingers clenched around the armrest as the shuttle lifted from the deck of the landing bay. Although I'd reluctantly learned to pilot a shuttle—turns out being able to fly yourself off a hostile planet is a good skill to have—riding in the back was not my favorite pastime. It required you to have faith in the person at the controls. And despite my defense of Derek "Nibs" Lee, I wasn't one hundred percent thrilled to have my life in his hands again.

"Don't worry, I'm sure he isn't in command for a mission like this." Joss patted my hand. "And I can always get us out of here."

"Why aren't you up front? I saw the call for a CEC pilot to join the Navy flight crew. Did they get that many volunteers?"

Joss smirked. "I'm not interested in sitting in a jump seat for the PR pics. But if I'd volunteered to fly, I'd be up there. You know I'm the best."

I scowled but didn't contradict him. Objectively speaking, Joss was the best pilot on this ship. Probably on any ship. He had the training and mission stats to back up that claim. But he didn't need me to feed his ego. "Too bad your head won't fit in the cockpit anymore."

"They make 'em large enough for the biggest of us." He shook his head. "Or something like that. My clever quips designer seems to be on the fritz."

G forces pushed us back in our seats as the shuttle surged away from the ship. A screen over the front bulkhead flickered to life, displaying our location relative to the *Verity* and the projected route to the planet.

The voice from the cockpit spoke again—it was definitely Lee. "Drop time to the target is twenty minutes. Please stay in your seats with your restraints locked. A flight attendant will not bring you beverages." He snickered, and everyone in the passenger compartment either groaned or ignored him.

"Just as amusing as always." Joss fiddled with his restraints. "And he doesn't trust us to keep our belts locked." He flicked the mechanism a couple of times, but the light continued to glow red.

"Apparently with good reason." I pulled his hand away from the controls. "So, why didn't you volunteer to fly?"

Joss scowled. "I told you, it's a PR stunt. The Navy won't let us fly their boats. I might get to ferry dignitaries to the meeting point, if I'm lucky. But mostly, I'm here to show that Earth is in alignment with the Commonwealth government on the Darenti issue."

"Seriously? They sent you along as a political pawn? Isn't your dad sending an official Earth rep to this 'historic occasion'? I can't believe the CEC allowed you to be used that way."

"Oh, he's sending a rep, too. Zina's on the other shuttle." He waved in what I presumed was the correct direction.

"Why didn't you tell me your sister was here?" I grabbed his arm. "Wait, Zina's representing the whole planet? Is she—"

Joss shook his head. "She's here for the Ancients. They decided to send one rep for each section of the population. Zina for the Ancients. A guy from India for the Earthers. And even one from the Dome."

"No way! The Insiders won't even go outside the Dome if they can avoid it. Who'd they send off-world?"

"Tiah, of course."

During the five hundred years Joss's dad—and thousands of others—had been in suspended animation, many generations of Insiders had been born, lived, and died within the sealed facility they called the Dome. After five centuries, the Ancients—the people in deep sleep—determined the atmosphere had regenerated enough to support life outside the Dome. Thanks to hundreds of years of brainwashing, the Insiders believed the surface would never be safe.

When the Ancients emerged, they discovered hundreds of thousands more had survived the environmental changes outside. Those people were now known as Earthers.

A few years later, the CEC rediscovered humanity's home world. My father had led that mission, and I had joined him. The Ancients had been eager to connect with their space-faring brethren. The Insiders preferred to stay isolated within their structure. The Earthers didn't seem to care one way or the other.

Eventually, the three groups had formed a triumvirate government that was frequently hindered by the fact that the Insiders refused to leave the "safety" of their facility. Only Tiah, who was barely twenty years old, had been brave enough to step outside.

"I can't believe she left the planet!"

"I know. I was stunned when Mom told me she was coming, too. But the Commonwealth government decided Earth representatives are the closest they've got to an indigenous species being discovered on a planet. Cause 'first' contact with us went so well."

I ignored his sarcasm. "Where are they?" I looked up and down our row of seats but couldn't see over the high backs in front of me.

"The other shuttle." He closed his eyes.

"How did you know all this? My dad didn't tell me anything!"

Joss's lips curved in a slight smile, but he didn't open his eyes.

"What else do you know?" I shook his arm again.

Without looking, he pulled my fingers from his wrist. "I was going to tell you—before you made that big head remark. Now you'll have to wait and see. Like everyone else."

CHAPTER TWO

THE SHUTTLE TOUCHED DOWN, and the crew ran their landing routine. The crew chief opened the rear doors, and a wave of heavy, damp air pushed in. Major Featherstoke strode down the narrow aisle between the seats and the side wall of the craft. He stopped beneath the now dark display screen. The media drones swooped over our heads, racing for the back opening.

Featherstoke peered around the shuttle hold. "Was that all of 'em?" After a few seconds, he nodded. "Good. This is the last time I'll be able to talk to you without media oversight." He pointed a finger at one side of the shuttle, then swept it across the seated explorers to the other. "I expect every one of you on your best behavior. The media are not our friends—they're here to catch us screwing up. This might be an historic occasion, but there are forces in the Commonwealth government who'd love to see the CEC defunded. If we screw up, that will be recorded, beamed to the universe, and used as ammunition."

He fixed his steely eyes on me and Joss. "They're gonna be on you two like dust in an Oort cloud. Do not mess up."

I nodded. "Yes, sir."

Featherstoke pointed at Joss. "I didn't hear you, Lieutenant."

"I will be a paragon of virtue, sir." At the major's raised eyebrows, Joss sighed. "I mean, yes, sir."

"Get to work, team. Dismissed." Featherstoke clapped once, and the lights on our harnesses turned green. A babble broke out.

"Do you even know what that means?" I whispered under the clatter of unlatching seat restraints.

"Usually, 'get to work' means we should do the job we were sent here to do." Joss stood and stretched as if he'd been confined to his seat for hours.

I widened my eyes until they hurt. "Really, sir? I don't know what I'd do without you to explain things for me."

"I know." He smiled smugly and followed the guy beyond him out of our row.

"They haven't let anyone near the Darenti in over a hundred years." Joss slapped his hand on the lock panel beside one of the doors in the brand-new officers' quarters. "Why now?"

My father discovered the Darenti when he was a CEC lieutenant. Since then, he'd explored three more planets and rediscovered Earth. Thanks to the deep sleep required to reach planets without jump beacons, his first visit to Darenti happened well over a hundred years ago.

The Commonwealth government established an "embassy" in a station orbiting Darenti Four but kept the planet restricted. Humans visited the planet annually to parlay with the locals. Every year, the Darenti invited the Commonwealth to establish a colony on Darenti and requested transit to the larger galaxy in return. Every year, the Commonwealth put them off for another year. Until now.

"Didn't you listen to any of the briefings?" I selected the room across the hall and registered my handprint to the door. Most of the team would bunk in the dorm, but as junior officers, we were entitled to individual rooms. The higher-ranking officers had suites on the other side of our module. I opened the door and looked over the narrow bed, three-drawer dresser, and tiny closet. It was better than a hammock in a shared bay, but barely. The bathrooms were still down the hall.

"Yeah." Joss tossed his bag on his bed. "They've had time to mature, we have a better understanding of their culture, yada, yada, yada. Still seems like it blew up pretty quickly."

"You mean after sensors discovered that promethium deposit on the western continent? I'm sure that's unrelated." I hung my dress uniform in the small cupboard. I'd have to find a steamer somewhere. Five hundred years after the Exodus, and our fabric still wrinkled as badly as the stuff from Earth.

Joss lounged in the doorway. "Be careful the drones don't catch you saying that."

"They're supposed to be forbidden from coming into our personal space." I gestured expansively, knocking my knuckles against the walls on both sides of the room. "And I still have the blocker Chymm wrote." I flicked my holo-ring. "Want a copy?"

He crooked his fingers in a "gimme" motion. "I had to delete mine—running out of memory. But I uploaded a lot of stuff to storage before we came down."

Thanks to the political situation, our holo-rings would connect to the planetary network—supported by satellites circling the globe—but access to the wider galacti-net was blocked.

I swiped the file to him. "I have a sneaking suspicion this mission is going to require a lot more paperwork than usual—you don't suppose they've given us anywhere to work on that, do you?"

He rolled his shoulder away from the doorframe and nodded toward the far end of the hall. "There's a junior officers' lounge down there. I'm guessing it's for working, not drinking."

I opened Liam's pocket. He popped out, nose twitching. The little guy had been squirming since we landed. I was fairly sure he could escape if he wanted, but he hadn't tried. The moment I let him free, he scrambled up my arm and launched himself from my shoulder. He landed on the doorframe, gave me a quick look that seemed to say, "I'll be back," and disappeared into the hallway.

Joss pointed. "Should we catch him?"

"He'll be fine. You know he always finds his way back to me. And he can't leave the compound." Or could he? He seemed to be able to pass through the force shields at will. I peered down the hall. "Too late now. He's gone." I pushed Joss out of the room. "Let's check out the lounge. No reason we can't use it for work and leisure."

"Except this is a dry mission." He looked up, then poked my arm and rolled his eyes toward the ceiling.

"Leisure activities don't always require alcohol." A faint buzz registered in my brain, and I followed his glance. A drone hovered in the corner of the hallway. I poked a finger at the drone, and the obligatory identification hologram appeared: G'lacTechNews. "Our old friends."

Joss snorted. "But not Thor Talon and Aella Phoenix."

"Probably not Thor." I glanced at the drone again. I couldn't remember if Thor's defection to Gagarin was common knowledge, so I didn't mention it. "And Aella's moved up to anchor."

Joss waited for me to precede him into the lounge, then slammed the door before the drone could follow us. His lips twitched. "That won't stop them for long."

"I'm not sure poking the bear is a good idea. I think that's what Major Featherstoke was talking about when he said you should be a paragon of virtue."

"I'm the one who said that. He just told me to stay out of trouble. And staying away from the drones is the best way for me to stay out of trouble."

"If they don't catch you it doesn't count?" I turned to look at the "lounge." A functional but not particularly attractive sofa sat against one wall, and a row of desks lined the other. A two-meter-long table filled the space between. A window looked across a clearing and into the steaming jungle. I dropped onto the couch. "As comfortable as it is beautiful."

Joss poked the stiff plastek, then wandered to the window. Three drones hovered outside, their cams pointed at us. He flicked his holo-ring and waved through a short sequence of icons. The window went foggy.

An androgynous voice announced, "Privacy shield engaged."

"You wanna start rumors, that's the way to do it." I flicked my own holo-ring and connected to the building's system. Controls for the privacy shield included audio, visual, and scans. When they were all engaged, no one should be able to tell how many people were inside or what we were doing or saying.

"Please. As soon as you and I were assigned to the same mission, the rumors started to fly. Closing the shades isn't going to make any difference." He drummed his fingers on the table. "Not even a decent shape for playing cards."

"That's probably intentional, since we're supposed to be on our best behavior." I flicked the building system app closed.

The door swung open. Two drones zipped in, followed by a Navy officer: Derek Lee.

G'lacTechNews

...LeBlanc Corporation spokesperson said the new source of promethium is promising, but difficulty in mining it will keep prices high. And now, with a report from Darenti Four, here's Starling Cross.

Thanks, Aella. The Colonial Explorer Corps has landed again on Darenti —providing support to the embassy during the initial treaty talks.

Although the official delegates won't arrive for several more days, many have sent staff to make initial contact. Yesterday, we saw the Kakuvian ambassador's staff, including the dreamy Sincheol Orion. My sources tell me the Earth contingent arrived a few days ago, including Zina Torres, daughter of the Earth Ambassador, Zane Torres.

We've also seen a few familiar faces. Lieutenant Serenity "Siti" Kassis, daughter of the Hero of Darenti Four, landed today with her bestie, Joshua "Caveman" Torres—one of the so-called "Ancients" from Earth, and twin sibling of Zina. Another notable: Navy Lieutenant Derek "Nibs" Lee.

Long-time viewers will remember Kassis, Torres, and Lee were involved in the expulsion of Gagarin spies from the Saha system five years ago. Kassis has also been linked with both men romantically.

This is Starling Cross, reporting live from Kassis Station orbiting Darenti Four. Back to you in the studio, Aella!

CHAPTER THREE

Lieutenant Lee swaggered into the room. "Not much of a lounge, is it?"

"Nibs." Joss frowned at the newcomer. "How long you staying?"

Lee grimaced at the callsign but didn't comment. He'd been our nemesis—and later, our reluctant savior—when we were cadets. He jerked his chin at Joss. "Caveman."

"Hey, Derek." I stood and held out a fist to knock knuckles with him. "I haven't seen you since graduation."

"Sorry to deprive you of all this." He threw back his shoulders and waved a hand down his own torso.

He looked good—he'd filled out substantially since the Academy, but I wasn't going to tell him that. I gave him an eye roll. "I don't know how I survived."

"Why are you still here? Shouldn't you be playing taxi driver to the VIPs?" Joss took my place on the couch but immediately jumped up again. "That's like lounging on a boulder."

"They've stationed us here. Lieutenant Commander D'metros and I have been assigned to fly the VIPs around." Lee puffed out his chest.

"Like my dad," Joss and I said at the same time.

"Yeah, yeah, big deal, your daddies are important." Lee's mother had been an admiral—until she was court martialed. "I got selected on my own merits."

Joss smirked and opened his mouth. With a quick glance at the drones hovering above our heads, he closed it again.

I tried not to smile. Biting his tongue was probably killing him. "I'm going to see what else is going on." As I skirted Lee, one of the drones jigged, clearly trying to decide which of us would provide better viewing. I gave them all—men and drones—a little finger wave and headed for the front door.

According to the embassy staff, Darenti had a rainy season and a more rainy season, with thick cloud cover year-around. The current muggy warmth would give way to cold, foggy weather in a few months. I hoped we were long gone before that happened.

Thick air pressed into my lungs as I exited the low-slung barracks, and I could almost feel my hair frizzing. A half-dozen drones slowly circled above the base, and one of them left its place to swoop down and follow me across a broad courtyard.

A plascrete pad separated the officers' quarters—or "Q"—from the other four CEC modules. The newly erected buildings bore signs indicating their functions: enlisted barracks, embassy headquarters, mission supply, and support. I strode across the courtyard to the support building and went inside.

Two sets of double doors formed an airlock. They weren't currently sealed but could be activated in an emergency with the flick of a control icon. The thick doors and higher internal air pressure helped keep the interior areas cooler and dryer.

This module was constructed on the same floorplan as the Q: one long hallway with rooms on either side. Here, those rooms were work spaces for personnel, operations, communications. The higher-level administrators would have plusher offices on the upper level. At the far end of the hall, I pushed through the door that read Mess.

This room stretched across the end of the building, with large windows looking out into the misty jungle. Here, a wide clearing separated the building from the blue-green foliage, and a pair of vehicles sat nearby. One had maintenance crew buzzing around it, while the other sat alone.

"Hey, Siti, over here!"

I turned away from the windows to see Zina Torres—Joss's twin sister—loading a tray at a small buffet. A white-garbed server refilled one of the trays, pausing to put something on Zina's plate. The dark-haired beauty said something in her low voice, and the man's cheeks flushed.

I waved but paused to survey the rest of the room before joining her. Tiah, one of the Earth "Insiders," and a small man I didn't recognize sat at a table on the far end. Across from them, a short, muscular woman wearing a formal suit spoke earnestly, effortlessly commanding their full attention. Ambassador Slovenska. I hoped to have that kind of presence someday.

"Zina! Good to see you." I exchanged a one-armed hug with my friend, then grabbed a tray for myself. "What's the specialty, chef?"

The white-clothed man ignored me, focused on placing small circular pastries into the tray in what I had to assume—based on the concentration required—was an intricate layout, although it looked kind of random to me.

Zina fluttered her eyelashes at the man, and he popped upright, the rosy blush spreading across his cheeks again. "Did you want more *firulan*, miss?"

"No, but my friend might like some." She took the plate he offered and plunked it onto my tray. "Thank you!"

"My pleasure." His cheeks went redder, and he returned to his careful stacking, eyes flicking to Zina after each morsel went into the tray. He ignored me.

I randomly added some items to the plate. I didn't recognize any of these bite-sized snacks, but they smelled of spices and caramelized vegetables. The brown sauce with meat chunks appeared on every CEC buffet, ever, and was usually the least tasty way to ingest calories. I added a scoop of white mashed something and a dollop of a lumpy, peppery white gravy. "Your brother's in the Q."

"I'm sure he'll find the food soon enough." Zina smiled at the server again, then carried her tray to a table near the windows.

I grabbed a beverage and set my tray across from hers. "Don't you have to join the delegation?" I jerked my head at Tiah's table at the far end of the room.

Zina picked up one of the small bites. "I've already heard Ambassador Slovenska's schtick. She's agitating for a Navy presence at Darenti. She doesn't have a leg to stand on, and frankly, I'm surprised the Commonwealth is letting her suggest it."

"Slovenska wants to bring in the military? Usually, the civilians want to keep the Navy well away from anyplace the CEC is exploring." I tried one of the *firulan*. At least I thought that's what it was. "Yum. I didn't think we considered the Darenti a threat."

"Try the green ones." She pointed at an item on my plate, then popped one of the flaky cubes into her mouth. "Apparently, she thinks the Navy should protect the Darenti from the rest of the galaxy, not the other way around. She doesn't really want them on the planet—just out there, like a blockade."

"I thought this meeting was so the Commonwealth government could start the negotiations with the Darenti. To open trade and communication, not close it. Wouldn't bringing in the Navy look bad?"

"Terrible." Zina cast a quick look at the server, then surreptitiously spit something into her napkin. "The pink ones are vile." She gulped some of her beverage. "That's one of the reasons Dad sent me rather than coming himself. I can listen to her demands, but I don't have the authority to make any formal declarations on behalf of the Ancients, just report back to him. It forces a little breathing space into any negotiations."

"I'm glad that's not my job." I made a face toward the ambassador's back, then poked my fork into one of the brown spheres. "Have you tried the meatballs?"

"Those aren't meat."

I sniffed at the sweet, smoky blob. "They smell kind of barbeque-y."

"The sauce is barbeque-ish, but all of the food here is plant-based. The Darenti don't eat animal flesh." She waved at the buffet. "It's all vegetarian."

I nibbled the non-meatball. "It's good, though. That chef knows what he's doing."

She laughed. "The Darenti do all the cooking. Franz just serves the food. Don't go into the kitchen—it's a madhouse."

"How do you know all this? How long have you been here?"

"We arrived yesterday. But you know me—I'm good at finding out all the details." She finished the last item on her plate. "I should probably go bail Tiah out. You wanna come say hello?"

"Sure." I grabbed my tray, but the white-coated server hurried to our table and took Zina's tray before she could. When she handed him mine as well, his face twitched, but he smiled at my companion and took the dishes.

Tiah jumped up when we arrived. "Siti! It's so good to see you!" We exchanged hugs while the ambassador and the dark man looked on with dour expressions.

When Tiah introduced me, the older woman's eyes flicked to my nametag, then my face. "Kassis? I hadn't heard you were assigned to this mission."

I ducked my head. "No reason you would, ma'am. I'm just part of the team."

Her eyes narrowed and roved over my face as if trying to read my mind. "I suspect that's not one hundred percent true. Like that one." She nodded at Joss who stood in the doorway.

"Yo, sis!" Joss gave the ambassador a wide berth as he hurried forward to throw his arms around his sister. When Zina made the introductions, he nodded and muttered, "Ma'am," then turned back to his twin. "How's Mom?"

The ambassador gave Joss's back an inscrutable look, then stood and straightened her uniform. "I must get back to work. Nice to meet you, Representatives." She executed a precise about-face and marched out of the room.

"Siti, Joss, have you met Mr. Arya? He's from India, on Earth. He's the Earther rep."

I turned to the table in surprise. Somehow, I'd completely forgotten he was there. "Hi, Mr. Arya. I'm Siti Kassis."

The short, slim, dark-haired man stood and smiled. "Very pleased to meet you, Lieutenant." His soft voice barely seemed to reach my ears.

"You know who I haven't seen yet?" Joss waved an arm around the room.

"Who?"

He waited, but no one said anything. I rolled my hand in a "get on with it" motion.

"The Darenti."

CHAPTER FOUR

THE THICK ATMOSPHERE almost choked me as we stepped out of the support building. The musky scent of the jungle wasn't unpleasant, but the dense air caught in my throat like syrup. Fine mist settled around me like a warm, wet blanket.

When I was a child, my father rarely talked about his mission to Darenti—probably because he spent two years on a public relations tour as the official *Hero of Darenti Four*. But the few times he mentioned the adventure, his description of the damp planet made an enormous impression on me.

The reality was even wetter than I'd imagined. Fortunately, technology had advanced in the hundred years since mankind's first visit. Improvements to our solar collection systems meant we could use our personal shields without worrying about depleting our power supplies.

As I debated activating my shield, Liam dropped to my shoulder. He rubbed his soft blue and white fur against my face and chirped.

"Good to see you, too." I reached up to stroke his back. He made a few more conversational sounds, then draped himself across my shoulder like a scarf. I gave the animal a quick look. This was unusual behavior for him—usually he was upright and alert. But he didn't appear to be sick. I made a mental note to keep an eye on him.

Zina moved closer. "Is that Liam? He looks bigger! Did he grow?" She slid a finger down the glider's spine, and he made a rumbling noise of approval.

"I don't think so." I twisted my head to check him out again. "He seems the same to me. Joss?"

The man shrugged. "I don't pay that much attention to the little guy unless he's stealing senidium or breaking into locked rooms."

Zina's brows went up. "Really? I'm not sure I've heard those stories."

I rolled my eyes at the drones hovering around us. "Some other time."

Zina led us across the paved courtyard and past the embassy headquarters. A line of familiar bollards topped by glowing blue globes delineated the perimeter of the base. Zina nodded to the guards at the gate, but they made no effort to stop us as we exited through the narrow gap. We crossed a strip of dirt to the thick jungle beyond. As we walked, Zina lifted a few centimeters off the path.

"It gets muddy ahead." She rotated so she was facing backward. "The Darenti don't seem to mind the mud."

Tiah sighed with relief as she lifted off. One of her legs was shorter than the other, so long walks through uneven terrain could be difficult for her. If she had grown up on any Commonwealth planet, she would have had the condition corrected as a child, but on Earth, that technology hadn't been available. Maybe now that she'd ventured out into the wider galaxy, she'd get her leg evaluated.

"I thought you just got here yesterday." I flicked my controls, and a sucking sound accompanied my feet pulling from the mud. "How do you already know so much?"

She shrugged. "I studied everything about Darenti before I came. The embassy sent us a lot of vid and commentary." She glanced around, her eyes catching on the drones following us.

An incoming group call pinged my audio implant. Tiah twitched, as if something had surprised her. I activated the call. The device announced the names of those in the call: Tiah, Joss, and Zina.

Zina's voice came through. "We don't want the drones listening in." Her lips twitched as she turned to face forward again.

"What are you worried about them hearing?" I activated my shield above my head to compensate for the increased drizzle.

"I'm not sure the embassy told us everything about the Darenti. Or they're not very good at their job. Their reports are completely superficial. They haven't allowed our scientists to examine them physically—fair enough. We wouldn't let them examine us, if they'd asked. No psychological analysis. The cultural descriptions are bland. Boring. They have examples of art and architecture, but none of it dates from before your dad landed here." She glanced over her shoulder at me and raised an eyebrow.

"That seems like a really obvious oversight. Why hasn't someone noticed the gap?"

Zina managed to imply a heavy sigh through the subvocal comm system. "I noticed it."

"True. But I mean someone else over the last hundred years. Surely, the Commonwealth has had cultural specialists studying everything."

She grunted. The drone swooped around us, hovering about a meter ahead of Zina, facing her. The woman flashed a brilliant smile at the tiny camera, then looked away with a shrug. "I'm sure someone other than me has noticed it. They haven't bothered sharing that information with Earth."

"Do you believe the Commonwealth government is monitoring us?" Mr. Arya gestured at the cloud of drones as he spoke aloud. One zipped toward him, and he flinched.

"They're news drones," I replied. "But I'm sure the government is monitoring their transmissions." I considered jamming the drone, then activated a side conversation. "Joss, do you have a way to access that drone's broadcast?"

Joss flicked his holo-ring and pulled up an interface. His primary specialty in the CEC was flying, but as a kid, he'd studied computer systems. When we started at the CEC Academy eight years ago, he'd picked communications and coding classes as his electives.

He flicked a code slip to me. "That's the official live broadcast of the news networks. The aggregator switches between channels depending on what search terms you enter. For example, you can put in your name and see anything they're broadcasting about you." My ring vibrated again. "That one will pull the feed of any drone currently within line of sight. There might be a slight delay—the program has to sync with their encryption. Fortunately for us, the rules of engagement mean the CEC gets live access to all feeds—if requested. I'm sure there are drones out there trying to stay unnoticed or using illegal encryption. But if we report any we find to the embassy, they'll be shut down."

I opened the program, and a small video appeared in my palm. It showed the five of us flying through the jungle above the muddy path. The feed shifted as the drone slalomed from side to side, focusing on each of us in turn. Arya's eyes narrowed every time it zeroed in on him. The audio caught his whispered comments clearly. "I will open discussions with the local embassy."

I flipped back to the group call and checked the participant list. "Does Mr. Arya have an audio implant?"

"No," Zina responded. "He refused to have your 'demon devices' installed. His community on Earth did not take easily to the technology of this century." She spoke aloud. "Mr. Arya, that drone is recording everything you say. Subvocal communications are the only way to ensure privacy with them watching."

"Thank you, Ms Torres. I will refrain from airing private information." He pressed his lips together as if he'd decided to refrain from speaking ever again.

"Good plan." Zina had clearly practiced—the drone didn't shift to record her until she added aloud, "It's a shame you didn't get an implant to ensure privacy."

"My people weren't sure we should send someone at all." The words burst from Arya, as if he couldn't help himself. He stared defiantly at the drone. "That is true, and not something we need to hide. We live on Earth—that is our concern. The activities of a species on a distant planet offer little interest to us." He held up a hand, as if waving off expected arguments. "I understand that certain factions on Earth feel differently. However, that is the view of the majority."

As the Earther delegate, Arya represented the vast majority of Earth's population. I didn't know how their decision-making process worked—or whether he wielded more power than Tiah or Zina who each represented only a fraction of people.

Tiah spoke for the first time since we'd left the mess. Her voice held the gravitas of a much older woman. "The Insiders agree with this view." She rubbed her forehead.

I spun to face her. "Then why are you here?"

A smile flickered across her lips. "I said the Insiders agree, not that I do. Besides, I wasn't going to pass up the chance to see another planet."

Joss snickered. "I guess your curiosity is the only reason any of you came, then."

Tiah nodded regally and pointed at Zina. "She owes me."

I flung up both hands. "Wait. What does that mean for any decisions that need to be made?"

Zina cast a dark look at the drone—which had been joined by a second one. "That will remain to be seen. But Earth only gets one vote on any decisions—like every other planet. And, of course, this is just a getting-to-know-you visit. If they were making any real decisions, Dad would be here. He's the official ambassador from Earth."

We floated in silence along the muddy path. Based on their body language, I suspected Zina and Joss were arguing on a private channel, but they said nothing aloud.

The vegetation stretched along either side in a perfectly vertical wall. Either plants grew very strangely here, or the path was manicured on a regular basis. Or maybe it had been created specifically for this visit.

Tiah rubbed her forehead again.

I moved closer. "Are you okay?"

She shrugged. "I've had a low-level headache since we arrived. Probably the barometric pressure or something."

We rounded a corner, and a clearing opened in front of us. I rose so I could see the whole facility. A smaller version of the Commonwealth base spread across the clearing. Six rectangles, made of a darker material—was that stone?—stood around a green courtyard. Like our base, but they looked like they had been built for much shorter people.

Unlike the human base, there were no gate, no guards, and no patrols. The jungle had been cut back only on the front. On the sides and back, green-blue foliage leaned toward the buildings, like spiky fingers reaching to pull them back into the trees.

Zina dropped toward the first building, and we followed. As we touched down, Liam scrambled across my chest and leaped to the plasphalt pad in front of the complex.

"Liam!"

Joss grabbed my arm. "He'll be back. You said so yourself."

As Liam disappeared around the end of the building, the door opened, and a group of five small people marched out. They wore clothing similar to ours, with two in military-style uniforms and three in more civilian-appearing attire.

Zina stepped forward and bowed to the delegation. "Greetings, friends. I have brought my companions from Earth."

I grabbed Zina's arm. "Shouldn't we have waited for a formal introduction?"

She shook her head. "These Darenti are all delegates—they've been briefed on human behavior and know not to take offense if we don't follow their customs. When this gathering was planned, the Commonwealth and Darenti ambassadors decided to make it as open and casual as possible. They believe it will be beneficial to all if we create personal relationships with the Darenti."

She introduced us to our hosts. We each stepped forward as she mentioned our names and affiliations. When she finished, the darkest of the Darenti followed her example. "I am Isaula Theomtimus. You many call me Isa." Isa turned to the being next to her. "This is Glaucia Ivengard, from Rovantu—the western continent." A small, pale-skinned Darenti with striking red hair nodded.

The tallest one saluted. This being wore a dark uniform with three red slashes on the sleeves and a sprinkling of ribbons on both sides of his chest. "Ricmond of the Western Seas." The voice was deep and masculine.

The other uniformed person also saluted. "Porcia Iordanus, from the Drusa Mountains."

The four moved to either side of the low step, allowing the last one, a tiny, pale individual in a long green robe, through. "And I am V'Ovidia

Demokritos, from—" A strange garble of syllables burst from the being's lips. "You humans call it the Lake District."

Zina bowed to the tiny Darenti. "I am most honored to meet you, Dar Demokritos." She straightened and turned to us. "V'Ovidia Demokritos is the Darenti ambassador. I hope our visit didn't interrupt important work. We have no wish to intrude or disrupt, only to visit."

Demokritos spread both hands in a strangely human gesture. "You are always welcome, Representative Torres. Interacting with our Commonwealth visitors is my primary duty. I have trained since my forming for this event. And please, call me V'Ov."

I raised my eyebrows at Joss and flicked to a private call. "These people are the first sapient non-human life in the galaxy. At least the first we've encountered. Why do they feel so human?"

"I'd guess they've studied us." Joss nodded at Porcia Iordanus and Ricmond, who stood a little behind the others. "Those uniforms look a lot like ours. Same dark, close-fitting shape. Pockets and belt pouches, like ours. They each have a ring on their left hand—like us."

"Except the redhead."

Joss raised his own right hand, just enough for me to notice. "Maybe she's a leftie, like me?"

"Do you think they selected people specifically to mirror us? Two in uniform. One left-handed. Ricmond is much taller than the others—like you. Isa is darker skinned—like you and Zina."

"Maybe they think there's some significance to those things, rather than random genet—" He broke off as Ricmond and Porcia Iordanus approached us. "Hey."

I hid a smile as the two aliens mimicked his raised hand and tone. "Hey."

"I'm Siti."

"Is this your preferred nomenclature, Lieutenant Serenity Kassis?" Ricmond asked. At my nod, he continued, "You may call me Ric, and Porcia Iordanus prefers to be called Danny. She and I would be happy to show you around our facility."

I filed the "she" away. Although they were barely a meter tall, the Darenti physiology seemed to match human in great detail. Danny had curves under her uniform, while Ric's broad shoulders and narrow waist looked similar to a typical human male.

My holo-ring vibrated, indicating an incoming link. I excused myself and turned away from the Darenti to check it. A message from Zina accompanied a connection to the embassy database. The five Darenti were listed, including preferred names and pronouns. I sent back a thumbs-up and returned to the conversation.

"—may have to bend." Ric leaned over, with his hands on his knees, to demonstrate whatever he was saying.

Joss tapped my arm. "You wanna go inside?"

I shrugged, casting a swift glance at Zina. She seemed to be the leader of our little mission. But she, Tiah, and Mr. Arya had already followed their escorts toward the building. V'Ov walked with a slight hitch in her step, similar to Tiah's limp. Were the Darenti mocking us or trying to put us at ease?

The cloud of news drones hovered over the steps but didn't follow us into the building. We ducked through the low door but were able to straighten once inside. My hair brushed the ceiling, and Joss had to hunch over. The building looked almost identical to the human base, with the exception of the name plates on each door. Those bore unfamiliar characters and pictographs. At the far end of the hall, we ducked through another door and climbed a staircase.

The top floor had even lower ceilings. Everyone but Tiah had to bend to fit. I briefly considered turning on my grav belt, so I could pull up my legs and simply float down the hall but decided that would be unnecessarily showy. When we entered the first door on the right, I was glad I hadn't bothered. Outside the window, the cloud of drones jockeyed for position.

V'Ov waved us toward a seating area where human-sized seats alternated with their Darenti companions. We sat, and I gratefully unrolled my spine. Isa and Ric sat on either side of me, with the other Darenti dispersed between the humans. Once we were seated, the smaller chairs telescoped to put everyone's heads level.

V'Ov's chair rose slightly higher. "Thank you for coming to my office. I welcome you to Darenti, and I look forward to getting to know you better. Our delegations will begin formal interactions tomorrow, but Ambassador Yarnel and I agreed these informal chats would create an opportunity for harmonious discussion."

Or a chance for unplanned hostility. But the CEC had chosen us for a reason, and each of the people in this room was level-headed and unlikely to cause offense on purpose. Mr. Arya was the only one I didn't know, but so far, he seemed deliberate, reasoned, and fairly unflappable.

As if he'd heard my thoughts, Mr. Arya jumped from his chair. "Nobody move, I have a bomb!"

G'lacTechNews

Breaking news!

This is Starling Cross, broadcasting from the Darenti Station. Isolationists from Earth have taken Darenti and Colonial delegates hostage inside the Darenti base. The hostages include two Earth representatives, Tiah Ross and Zina Torres, as well as CEC poster couple Siti Kassis and Joshua Torres.

Naval Lieutenant Derek Lee offered no comment.

CHAPTER FIVE

We stared at the short man in shock.

"Why do you have a bomb?" Tiah stuttered.

Arya stalked to the center of the room, turning on his heel to look at each of us. "The Darenti are an abomination! Look at them, pretending to be human! You think I didn't notice their mockery? That one—" Arya stabbed a finger at Isa. "That one was aping my accent!"

Zina lifted her hands in a placating gesture. "They are trying to set us at ease through familiarity. Didn't you view the briefing materials?" Her eyes darted past Arya to Joss.

A call from Zina came through my implant as Arya went into a rambling rant. "Be ready to jump him."

"If he has a bomb, that could set him off." Joss eased to the edge of his seat.

"I don't think he has one." I shifted forward, ready to spring up. "Even the most sophisticated explosives require bulky equipment and would have been picked up by sensors on the ship. Unless it's a biological—but he specifically said bomb. And where would he get it? Weren't he and his luggage screened before leaving Earth?"

"And before dropping to Darenti. At least they checked all my stuff." Zina raised a hand and her voice to interrupt Arya's monologue. "Mr.

Arya, I'd like to see some evidence of this bomb. Because right now, you just sound crazy."

Arya surged toward Zina. Joss exploded out of his chair, launching himself at the small man. I leaped up, throwing myself at him, too. Tiah squeaked and pushed herself away from the conflict.

Before Joss or I touched Arya, something hit him, taking him down. In the split second before he hit the floor, it appeared to be a blob of brown. Then Arya crashed to the floor, with Isa and Ric across his back. They grasped his arms, pulling them behind his back, and Ric affixed something to them. Then they dragged him to his feet.

V'Ov went completely still, staring statue-like at the man for several seconds. Then she moved, her body almost rippling as she relaxed. "You are not Hari Arya."

Arya's eyes burned in his face, then his features seemed to melt. "No, I am not." His face changed, like clay being remolded by a sculptor. His skin lightened, his hair shifted and grew, becoming a curly, graying shag, softening his pointed chin and prominent nose.

I glanced at Joss. "He must have a programmable visual disruption device."

"How would an Earther get a PVD?" Joss straightened, his head thudding dully against the ceiling. He hunched his shoulders and reached for Arya. "We should take him back to the embassy."

"Someone should search him first. If he really has a bomb…"

Ric held up a hand. "We searched. He is clean."

"Searched when?" Joss moved closer. "You just grabbed him. I didn't see you search!"

V'Ov lifted a hand, cutting him off. "No search is necessary. Ricmond of the Western Seas is correct. There are no explosives. And this is not Mr. Arya."

"But he—"

"This is not a human. He is a Gothodi—an isolationist from the Gothod region—impersonating a human."

We all stared at the little man in the middle of the room. He stood quietly between Isa and Ric, his hands behind his back. With his PVD turned off, he looked shorter and even slighter than Arya had. His graying curls hung around the pointed face, giving him a kind of elfin appearance.

"Give me his grav belt. That technology is not cleared for Darenti use. Or accused terrorists." While Isa fumbled with the buckle, I turned to V'Ov. "If he's a Darenti, how did he get a Programmable Visual Disrupter? Do you have those?"

She blinked, the rest of her face still. Then her eyebrow went up, looking weirdly separate from the rest of her face. "Do you refer to the ability to change his appearance? We have that capability." She turned to Isa and Ric. "Take him away. I will deal with him later."

"Wait." Tiah slid off her chair. "He is not Darenti. Hari Arya traveled with me from Earth. I have a responsibility to my... planet-mate, to ensure he is returned home for disciplinary action. I can't allow you to take him away to some unknown location to be 'dealt with' unless you can prove he is indeed Darenti."

The five Darenti looked at each other, and I got the feeling they were communicating. According to our records, they didn't have comm technology like ours, but perhaps those records were wrong? As Zina had pointed out, we knew so little about the Darenti. After a long moment, V'Ov turned to Tiah. "If we can find the real Hari Arya, will that satisfy you?"

Tiah thought for a moment. "I do not relinquish control over this being at this time. If and when we locate Hari Arya, we will revisit the decision."

"Did Tiah go to law school?" Joss asked through the private call.

I rubbed the back of my neck. "What's law school?"

V'Ov bowed. "That is satisfactory. I understand and acknowledge your concerns. I would not leave one I believed to be Darenti in the control of humans." Her chair lowered, and she stood, gesturing for Isa and Ric to precede her. "I suggest we take him to your embassy."

The two Darenti guided Arya out of the room, with V'Ov in their wake. Glaucia and Danny disappeared down the hall as we humans followed the other Darenti down the stairs. I didn't know about the others, but my brain was having trouble processing what had just happened. A human delegate—an Earther human—tried to blow up the leader of the Darenti delegation but turned out to be a Darenti separatist? I reactivated the private chat. "Is that why Arya didn't have an implant? Because he's a Darenti?"

Tiah shook her head. "The real Arya is human. It was his decision to forgo the implant."

"If this Arya is an imposter, that's true. But maybe he refused the implant because he's Darenti? Audio implants require installation. A doctor would have noticed the physiological differences," Zina said as we exited the building. "That is one area the Darenti have refused to exchange information on. We know nothing about their physiology. We've tried scanning them, but nothing registers. I suspect they know more about us than we do about them."

Zina shook her head. "Tiah and I met Hari Arya on Earth and traveled here with him."

Tiah nodded in agreement.

We paused on the front step. The drones swooped down, buzzing around us like mosquitos. Glaucia hurried out a few seconds later, with a pair of larger Darenti carrying a spindly golden structure between them. They were the biggest of their species that I had seen—each of them well over a meter tall, with broad shoulders and strong arms. They lowered the stretcher-like thing to hip level, and V'Ov sat on it. She twisted around and folded her body, sitting almost—but not quite—cross-legged. The two large Darenti lifted the litter to rest on their shoulders and carried her off the step.

I cast a speculative look at the Darenti. Being the highest seemed to be important to her. After a quick, silent conference, we set our grav belts to five centimeters—so our toes barely cleared the mud, but our heads would be lower than V'Ov's.

The other Darenti—and Arya—slogged along the muddy path. We followed behind the litter, with Glaucia bringing up the rear. About halfway back to the base, a rustling in the foliage beside the road caught my attention. I put a hand on my stunner and noticed Joss doing the same. The rustling got louder, and spiky leaves just above head height quivered as if something were forcing through. The litter bearers stomped past, not bothering to look. Perhaps this was a common animal on Darenti?

As I came even with the quivering leaves, a little blue head poked through. Liam dropped his jaw in a sair-glider grin and launched himself through the foliage to land on my shoulder.

"Where have you been?" I rubbed my cheek against his head. "I know you can take care of yourself, but this is an unknown planet. I wish you wouldn't disappear like that."

He cheeped at me, his tone conciliatory, then draped himself over my shoulder again. A drone did a flyby. Liam's head popped up, his dark eyes following the tiny flying camera until it buzzed away.

Ambassador Slovenska met us at the front gate with a dozen CEC security personnel ranged behind her. Zina must have called ahead. Or the Darenti had. I gave myself a mental head slap—I should have reported the unusual situation to Major Featherstoke as soon as it happened. I glanced at Joss.

"Oops." Joss's lips twitched as the comment came through my audio. "I guess we shoulda called."

The litter bearers lowered their burden, and V'Ov stepped to the plasphalt pad. The drones swarmed above her head.

Slovenska hurried through the gate and bowed to V'Ov. "Dar Demokritos, I can—"

V'Ov cut her off. "You have been informed of the incident. This person is Darenti, although he masqueraded as a human. We would deal with his threats ourselves, but your Representative Tiah of the Dome demanded we prove he is Darenti, not human. We cannot do that—as you know the treaty forbids physical examination of the other species."

Slovenska's gaze traveled over the group, pausing on me longer than I liked. When her eyes returned to V'Ov, she nodded. "I understand the treaty and will not suggest a remedy that runs counter to it. Has the suspect been searched?"

I shot a look at Joss and flicked on a private call. "Why didn't we search him? Ric and V'Ov said we didn't need to, and we just—what, gave up?"

The puzzled look on Joss's face must have mirrored my own. "It's like I forgot it was a thing? I was going to, then they said we didn't need to… and I believed them."

I glanced at Tiah and Zina, but they were focused on V'Ov and the ambassador. The matter of the search seemed to have been passed over. I'd have to ask Zina what I'd missed.

"Very well." V'Ov swept toward the gate, and Slovenska fell in beside her. "Thank you for welcoming us to your base. This being will be held in your facility until his identity is confirmed."

The two leaders marched into the facility, with the rest of us falling in behind. Isa and Ric followed a young security guard to the support building. There was a small cell in the security office—no doubt that was their destination.

As the others went inside, I grabbed Joss's arm and pulled him aside. "What are we going to say when the ambassador asks why we didn't search him?"

"I don't know." Joss ran a hand over his face. "I can see my career flashing before my eyes."

My audio implant pinged, and I connected to the call. "Kassis."

The readout indicated a three-way call had been initiated by the ambassador's aide and included Joss. "Lieutenants, report to my office."

CHAPTER SIX

Joss and I stood at attention before Major Featherstoke and Major James, the ambassador's aide.

Featherstoke waved at the chairs in the waiting area of the ambassador's office. "At ease. Take a seat. This meeting is being recorded." He gestured to a drone hovering in the corner. This one was larger than the news drones and bore a very obvious CEC shield. "That's ours—media aren't allowed in here. What happened over there?"

Joss and I exchanged a look. When I opened my mouth, he nodded for me to answer. I turned to the two majors. "Hari Arya threatened to blow us up. Two of the Darenti, Ricmond of the Western Seas and Isa—Isa-something—"

James raised an eyebrow. "Isaula Theomtimus?"

I snapped my fingers. "Yes. Isaula Theomtimus and Ricmond took him down before Lieutenant Torres and I could respond. They're fast, sir. Ricmond searched the assailant but found no threats." I held my breath, waiting for the outburst.

It never came. "And you insisted on bringing Arya back to the human compound?" James made a note in a file on his holo-ring.

"That was Tiah." Joss fidgeted in his seat. "The Darenti wanted to take him away—they said he was one of theirs. But Tiah insisted he come back here because they couldn't offer any proof he wasn't human. How can you tell human from Darenti?"

"Most of the time, our size gives us away." The burly Featherstoke gestured to his own body then held out a hand, measuring about a meter from the floor. "They're tiny."

"Arya is short for a human male but taller than any Darenti I've seen yet." Joss raised his eyebrows, looking to me to confirm.

I nodded. "Agreed. But when he turned off his PVD, he seemed to shrink. I didn't know those things could make you look bigger."

James's hand froze, mid-swipe. "PVD? No one said anything about a PVD."

"V'Ov said it was their tech, not ours." I rubbed my forehead. We'd taken Dar Demokritos at her word on so many things. How had we been so gullible?

The aide grunted and went back to his file. "If the Dar said it was their tech, it must have been."

I glanced at Featherstoke. "We take her word for it?"

"They don't lie." James shut down his file. "Deceit is a foreign concept to them."

Joss tapped his finger on the chair arm. "Then Arya can't be Darenti because he lied about having a bomb."

"Wouldn't pretending to be someone else be considered deceit, too? And V'Ov said they have the PVD capability—which is also deceitful." I rubbed my forehead again. "Everything about this situation contradicts the idea that they don't lie."

James stood. "That's above my paygrade. I'll make sure the ambassador sees this meeting vid. You're dismissed."

"She doesn't want to talk to us?" I asked in disbelief.

Joss made a frightened face at me and gave a tiny head shake.

The aide cleared his throat. "She doesn't have time—that's my job. And I think we've got enough. I can always call you if something comes up. Not like you're going to leave." He laughed at his own joke. "Why, is there something you want to tell her?"

I sucked in a breath, but Joss didn't hesitate. "No, sir. We're good."

"Excellent. You're off duty until tomorrow." James waved at the door, then stalked to his desk. Featherstoke gave each of us a brief nod and hurried out the door.

Joss and I exchanged a look and followed the major. As the older man disappeared down the stairs, Joss punched my shoulder lightly. "Time to hit the gym."

I rolled my eyes. Joss would live in the gym if he could. "Is there one?"

"This is the CEC. There's always a gym. Back of the support building." He jutted a thumb over his shoulder. "You coming?"

"I think I'll go for a run instead. I don't want to be cooped up in a building."

We hurried to the Q to change clothes. I waved to Joss, then checked the virtu-board for advisories. A couple of jogging paths had been laid out by the embassy staff, so I pulled up an easy five klick run and headed out. Liam flew to my arm as I left the building. A news drone hovered over my shoulder for a few minutes, then buzzed away. A junior officer taking a run was not newsworthy—especially since they had a juicy story to follow.

The guards at the gate waved me through. "Be back before sundown!" one called.

I flashed a thumbs-up as I pounded down the trail outside the compound. I'd read the warning on the virtu-board. Thanks to the lack of moon, nights on Darenti were dark. The Darenti recommended staying within the force shield to avoid fierce nocturnal predators. "Reminds me of Saha."

Liam grunted in apparent agreement, then launched himself from my shoulder. The thick, damp atmosphere of Darenti seemed to give him more lift than usual—he soared above me like a bird. We made our way around the base, then turned onto a tunnel-like path leading away from the compound. After a few meters, the path widened and traveled beside a small stream. Shredded wood covered the surface, protecting my running shoes from the mud beneath. Light filtered through the canopy of blue-green fronds overhead, leaving us in a thin twilight.

About a klick from the base, the path curved away from the stream and entered a wide clearing. Low-growing blue foliage covered the ground in a thick carpet, except where the sawdust-covered path cut through. The clouds overhead broke as I jogged into the open area, illuminating the circle with faint sunlight. The sun seemed to burn through some of the thick, misty air and warmed my face.

As I reached the center of the clearing, Liam landed on my shoulder and chirped—the sound he usually made when we encountered a friend. But the clearing was empty.

Then it wasn't.

A pair of Darenti stood on the path at the far side of the little meadow. They wore dark uniforms that looked subtly different from Ric's and Danny's. Based on body shape, they appeared to be one male and one female. The man wore three blue stars on his collar, and the woman had two green crescents.

I slowed as I approached, but they didn't move out of my way. I stopped a few meters from them and nodded. "Greetings."

"Greetings." They spoke together, but just out of sync, so the word echoed.

The three of us looked at each other, but no one spoke again. Liam chirped, then pushed off my shoulder and soared across the intervening space to land at the strangers' feet. He chirped again, as if speaking to them.

The man stared at Liam for a moment, then looked at me. "You are the progeny of *the* Nate Kassis."

"Yes," I said slowly. "I'm Siti Kassis. May I have your name?"

"You may call me Gara." The woman gestured to her companion. "This is Verdat."

"Did you meet my father?" He had discovered the Darenti over a hundred years ago—if they knew him, they were old.

"Father?" Verdat repeated. "Does that not mean direct progenitor?" At my blank look, he went on. "The being who sired you, rather than—" He moved his hand in a backward stair-step fashion. "You are young. We did not think humans lived that long."

"We live about a hundred and fifty years." I considered explaining that my appearance didn't necessarily correspond to my age—thanks to rejuvenation treatments, many people looked to be in their middle twenties who were actually much older. My reason was more common in the CEC.

"And, yes, he is my direct progenitor. CEC travel used to require decades in deep sleep."

The creature nodded, as if he understood this term. "Welcome to Darenti, Siti Kassis. We need your help."

"My help? Is someone injured?" I turned in a circle but saw no one else. "No? Something else, then?"

"We need you to save the Darenti." Verdat stepped off the path into the lush blue clover. The sunlight through the mist created a halo effect around his body that dazzled my eyes.

I held up a hand to try to minimize the glare, but the mist dispersed the sunlight, and the bright aura filled the clearing. "Save the Darenti? Don't tell me I'm the chosen one." I tried for sarcasm, but it came out as a plea.

"You're the chosen one." Verdat nodded, as if this were a normal conversation to have with a new acquaintance. "We chose you because we trust the daughter of Nate Kassis. He has kept our secrets." He moved closer.

"Secrets?" I took a step back. With their tiny stature, the Darenti weren't physically threatening, but something about the combination of matter-of-fact voice and over-the-top word choice—not to mention the weird glowing effect of the sunlight through the mist—put me on edge. I toggled my audio implant and put a call through to Joss.

It went to voice mail, of course. He never answered when he was in the gym. "You got Caveman Torres. I'm busy flyin' or workin' out. Leave a message."

"It's Siti. I'm running—just met some weird Darenti named Verdat and Gara."

As I left my subvocal message, Verdat moved closer. "Are you communicating with your tribe? That is not allowed." His arm seemed to stretch —long enough that he could touch my head.

I stumbled back, hitting a boulder I didn't remember. I glanced over my shoulder. Not a boulder, but Gara. Her legs seemed to have merged into the ground in a single, immovable lump, stopping me. Her arms came out, blocking me on either side.

"I need some help, Joss! I'm—" Verdat's fingers pressed against my temple, and the words drained out of my head. I could still think them, but something kept me from articulating them.

"We need your silence. Like your father." Verdat's other hand pressed against the right side of my face, and a sizzle passed through my brain from one side to the other. It didn't hurt, but my audio implant went cold. Had he shorted it out? His hands left my head.

I pulled away from the two Darenti, backing until I could see both of them. "What did you do? What do you want?" My hand drifted toward my stunner, but I felt nothing.

I looked down. CEC regulation required explorers to wear defensive weapons whenever we went outside the base on an unsecured planet like Darenti. My belt held a field-med device and a water pac, but the stunner was missing. "Where's my stunner?"

Liam chittered. He perched on the remains of a fallen tree near the edge of the clearing, with my stunner beside him. His paws waved as he chattered, as if explaining that he'd disarmed me. Despite his complete lack of comprehensible speech, I got the impression he wanted me to help these Darenti. That they wouldn't hurt me, and I could save the day.

That I was, in fact, the chosen one.

Traitor.

"Please, come with us." Gara took my arm and urged me across the blue field, moving perpendicular to the path.

I considered running—surely, the Darenti's short legs would allow me to outdistance them easily. For some reason, that seemed like a bad idea. I should go with Gara and Verdat and find out what they wanted. Then I could report back to the ambassador.

It never occurred to me that taking instructions from a sair-glider was not a great plan. Or that disappearing into the jungle with an unknown group of aliens was against protocol. That all of this was a really stupid idea.

CHAPTER SEVEN

GARA AND VERDAT led me to the edge of the clearing. They pushed aside some of the thick, curly fronds, revealing a narrow path. I had to double over to avoid the foliage above the track, since it had only been cleared a meter above the ground. Perfect for the tiny Darenti, but not so great for a human.

Tall blue-green shafts rose from the ground, with curly fronds poking out at all angles. Thick vines wove between these shafts, forming impenetrable walls on either side. The vines weren't cut—they seemed to have been woven away from the path, creating a tunnel with a vine ceiling and walls. In places, the path curved around wider shafts of the tree-like spikes that bore the huge curly leaves.

As we walked, the path widened, and the headspace increased until I only had to duck when we encountered a particularly thick patch of jungle. Liam followed, jumping from branch to vine, clearly enjoying the excursion.

"How far are we going?" I pushed aside a frond that drooped across the path and ducked under the half-meter thick vine behind it.

"Far." Verdat's short legs moved quickly along the muddy trail. "We have transport waiting."

"Transport?" None of the reports I'd read had mentioned transportation. As far as I knew, the Darenti walked everywhere.

Which, now that I thought about it, didn't make a lot of sense. We had met Darenti from all over the planet. Ric came from the Western Seas. Danny represented the Drusa Mountains. Both those locations were thousands of klicks from here. Had they really walked that far on their tiny legs? Sure, it was possible, but was it likely?

The tunnel of foliage widened into a small glade on the edge of a wide river. A thick blue-gray log floated near the edge. I looked closer—it was a boat, hewn from a single tree bole, like an enormous canoe.

Glaucia Ivengard had said she hailed from the western continent which implied some kind of ocean travel. On a planet this wet, I should have expected a boat. But none of the reports had mentioned them. As Zina had pointed out, those reports seemed to leave out a lot of details.

Small vines rose from the interior of the canoe, creating a living canopy over the open top, with an arched gap near the center. Gara gestured toward that space. "Please, after you."

Liam raced across the clearing and leapt into the boat. I lifted a leg and climbed over the side, ducking under the overhanging leaves. Inside, the roof arched high enough for me to stand upright, with the lowest leaves brushing my head.

Five benches spanned the width of the craft, apparently carved from the original tree. Gara followed me into the boat and indicated I should sit on the center bench. She and Verdat then took places on the bench behind me. Liam jumped to my shoulder, chirping softly in my ear, as if reassuring me this excursion was completely reasonable. Strangely, I felt no concern over leaving the base without alerting my superiors.

The boat swayed under my rear end. I leaned down to peek through the doorway as we pulled away from the shore. I hadn't seen anyone outside the boat, nor had I noticed whether it had been tied to anything. But somehow, we were underway.

The wind rattled through the leafy cover, creating a pleasant white noise. I drooped on my bench, trying to stay alert but failing miserably. After a while, Gara appeared at my side. "You are tired. Sleep. It is a long journey." She handed me a length of thin material.

The variegated green fabric had a nubby texture, like rough silk. I placed the folded bundle on the bench like a pillow, lay on my side, and went to sleep.

WHEN I WOKE, it was dark. The rushing of water underscored the white noise of the canopy, and the boat shook as we sailed through rougher water. I peered through the door but could see nothing.

I rolled onto my back and stared at the leaves overhead. Some of them glowed softly, providing dim illumination. Was that a natural phenomenon? I didn't recall any reports of glowing foliage. In fact, I didn't remember any reports beyond a cursory description of the major plants. We'd supposedly had access to all available exploratory data.

The dearth of information available about Darenti had never been so obvious to me. How could we have had people on this planet for a hundred years and know so little about it? And why had no one questioned the lack of data? We were the *Explorer* Corps. Our mission was to learn about other planets. It was as if we'd decided since Darenti was occupied, it was none of our business.

But we had a base there. For over a century, CEC personnel had lived and worked above the planet, taking annual excursions to the surface. If they had so little information about the world, what had they been doing?

My mind raced. When I was a cadet, we'd uncovered a gang stealing valuable elements from Sarvo Six—a gang run by members of the CEC leadership. My father had made it his mission to clear out the corruption in the Corps, and I thought he'd succeeded. Maybe Darenti had fallen through the cracks? Were members of the CEC leadership hiding something? And if so, why had they allowed us access to the planet now—in such a public way?

My head came up. Public. The news drones had dogged my steps from the moment I landed—they hadn't followed me on my jog, but maybe they'd picked up the unusual boat. Were they watching now as I floated downriver with my Darenti crew on what felt like a secret mission?

I scanned the interior of the boat. Liam slept in a nest of fabric on the floor near my bench. Gara dozed on the bench at the rear of the boat. No drones were visible. I flicked my holo-ring and did a quick scan—no electronic emissions within range—none at all. No holo-rings, no satellites, no shuttle craft or ships. Even the small space station that orbited the planet didn't register. Was my ring broken? I flicked the VidTube icon and got nothing. I was completely off the grid.

I rolled up to a seated position. Behind me, Gara startled, then went back to sleep. Liam snored softly by my feet. Water lapped against the boat—soft splashing that matched the lateral roll of the craft.

"Where's Verdat?" I swung around to face Gara. "Did we drop him off somewhere?" Could I have slept through a stop?

Gara blinked at me, her eyes large in her small face. She lifted a hand and pointed past me. "He's there."

I spun around. Verdat sat on the front bench. I squinted through the darkness. Was he wet? "Were you swimming?"

He shook himself, like Liam did after a dip, water flying from his clothing. The cold spray splattered across my face. "Swimming?"

"In the water?" I mimed diving and swimming. "Why are you wet?"

"I help moving the boat."

"Help moving—you were pushing? But we were going downstream. Why do you need to push the boat?" I scrambled to the door. The boat tilted as my weight shifted the center of gravity, and water splashed through the opening.

"Please, sit." Gara scrambled to the far side of her bench, providing a counterbalance that offset my weight very little.

With a grumble, I returned to my seat. Gara did the same, and the boat stabilized. I glanced at Verdat, but he'd disappeared again. Muttering under my breath, I activated my grav belt and slowly lifted a few centimeters above the bench. Pulling my feet up, I moved toward the door.

"Where are you going?" Gara squeaked. "Do not leave the boat. We are far to sea. You will be lost."

"We're at sea?" Panic squeezed my lungs. How had we gotten this far? The base was hundreds of klicks from the sea. "Where are we going?" I set a grav belt tether to the center of the ship with a five-klick radius. If I flew away from the boat, the tether would allow me to find it again, but if it sank, the tether was long enough that it wouldn't drag me under. Then I moved to the door again.

A thin line of light glowed along the horizon. The sky there had lightened to gray, although it was still completely black overhead. The usual thick cloud cover dissipated the light of the rising sun.

The sea was calm. Without a moon, this planet had no tides, which decreased the volatility of the ocean. Weather patterns were stable and predictable: heavy clouds, rain, and more rain. I lifted above the boat. Ten meters, then twenty. There was no land in sight. Even at fifty meters, I could see only ocean. And far ahead of us, a break in the cloud cover that allowed stars to peek through.

I returned to the boat. "Where are we going?" I dropped to my bench, and Liam scrambled up my leg to sit on my shoulder.

"We go south, then west. Our destination is Rovantu, the western continent. That is where we live." Gara waved around the boat, as if including a vast crew. "Where most Darenti live."

"Most Darenti? Why would the CEC build a base so far from the center of populations?"

Gara's shoulders rippled in an odd parody of a shrug. "That is where V'Ov told them to build. They speak only to V'Ov."

"Of course. V'Ov is your planetary representative."

"There is no representative on Darenti. Do you have a single person who speaks for all inhabitants of your planet?"

"Not—well, yes and no. We elect representatives to speak for us. That's why Tiah and Zina are here. And Mr. Arya. They represent Earth. And delegates from other planets are arriving soon."

"They are more than one." She crossed her arms.

"Yes."

"And 'elected' means what?"

"The people voted." I waved my arms in a circular motion, to imply a group. "They chose these people to represent them. Are you saying you did not choose V'Ov?"

She scowled. "V'Ov chose V'Ov. She rules the eastern continent. None question her authority. But she does not represent us." Her hand slapped against her chest.

I nodded. This arrangement sounded like some of the dictatorships we studied in history class, but I wasn't sure the CEC wanted to get involved in Darenti politics. Even if they did, it was well above my pay grade. "Why are we going to Rovantu?"

"You are the daughter of Nate Kassis. You will help us."

Uh oh. I cocked my head. "Help you how?"

"The Kassises are skilled explorers. You will help us find the Stone of Avora."

I rubbed my forehead. This was starting to sound like a video game. "And why do you need the Stone of Avora?"

"The one who possesses the Stone is the ruler of Darenti."

I groaned. Had I really been recruited to find a magical kingmaker? "How is that any better than V'Ov making herself the ruler?"

"It is a story, told to children. Not magic. But if we can find the Stone, it will encourage the people of Perista—the eastern continent—to defy V'Ov. She has convinced them she has the Stone. If we bring the real Stone back, they will not follow her. That will allow us to install a democratic government."

I gaped at Gara, then gave myself a mental head slap. Gara's command of Standard was excellent though stilted on occasion. But odd word choice didn't indicate inferior intellect.

"Why not just make one? Find a rock. Paint it gold. Add a few sparkles. Voila, Stone of Avora!" I raised both hands, lifting an imaginary rock.

Gara fixed me with a mocking glare. "This would not work. We see deception."

An image of Arya crossed my mind. "We've been told the Darenti don't lie—that you don't *understand* deception. But if Arya was a Darenti, then he was lying. And if he is human, V'Ov was lying."

Gara started nodding before I completed the thought. "We do not deceive because other Darenti know when deception occurs. If Arya—or V'Ov—deceived you, then other Darenti knew of this deception."

I sagged on my bench. If Arya was a Darenti, the others would have known. And if Arya had really had a bomb, they would have known. Surely, the guards would not have allowed him into V'Ov's office? If Arya was human, V'Ov had lied, and the others would have known. Either way, if what Gara said was true, V'Ov and her entire team had deceived us.

The question was, why?

CHAPTER EIGHT

I DOZED a good part of the morning—there's nothing more boring than a sea voyage inside a giant log. After sunrise, Verdat had returned to the boat, and Gara disappeared—presumably to "help moving the boat." Neither of them had explained that in greater detail. Verdat had shaken the water from his body and clothes, then curled up in the bow of the boat and gone to sleep. With no one to talk to, Liam and I had both caught up on our rest as well.

About mid-morning, I glimpsed the Rovantu coastline in the distance. The smudged gray line grew into a rocky, forbidding cliff, stretching as far as I could see. I lifted out of the boat to get a better view, but even at the grav belt's highest altitude, only rocky coastline and foliage-covered jungle met my eyes. Rovantu looked exactly like Perista as far as I could tell.

When I returned to the boat, Verdat offered me food. The small squares and circles topped with colorful slices of fruit looked very similar to the food served in the officers' mess yesterday. I ate everything Verdat offered, my stomach rumbling greedily. With land in sight, I risked finishing the water in my belt pac. Verdat offered me a fuzzy brown globe, about the size of both of my fists together. The top had been sliced off, and it was full of liquid. A quick sniff told me it was water.

As if sensing my concern, Liam scrambled down my arm and stuck his muzzle into the cup. When he straightened, his whiskers twitched, flicking a spray of water across my face. Sair-gliders had a built-in ability to avoid contaminated water—it was one of the reasons CEC explorers took them on missions. I considered testing it for additives—something my rudimentary med-kit could do—but since they obviously wanted to keep me alive, I decided to skip it.

"Would you like more food?" Verdat held out a wooden plate covered with more tiny morsels.

"Where did that come from?" I peered around him, but there was no evidence of food preparation. The fruit was fresh and juicy and the crispy pastry beneath crumbled easily, so these weren't travel rations. And I would swear that plate had been empty just a few minutes ago. Maybe they had an Autokich'n hidden somewhere in the boat? I peered under the seats but saw nothing.

"There is plenty, if you desire it." Verdat pushed the plate at me again.

"No, thanks, I'm good." I patted my stomach. "When do we land?"

Verdat whisked the plate away somewhere. "Soon." He stepped onto the front bench and reached up to the leafy canopy. His arms appeared to stretch again as he flipped the woven vines toward the stern, opening the front of the ship. "See—the coast approaches."

I stepped over the bench we had used as a table and stood beside him. Even standing on the seat, his head only reached my shoulder. I gripped the edge of the boat and stared toward land.

Rocky cliffs several hundred meters high towered above us, the gray stone blending into the gray sky. High cloud cover obscured the sun, leaving us in a shadowless, monochromatic world. There was no vegetation in sight from this angle, but the warm, damp air carried a whiff of growing things above the tang of salt water.

Waves splashed over a narrow gravel beach at the base of the cliffs. The boat surged forward and drove across the pebbles, grating loudly as we slowed. The cliff face loomed large, and we shuddered to a stop a few meters from the rocky wall.

"You may exit." Verdat seemed to compress, then sprang over the side, landing with a faint splash on the stony shore. I whistled to Liam, who scrambled up my back to his customary perch on my shoulder, then used my grav belt to lift over the side. A wash of foam drained away under my feet as I landed, and my holo-ring pinged.

I flicked it, bringing up an alert—my grav belt power was nearly depleted. Normally, it would have recharged during the morning, but the foliage of the boat's roof must have reduced the efficiency of my jacket's built-in solar panels.

I tipped my head back to gaze up the cliff. Climbing that without the belt would make for a long, strenuous afternoon. Of course, the Darenti had no grav belts, so they must have a way to ascend. I turned to Verdat. "How do we—"

Fourteen pairs of eyes blinked at me. And one trio. I stared at the Darenti gathered around my legs—the smallest one barely reached my knees and had a third eye in the middle of his—or her—forehead.

I stepped back in surprise. "Where did you all come from? Where's the boat?"

Gara circled around me, shooing the rest of the Darenti away. They dispersed like the foam under my shoes, seeming to disappear into the gravel.

I rubbed my eyes. Had I been hallucinating? Only Gara and Verdat stood on the beach with me. I gaped at them. "Where did the others go?"

"They have work to do." Gara started across the beach, the rocks grinding softly under her feet.

Another small wave washed up the shore, sending a mist of sea spray across my face. The constant ebb and flow of the water created a soft, rhythmical grate that flowed across my mind in a soothing wash. I shook my head, trying to focus. "There were others here—where did they go?"

Gara stopped and faced me. "There is much you do not know about Darenti. We are not what you see." She gestured to the beach behind me.

I turned. Verdat stood beside the boat—or rather part of the boat. As I watched, the craft I had crossed the ocean in—little more than an enormous carved log—shifted and split apart into a dozen rough blobs. Each of those reformed to become a small humanoid. One of them had three eyes. They stacked a small pile of items on the beach—the blanket, the plate, a wooden box.

I staggered against the cliff and dropped to my butt on the damp gravel. "What—was that—what?"

Gara squatted beside me, somehow transitioning from standing to sitting without the usual folding of legs. "We are not fixed."

Something in the way she said the word "fixed" made her meaning clear. The Darenti's physical forms were not constant. My mind tried to make sense of this idea but seemed to spin in an incoherent whirlpool. Not fixed.

"I will demonstrate." Her body seemed to melt into a lumpy brown puddle which transformed into a pile of small, round stones. In seconds, she disappeared into the beach.

"Are you still here?" I reached out a tentative hand but didn't dare touch the low mound of pebbles—how rude would it be to poke a finger into her ear or nose? "You're shape-shifters?"

Gara's face reformed beside me, gazing up from the flat pile. I swallowed hard, trying to convince my stomach the sight should not make me queasy. Then she extruded from the beach, reforming into the tiny humanoid I'd traveled with. "We can take on any shape required."

I sucked in a breath, and my stomach settled. "So, when you were helping to move the boat—you actually became part of it?" I rubbed my eyes again. This was going to take some time—and possibly some counseling—to get through.

She rocked her hand back and forth, in a very human gesture. "We become part of the boat and part of the water. I'm not sure I can explain in words. May I?" She reached toward my head.

I reared back. "May you what?"

"I can implant the understanding." She wiggled her fingers at me.

I held up both hands. "Like telepathy? No thanks. I'll just—I'm good. Hey, wait—is that why I'm here?" I did a mental review of the last few hours. I had been unusually cooperative when they essentially kidnapped me yesterday afternoon. My eyes narrowed. "When he touched my head—is that what Verdat was doing? Implanting a suggestion that I should come with you?"

Gara's eyes slid away from mine, and she nodded. "Yes. He was suggesting. We do not like to use this technique—it is something V'Ov uses on humans many times. We are not like her. But we needed you to come."

I jumped to my feet, backing away. "V'Ov has been using *Jed-eye* mind tricks on the humans? For how long? And to what end? I need to get back and warn them! How can we stop it?"

Gara held up a hand. "Please, we wish to stop, too. This is why we need the Stone of Avora. With the Stone, we will convince the Derenti of Perista to join with us. Then we will cease the deception of the humans."

I crossed my arms and stared down at the small woman. "You won't lie to each other, but you have no problem doing it to us."

"Not 'won't lie.' Can't lie. Just as Verdat was able to implant a suggestion in your mind, Darenti can see into the minds of others. We cannot hide an untruth from each other. This is why the Stone is important—it will destroy V'Ov's credibility. She believes she is doing what is best for the Darenti, but if we have the Stone, they will listen to us. And we can protect you."

"If you can't hide an untruth, how can she lie about having the stone? And how can you protect me from mind reading?" I shook my head. "Or from being influenced by your little tricks?"

"Both. I can show you how to protect yourself from unwelcome suggestions and incursions." She raised her hand to her own temple and wiggled the fingers. "We need a thin sheet of metal." She pressed her hands over her scalp.

I snorted. "You want me to make a tin foil hat."

Her head cocked as she considered, then she nodded. "Partially. Any conductive metal will work. Gold, silver, copper. And you don't need hat. Just here." She placed her fingers above her temples.

"Is this another mind trick? Convince me I'm protected so I won't realize I'm being controlled? I'm not sure how you expect me to trust anything you say."

"We will create a protection device, and you will test it." She picked up a handful of rocks. "Do you have any metal?"

I patted my belt. The grav belt had metal components, but I wasn't going to cannibalize it. My stunner contained metal, but it was gone. My med kit might be necessary. Likewise, my holo-ring. I shook my head. "I knew I should have brought snacks."

Gara chuckled. "Because human food has metal in the wrapper? Very good. But in the absence of snacks, we must improvise." She sifted the rocks through her hands, letting most of them fall back onto the beach. Selecting one of the stones in her palm, she fingered it, then handed it to me. As she worked, the other Darenti began imitating her movements, each of them coming forward to deposit a pebble in my palm from time to time.

They continued to work, picking out rocks and adding them to the small pile in my hand. After a while, I stripped off my jacket and deposited the stones on it. None of the Darenti said anything, so I stretched, then walked up the beach.

A few meters away, a small stack sat against the cliff face—items left from the boat, including the blanket I'd used as a pillow and the plate on which Verdat had served my breakfast. These things sat on a small wooden box that must have held the food. On top was my weapon. I checked the charge and pushed it back into its holster.

"Siti Kassis!" Verdat stood over Gara, beckoning me. The other Darenti sat around them, still sifting rocks.

I jogged across the shifting stones. "Yes?"

"We have enough." Verdat scooped a few of the rocks from my jacket and gestured for the others to do the same. Each of them took a few and closed their hands around them. They shut their eyes and pressed their hands together.

After a few minutes, Gara opened her hands and blew on the contents. Dust billowed from her hand and sifted through her fingers, leaving a pile of metallic flakes. She stared at these, and they seemed to liquify, melt together, and reform into a small blob.

Verdat took the bit of metal and collected similar pieces from the others. He closed his hands around them and squeezed again. Then he opened his hand to reveal a thin, rough oblong about two centimeters long. "That will work. Do you have something to hold this to your head?"

"Does it have to press against the skin?" I took the blob and pressed it to my cheek. "Or just dangle?" I demonstrated, holding the oblong from one end.

"Either will work." Gara gestured toward my jacket. "Perhaps a piece of fabric? We can design something more refined when we get to the city."

I looked up, my coat hanging limp in my hand. "There's a city?"

CHAPTER NINE

THE DARENTI LED me to a cleft in the cliff wall, where the stones had broken to form a natural staircase. The steps were uneven, ranging from a half meter to a little over double that height, and the Darenti's legs stretched and contracted to accommodate. I climbed with them, saving my grav belt's power. I had connected it to the charging panels in my jacket, but I wasn't confident in the material's ability to recharge in the shadows from the cliff.

Before we'd left the beach, I had woven the pieces of metal into the braids at my temples and secured them with some thread from the emergency repair kit I carried in my belt. I considered duct tape but didn't want bald spots when I removed them.

As we climbed, Gara and Verdat attempted to prove the hair ornaments were protecting me, but there was no way to prove their attempts to infiltrate my mind were real. Before long, the climb made talking difficult. The crevice widened as we rose, and a rustle of leaves beckoned us onward. A faint gurgling reached my ears, but if there was water, the arid stones hid it. A breeze wafted through the cleft, bringing earthy scents from above.

More clouds rolled in as the sun reached its zenith, a faint bright spot in the overcast sky the only indication of time passing. A thin fog settled into the gorge. The gray seemed to press on my mind, leaving me dull and depressed. I stumbled up the steps, now only a few centimeters each, but the uneven heights required me to keep my eyes on my feet.

Another little breeze ruffled my hair, and I stopped for a breather. As I watched, the mist parted, revealing a wider valley at the top of the stone steps. Behind us, the rock dropped away to the shore, and the sea stretched to the horizon. Ahead, low, greenish-blue shrubs covered the ground and sides of the gorge and steep hills that formed the sides of the valley. Tall trees speared into the mist, with vines dripping from their broad branches. Huge curly fronds—similar to those on the northern continent but even larger—waved from the branches under a lacy drapery of vines.

I reached for my water pac, then remembered I'd finished it in the boat. "Where's this city you're talking about? We've found no evidence of a city on Darenti."

"The city is still some distance." Gara held out a hand. "I will get you water."

I handed her the empty water pac. She stepped off the path, her feet barely ruffling the mossy plants covering the rocky ground. A trail of dark blue vegetation rose up the side of a two-meter-high block of stone. Gara stretched, her body becoming thinner as she grew taller until she resembled a piece of taffy. Liam jumped from my shoulder and scrambled up Gara's back, disappearing over the top of the stone. Gara dipped the water pac below the top of the block, then removed it and contracted to her former height.

I took the pac—it was full of water. "Is there a pool up there?"

"Yes, built for refreshment." She gestured broadly, and the horde of Darenti accompanying us surrounded the block. They all stretched out, their heads disappearing as they leaned over the stone. When they pulled back, water flew from their hair.

Three smaller Darenti elongated but could not stretch tall enough to reach the pool. Once the larger ones had drunk, they lifted the smaller ones.

Except they didn't really lift them. The small ones stretched out to their full length, then grabbed onto the bigger ones. Then they compressed again, their feet leaving the ground and springing up like a rubber band released from tension. They settled their feet in the new location—the taller creatures' hips or shoulders—and stretched upward again to disappear over the top. It was kind of creepy.

After my water filtration sequence ran, I drank, and Gara refilled my pac a second time. Then we continued into the valley. Before long, the thick foliage closed in over our heads, leaving us in a dim jungle similar to that on the northern continent. The thick weave of vines and trees hid the valley walls from us, but the path continued at a gentle upward slope.

Unlike the mostly silent jungle around the base, our ears were assaulted by chittering, whistles, slithering, and the occasional rumbling roar. "Are any of those animals dangerous?"

Gara tilted her head to one side and rocked her hand in a good imitation of the human gesture. "They are afraid of us. You are unknown, so…"

I got the message—stay with the Darenti if I didn't want to be lunch. Was this more fabrication or truth? I wasn't ready to find out.

Liam rode on my shoulder for a while, then launched himself into the foliage. He reappeared at intervals, chattering about what he'd seen, then disappearing again. Over the eight years we'd been together, I'd learned to trust the glider's ability to take care of himself. Other explorers didn't give their gliders as much freedom, but Liam seemed to be much smarter than average.

"How far is the city? And why didn't we know it existed?" CEC satellites orbited the planet, observing weather patterns, animal migrations, and more. Thousands of small settlements had been documented but no urban centers.

"It is protected." Gara raised her arms in an arc over her head.

"By your *Jed-eye* mind tricks?"

"I do not understand '*Jed-eye*.' May I?" Her hand stretched toward my temple.

I held up a hand and stumbled to the far side of the wide path. "No. '*Jed-eye* mind tricks' is a saying I picked up on Earth—I'm not sure where it came from, but it means controlling others' thoughts. Like you do."

"Ah, so. No, the city is protected physically, not mentally. Although we do not speak of it to humans." She grinned. "Except you."

"Yeah, why is that again? And don't tell me I'm the chosen one."

"Is that another Earth saying? Because we *have* chosen you. Your father knew one of our secrets, but he did not share it. Now you know another, and we trust you to keep it." She held up a finger. "Without *Jed-eye* mind tricks."

My hand strayed to the metal woven into my braids. "You pick up our figures of speech way too easily. I don't think these things are working."

"My ability to understand humans is one of the reasons I was the chosen one" —she gave me a wicked grin— "for this mission."

"The mission to get the Stone of Avalon? Or to grab the human?"

"Avora, not Avalon. And my mission is to interact with the humans. I have been working at the base for a long time. But when you arrived, we decided I should contact the daughter of Nate Kassis."

"Humans have been coming to Darenti for a hundred years. Why did you wait so long? Or is this whole V'Ov thing a new deal?" I watched her carefully to see if she understood my questions. Even after "a long time" working with humans, she might not understand human idioms. Unless she could still read my mind.

"V'Ov is not new." Her twinkling eyes made me think she knew I was trying to test her abilities. "Did your CEC not provide the historical background for Darenti?"

I rubbed my arm. "Ouch. You don't pull any punches."

Her brows drew down. "I did not punch you." Real misunderstanding or faked?

"Not physically." I'd let her figure that one out. "The CEC provided a brief overview. The Darenti were discovered a hundred and seven years ago by my father. The CEC built a station here. Every year, the ambassador comes down to meet with the Darenti leader. Over the last century, there have been many human ambassadors to Darenti. In recent years, your people have asked to see the rest of the Commonwealth, so this meeting is the beginning of negotiations to discuss off-planet travel."

A tiny smile crossed Gara's face. "That is indeed very brief. During that same time, there has been only one Darenti 'leader.' V'Ov. In the beginning, the council selected her to be our speaker—with the understanding that she would answer to them. Over the years, she has refused to relinquish the position and has stopped deferring to the council. She is the one who has requested off-planet travel. And she wishes to control that travel."

"Why hasn't she simply used her *Jed-eye* mind tricks to convince the ambassador?" I stopped to take a drink. I offered my pac to Gara, but she declined.

"Some of us are better at those than others. It is not V'Ov's primary skill. She requires direct physical contact for a prolonged period to bend another's will. Which may be why she has developed her skill at deception."

"Why haven't the other Darenti outed her to the human ambassador?"

"Outed?"

"Told the truth. Undeceived. Clarified."

"Ah. We have tried." She looked away, as though bewildered. "The humans trust only V'Ov. And she has replaced most of the Darenti staff with her own supporters. They keep us away from the humans—and influence them on her behalf. I have managed to stay—only because I understood how to hide my inner thoughts from her inquisitors." She tapped her temple, and for the first time, I noticed a glint of metal. It seemed to be embedded in her skull. As I stared, her skin closed over it.

Shape-shifters. I suppressed a shudder.

"Are you wearing the same protections I am?" My fingers strayed to the metal in my hair.

"I am. That's how I know they work. I am a strong messenger—that's what we call those who can implant ideas—as is Verdat. Most strong messengers do not support V'Ov because we can read her intentions. She doesn't trust us because we can hide our thoughts from them." She tapped her temple. "The talismans protect us, so we need not be on guard at all times."

We continued in silence for a while, walking side by side up the dim path. There was a lot to understand. Aliens with the ability to implant ideas in human minds was the stuff of fantasy. Or horror. What kind of havoc would they wreak if they were allowed into the wider galaxy? And shape-shifters who could implant ideas were even more terrifying.

"What about this shape-shifting ability? Why didn't we know about it?"

"This was the secret your father protected. He saved Lei-hawm and his tribe from a mudslide. He was the first human our people had encountered, and we took on his shape."

"What is your natural shape?" I ducked under a low-hanging branch.

"We don't have a 'natural' shape." She paused for a second, then continued. "I suppose 'formless blob' would be a good description. Young Darenti choose a shape which pleases them. Some may change shape frequently, but most maintain a shape for many years, shifting only for expedience."

I pointed my thumb over my shoulder. "Like getting the water."

"Exactly." She nodded and stretched out her hand. Her fingers fused and flattened into a paddle, then reformed into a cup, and she mimed scooping up water. Then her fingers uncurled into a normal-looking hand.

"Is it painful?"

"Not at all. But change requires energy, so older Darenti tend to maintain a single configuration, often for most of our lifetime. This one is not the most efficient, but it is not bad. And my mission required me to appear humanoid."

"Is that V'Ov's requirement?"

"It is the will of the Darenti. We all recognize the usefulness of this form." Gara glanced at the path ahead, and at the sky. "We'll be at the city soon. Are you hungry?"

I looked over the small figure, then at the others. "Where would you find food? I don't see anyone carrying it."

"We can make food as we made your talismans." She pointed to her own head. "It requires only the appropriate materials." She waved at the landscape. "Any of these plants can be reformed to suitable food. If you wish?"

I held up both hands. "No, I'm good." This explained the Darenti chefs at the base and how Verdat had fed me on the ship. Presumably, his box had held the raw materials. Or maybe he'd pulled something from the sea. I was probably better off not speculating.

A few minutes later, the tunnel of green that had surrounded us since we left the stone steps fell away. We stood at the top of another rocky cliff, staring down at a wide, fertile valley. Greenish-blue plants with wide leaves covered the floor and climbed the steep sides, merging with the jungle at the top.

Before us, a narrow, uneven stone staircase led down the side of the cliff to the valley. Our companions scrambled over the edge and down the steps. In places, it looked barely wide enough to hold a single small Darenti. My comparatively big feet would hang off the edges. I checked my grav belt charge. Despite the jungle, my panels had managed to bring the power reserve back to fifty-seven percent. Enough to drop safely to the base of the cliff.

"Would you mind if I meet you at the bottom?" I tapped my belt controls. "That path doesn't look—" I stared, aghast, as one of the Derenti changed his mind and started back up the steps, stretching over and around those coming down.

Gara chuckled—at least I think it was a laugh. The rumble started in her belly and worked its way up her body in a kind of wave, erupting from her mouth as a low grinding. "Or I could implant the idea in your head that the way is safe?"

"You can do—never mind, of course you can. And, no, thank you. I'd rather *be* safe than think I am."

"Stay close to the cliff. There are aerial predators who might think you look tasty. We shall meet you at the bottom." She pointed down and to the right. "The back-and forth ends below the tree line, and the path goes that way."

I started to lean over the edge to look but knowing my grav belt wasn't yet engaged gave me vertigo. "I'll find you." I whistled to Liam, and the little glider jumped to my shoulder. With a wave to Gara, I tapped the controls and stepped off the edge.

As I dropped, I let my mind drift. The sheer volume of new revelations had me thinking in circles.

The Darenti bounced down the narrow stairs, almost like rubber balls, seeming to enjoy the adventure. If one of them fell and plummeted to the ground, would they be hurt? Or would they just reform at the bottom? I made a mental note to ask Gara sometime.

My feet brushed the leafy canopy, and I adjusted my descent, angling toward the point Gara had indicated. The fastest of the Darenti were still halfway up the cliff, so I drifted to the steps and followed them down into the overgrown valley.

As the foliage closed around us again, Liam pushed off and soared ahead of me, flying on a current of air I couldn't detect. After a long, shallow descent, he landed on the steps and raced ahead into the jungle.

The steps flattened out as the base of the cliff changed to steep hillside, then gradually levelled off. I pushed through the drooping leaves, bending almost double to keep from getting slapped in the face by the foliage. The thick leaves were flatter and broader than those in the jungle above, and smaller plants filled in the spaces between the big trees, rather than the vines I'd seen on the eastern continent.

I turned off my grav belt and strolled along the path, looking for a comfortable place to wait for Gara and the others. Rounding a broad tree, I came face-to-face—or rather, face-to-belt-control— with a small Darenti.

"Hi." Would he understand me? The CEC hadn't added Darenti to our translators—perhaps because V'Ov and her team didn't want us to understand them. Every Darenti I'd spoken with had passable Standard. Of course, if they could read minds and implant suggestions, it would have been child's play to learn our language and correct themselves on the fly.

The others in our party hadn't attempted to speak with me—I wasn't sure if they didn't understand Standard or if they'd been warned off by Gara and Verdat. And this one was small. I hadn't met any young Darenti, yet, but surely, they would have no reason to learn Standard.

"Hi, Siti." The voice was deep and gravelly—not at all what I expected from a child. But maybe small size didn't indicate youth? I hadn't asked.

"How do you know my name?" I found a large chunk of rock and sat, so the being wouldn't have to stare at my belly.

"We've been traveling together for a long time." He smoothed back blue and white striped hair that flowed to his shoulders. It was his most prominent feature—all the other Darenti had very short hair. Even those who appeared female. He couldn't have been traveling with us—I would have noticed the hair.

"Were you on the boat?" Overnight might seem like a long time to a child. If he was a child.

He grinned, and the smile looked familiar. "I was. But I've been around a lot longer than that."

"That would explain your excellent Standard. Do you work at the embassy?" I pulled my water pac from my belt and took a sip, then offered it to him. "I don't remember seeing you before."

"No, I have only been at the base for a day. Do you not recognize me?" He stood in front of me, bouncing on the balls of his feet.

I stared closely at him, then shook my head. Why would I recognize him?

The being melted to the ground as Gara had done on the beach, but incredibly fast. Then the blob shifted and reformed.

As Liam.

G'lacTechNews

This is Starling Cross, with G'lacTechNews.

Thanks to the debunking of the bomb scare, I have received permission to descend to the surface to cover the treaty negotiations. My next report will come directly from the Commonwealth embassy.

In other news, Serenity "Siti" Kassis has disappeared. Major Calyx James, aide to the Commonwealth's official ambassador, says Kassis is performing normal duties as assigned, but our news drones have not spotted Kassis in several hours. Oddly, neither Lee nor Torres seem to be concerned.

CHAPTER TEN

My heart spasmed, and I clutched at my chest, like a fainting woman in an ancient vid. This couldn't be Liam. This child must have figured out how to imitate him. "That's a very good impression of a sair-glider."

The creature chittered at me, like Liam. *Exactly* like Liam. Then he leapt at me.

Before I could scream or bat him away, he launched himself off my shoulder and into the closest tree. He performed an acrobatic display reminiscent of Liam's antics on Saha, jumping from plant to plant, flying and looping. After a last amazing flip, he landed on the ground before me.

If this wasn't Liam, it was an excellent imitation of the glider.

The blue and white creature jumped to the boulder, landing beside me, and put his front paws on the pocket of my jacket. The pocket where I usually carried a protein bar that I often shared with Liam.

How would this Darenti know that?

The glider chirped and patted the pocket.

"Sorry, I'm out. Why are you pretending to be Liam?"

The glider jumped to the ground and did the melting thing in reverse, reforming into the small Darenti.

"I can't speak when I am Liam. I have to—" He paused, as if trying to articulate a difficult concept, and his nose twitched in a way I'd never seen a human—or Darenti—nose move before. But it looked remarkably like Liam's expression. "When I shift to a smaller size, I have to leave parts of myself elsewhere. My ability to talk is one of the things I leave behind. It aids in my subterfuge if I can't inadvertently speak."

"Are you seriously trying to get me to believe you *are* Liam? That instead of a sair-glider, I've had a Darenti stow-away with me for the past eight years?"

"Yes."

"That's it? Just 'yes'? And I'm supposed to believe you why?" I jumped up from the boulder and stomped across the tiny clearing. "That's insane! How did you get onto the *Return in Glory*? Why would you pretend to be a glider for eight years? And—" I threw my hands into the air as I spun around to face him. "I don't even know what to ask! This is impossible!"

But was it? He had just demonstrated he could physically do it. And there had been so many little hints. Liam had proven time and again that he was smarter than any other sair-glider.

I'd found him on the ship after a twenty-year deep sleep, and no one seemed to be missing a glider. Unregistered gliders didn't get onto CEC ships.

He was male, despite the fact that every other glider in CEC service was female. And somehow, he'd passed the CEC medical exam after I found him. A male glider should never have gotten through.

Unless he could influence minds?

I stared at the little Darenti. "Convince me. Without your *Jed-eye* mind tricks."

He jumped to a low branch and swung himself up so our eyes were level. It was an impressive leap for the tiny being, but easy for a sair-glider. I thought back to the beginning of the walk—how the Darenti had stretched themselves to reach the pool at the top of the block. The smaller ones had done that weird climbing thing. Thinking back, I'd *never* seen one of the short, squat Darenti jump.

This being swung his legs like a child and rubbed the top of his head. Like Liam scratching an ear. Then he dropped his chin in that familiar glider grin. "I got that piece of senidium for you on Sarvo Six. And destroyed the Gagarin drones on Saha."

I swallowed a gasp. How would a Darenti know any of that? "You must have overheard Joss talking about those things—he was with me on both those trips."

The creature laughed. "True enough. How about when I found you in the caverns on Earth? When Marika kidnapped you. Joss wasn't there."

He jumped to his feet, then swung around the branch, dropping to the ground with surprising grace. "Or this. You found me in a potted tree outside the mess hall on the *Return in Glory*. Do you remember? You hid me in your pocket and fed me a protein bar."

No one knew that. I'd had to explain where I found him, of course, but I didn't tell anyone I'd hidden him in my pocket and fed him a protein bar. "Good guess?"

"And you hid me for days. It was only when your father noticed me in the shuttle to Earth that you took me to the medics for examination and certification."

How would he know that? "How did you pass the exam?" His mischievous grin sparked an urge to smile back, but I suppressed it.

He chuckled. "I was lucky I didn't end up being shipped to Kepler Three. I should have worked harder to hide my gender from you. But I was able to convince the vet-tech to fudge the paperwork."

I flushed. "I never checked your gender." There was a sentence I never hoped to utter again. "I left that to the vet. Speaking of which, how did you do that? More *Jed-eye* mind tricks?"

"I believe the term is *Jedi*." At my raised eyebrow, he went on. "We saw the vid on Earth, remember? The story about the farm boy and the princess? The one with the laser swords, not the one with the six-fingered man. I was able to convince the vet-tech to list me as female—he just about lost his mind, since I'd had different 'accoutrements' the first time." He waved downward. "I feel bad about that. I don't like deceiving people."

His revelation stunned me. It was the mention of *Star Wars* and *The Princess Bride* that convinced me more than anything else. That was information no one would think to pass on if this were a prank—or something more sinister. My mind spun with the implications. I dropped to the boulder again with a thump. "What's your real name?"

"Humans call me Lei-hawm. It's as close as you can get to—" He said something that sounded not quite like "Lei-hawm."

My eyes bulged. "How did I—oh. *You* told me your name was Liam. Through the mind-meld."

"That was also how you knew I was male. I should have been more careful, but it was such a pleasure to be called something close to my real name." His smile turned apologetic. The variety of his expressions convinced me as much as what he'd said. Not only did they look strangely similar to Liam's, but they were also much more nuanced than anything I'd seen other Darenti produce. Even V'Ov and her crew hadn't looked this human. But they hadn't lived with one for eight years.

"How did you get onto *Return in Glory*? And how long have you been away from Darenti? You're restricted to the planet."

He glanced toward the path. "The others are coming. I think it's best if I resume my other form."

I jumped up and leaned down to grab his shoulder. "Why? Do they not know about you? Are you working with V'Ov?"

"No, it's not that—"

"I think you should stay here and explain to Gara and Verdat what's going on. Unless they already know?" I tightened my grip. Could he shift back to Liam while I held his shoulder?

He lifted his other hand. "So be it."

The babble of the approaching Darenti sounded remarkably like a coterie of sair-gliders. How had no one noticed the similarities before? "Are all gliders actually Darenti?"

Lei-hawm snickered. "Definitely not. The real ones are not particularly intelligent."

The crowd rounded the corner and caught sight of us. Immediately, they surged forward, sweeping around us like the sea, chattering happily, stretching their arms to touch Lei-hawm and comment. Within seconds, they had separated me from the little Darenti and relegated me to the outer edge of the group. Even Verdat and Gara ignored me, clamoring for Lei-hawm's attention.

I dropped to the boulder again, waiting for the excitement to subside. While I waited, I tried my holo-ring again—still no satellite connections.

How was that possible? The CEC comsats were deployed to cover the entire globe. I fiddled with my settings and tried again.

Nothing. It was as if I'd been dropped onto an undiscovered planet.

What felt like hours later, Verdat approached. Behind him, the other Darenti continued to chatter and mingle. Many of them chewed on leaves they'd torn from nearby plants—it looked like a party.

"What's the deal? Aren't we supposed to be getting to this city of yours?"

"Lei-hawm has been gone. We are happy to see him again on Darenti." Verdat lifted his hands in an awkward shrug, reminding me how human Lei-hawm's gestures looked.

"How long has he been gone?" The *Glory* had left Grissom about twenty years before I found Liam. We'd been in deep sleep for most of that. And it would have taken time for him to get from Darenti to Grissom, so maybe thirty years?

"He has been gone since the beginning."

"The beginning of what?"

Verdat waved an arm in a broad, all-encompassing gesture. "Since the humans arrived. Lei-Hawm departed with Lieutenant Nate Kassis."

"He left with my dad?" I sat upright. "My dad smuggled him off the planet?!"

CHAPTER ELEVEN

VERDAT SHOOK HIS HEAD, jerking it from side to side in a mechanical way. I hadn't noticed before how manufactured the Darenti's "human" gestures looked. "No, your father knew nothing."

"You're saying Lei-hawm snuck off Darenti a hundred and seven years ago and is just now returning." I scratched my head, my short fingernails clicking against the metal plates woven into my braids. Did they really work? If they didn't, Lei-hawm would have had an easier time convincing me.

Or maybe that was the point—to "prove" they worked by manufacturing this ridiculous story and convincing me "without" the mind meld. Could they be that devious? They said Lei-hawm had lived in the human world for a century without detection. That was deceit—something the Darenti claimed to abhor in V'Ov.

"Correct." Verdat nodded.

Across the clearing, Lei-hawm jumped to the branch again, and the crowd cheered. He perched above them and spoke, his arms gesticulating widely. His gravelly voice rumbled in my ears, but the words were unintelligible.

"Why do they all seem to know him?" I waved at the crowd still surrounding the shortest Darenti. "And why is he so small? Sorry, is that an offensive question?"

"Not at all. Why are you so big?" Verdat bared his teeth in an awkward facsimile of a smile.

"I'm tall, not big." I held my arms out in a body-builder pose to indicate the difference. "Joss is big. And among humans, our size is usually a genetic thing. My parents were both tall and thin, so I am, too."

"I met Lieutenant Nate Kassis." Verdat nodded again. "Is he still as tall?"

I shrugged. "He might have lost a centimeter over the years. Humans tend to shrink a bit as they age." I held up my fingers to indicate the amount.

"Darenti also shrink as we age." Verdat held his hand above his head, then dropped it to his waist. "The young are tall. Over the centuries, we decrease in size. Lei-hawm is very old, even for *enti*."

"Centuries? How long do you live?"

"Many years. Exact age is not important to us. Lei-hawm can tell you how many seasons he has enjoyed. I have seen four hundred and seventy-three revolutions of the planet. He is much older. This is one reason all seem to know him—he has always been here. Except the short time he was with the humans."

"Come, Siti Kassis!" Lei-hawm waved from his branch. "We must go to the city, then find the Stone of Avora." He executed one of his spectacular leaps, twisting and landing lightly beyond the crowd. The Darenti cheered and surged around him, scooping him up and carrying him on their shoulders as they rolled out of the clearing like water draining from the beach.

"Come." Verdat stood. "We must stay with them. There is safety with the Darenti."

As if it had been listening, something roared deep in the jungle. I hurried after the crowd, wondering why something that sounded so ferocious would be afraid of these tiny beings. Of course, for all I knew, the animal who made the sound was as tiny as them and not at all hazardous. I only had their word those native creatures might be dangerous. And they'd already proven to be less than one hundred percent trustworthy. Which made a species that "could not lie" even more suspect.

WITH THE OVERCAST SKY, it was hard to tell time. The reflected light created almost no shadows, and the sun was just a dispersed glow behind the clouds. Fortunately, my holo-ring kept time without being connected to the net.

Just after four, we reached a side path. The main trail continued onward, but we took the turn. Few of the Darenti had spoken to me since we left the clearing—they continued to jabber at Lei-hawm without seeming to listen to his responses.

"How can anyone understand all of that?" I asked no one in particular.

Gara appeared beside me. "Most of the discussion is silent."

"What do you mean?"

"They speak mind-to-mind. What you hear is mostly... emotions. Non-verbal responses."

"Like 'ah' and 'mhm'?"

She thought for a moment, then nodded. "Yes. I have witnessed humans making these noises. I'm sorry I have ignored you—seeing Lei-hawm has been—" She waved her arms and made some wordless noises.

I nodded. "I get it. He was gone a long time. Did you know he was here?"

"No. We have heard no word of him since he left—how would he communicate? Even the most powerful messengers cannot speak to those off the planet." She tapped her temple. "We didn't know what form he would take to facilitate his travel. He says he was with you."

I blew out my cheeks. "That's what he says. And it appears to be true. He was my glider, Liam." I lifted a hand to my shoulder. "Little blue and white guy?"

Her eyes bulged. "That was Lei-hawm? He is very skilled to take on such a shape. I have never heard of an enti who can compress their being into so little space."

"He said something about leaving part of himself somewhere else? What did he mean?"

"I'm not sure I can explain. According to our legends, skilled Darenti can move part of their being to another reality, which allows them to appear smaller in this one. But I have never heard of anyone who actually did it."

"Like to another plane? Or an alternate universe?"

She lifted her hands. "I do not know. I cannot do it. The skill requires much experience to achieve. And even if I could do it, I could not become a being as small. I contain too much mass. Perhaps in a few centuries…"

I bit my lip, not sure if I should pose my next question. "Do you know why he went… traveling?"

"He wanted to see beyond the world. We agreed sending one Darenti would be a wise choice, and Lei-hawm is the most flexible among us. He was the most likely to go unnoticed."

I eyed her suspiciously. "You say 'we.' Who is we? I thought you didn't have a representative government."

"We do not have representation. We make major decisions in concert with all others." She tapped her temple again. "Everyone can contribute to the discussion, and consensus is reached."

"Are you saying some Darenti didn't want Lei-hawm to go?"

Her head jerked side-to-side. "No. Most Darenti did not care. A few voiced concerns but chose to withdraw them after discussion."

A truly democratic society? Where everyone weighed in and the majority ruled by convincing the minority? Or at least convincing them to give up.

She growled a little. "But V'Ov makes decisions for the Darenti without consultation. This is why she must be stopped."

"Why don't you send a delegation to speak with the humans?"

"We have tried. V'Ov does not allow us to speak. Or discredits us later. And for the humans, V'Ov is like Lei-hawm. She has always been here."

The group shuffled to a halt, gathered around a hole in the ground. A few at a time, the Darenti stretched their legs and stepped into the hole, then shrank into the darkness as if riding a grav panel down. Lei-hawm stood by the lip of the hole, speaking with each Darenti as they entered.

Gara and I waited at the back of the crowd, moving forward a few steps at a time until all the others had descended.

Lei-hawm held out a hand. "Siti, will you join us?"

"I guess that's why I'm here." I flicked my grav belt and stepped over the void. "But you and I need to have a long talk."

He grinned. "That's why I didn't want to reveal my identity to the group. I knew they would monopolize me."

His command of Standard was the final nail in the coffin. The Darenti were fluent but still used awkward phrasing from time to time. And their facial expressions were—now—obviously imitations of ours. Lei-hawm spoke and responded like a human. After living completely in our company for a hundred years, it made sense.

"You were right." I pointed at him as I dropped. "But we still need to talk."

My feet hit the ground faster than I expected. My head still stuck out of the hole—I must have looked ridiculous. I turned off my grav belt and dropped to a crouch, clearing the way for the remaining Darenti.

Lei-hawm stretched his legs to their full extent, but they only got halfway to the ground. I rocked forward onto my knees and reached up to help him, but he let go and dropped the rest of the way. He crooked his fingers at me and moved into a low tunnel.

I followed on my hands and knees. The tunnel had smooth sides, as if it had been carved from damp clay with a sharp circular cutter. Overhead, a glowing line of a fuzzy, spongy substance provided light. My fingers itched to pull a specimen container and take a sample, but I refrained. Perhaps I could get one later. "I noticed most of the Darenti don't jump like you do."

He shrugged. "We have no need. Stretching is more efficient—at least for younger enti."

"Enti?"

"It means 'people' in our language. Now, you have questions. I will tell you the beginning, and you can ask." He paced beside me, his head level with mine as I crawled. "Your father rescued me and my tribe from a mudslide that covered the entrance to our city." He jerked his head toward the entrance.

"He's told me the story many times. How he met a tribe of tiny humanoids in a tunnel like this and helped them get out. He never mentioned shape-shifting. And if you can shape-shift, and convert things into food, why couldn't you just make a new hole?"

"Yes, we would have eventually dug out, but not before Lieutenant Nate Kassis expired from lack of water."

"Couldn't you have made some water? Or pulled it out of the dirt like you did the metal from the pebbles?" I dropped back on my heels to pull a pair of gloves from my pocket. The floor of the tunnel was covered in sharp bits of loose rock.

"We can pull water from the dirt and mud, but even with all of us working, it would not have been enough for a human. And there are limits to what we can shape. We cannot convert iron and silicon to food. But he had the tools to remove the stone covering our entrance." He pointed at my grav belt. "He lifted the rock, and we escaped. I am surprised he didn't mention the shape-shifting—even to his own daughter. We did not ask him to hide this fact."

Gara, who had been walking behind us, spoke up. "From what I have learned at the base, he may have mentioned it to his people. But without evidence, he was not believed."

"Did he get any vid of you changing?" With my gloves on, I started crawling again.

"He seemed upset by our shifting appearance, so we decided to present one that would look familiar to him and his peers." Lei-hawm's face shifted until he looked like a younger version of my dad. On his tiny body, the effect was kind of comic.

"Oh, I'm sure that didn't freak him out."

The little enti cackled, and his features shifted back to his human-Lei-hawm aspect.

"Hey, how did your friends know it was you? You can change your shape. They didn't recognize you as a sair-glider, so it can't be the mental thing."

"Oh, but it is. I told you I had to temporarily put aside part of myself to become Liam. By removing those attributes, I become unrecognizable to those who know me. It's why none of the enti in Perista noticed me."

The tunnel had been sloping gently downward, but now it flattened out. Based on my memory of the terrain above, we had to be under the hills that formed the west side of the valley. Ahead, the way brightened.

The Darenti around us had been so quiet, I'd forgotten they were there. As they caught sight of the light, they began chattering again, and they moved faster. I tried to increase my speed, but I wasn't used to crawling for long distances. The tunnel emptied, revealing an opening.

The tunnel exited into a vast cavern with walls covered by more of the glowing fuzz. It illuminated a huge structure topped by domes and spires. Brilliant colors covered every surface. Stripes of green and blue twisted up one spire. Jagged red spots on a white background covered another. Row upon row of narrow balconies wrapped around the various levels with wide window openings above each. The roofline undulated in a way that looked impossible.

And enti swarmed over the structure like ants. They raced along balconies and moved from level to level using their odd stretching maneuver. From this distance, I couldn't discern details, but many of them did not appear to be humanoid. As we got closer, one of our party morphed into a three-legged creature and put on a burst of speed. Several others changed as they walked, growing limbs, elongating or shrinking. One became a pink ball that bounced down the gentle slope toward the city.

"You'll see very few human-shaped enti here. And no, I didn't read your mind, but it's the logical next question." Lei-hawm still walked beside me, but his blue and white hair now covered his entire body. "I can retain my ability to speak if I stay this size. How would you like a giant sair-glider?" His jaw dropped in his familiar grin.

"Have you done this before?"

"Become a giant glider? No, I wanted to remain undiscovered."

I thought back to the many times Liam had saved our bacon in the field, doing things no other glider would think to do. "You probably should have played dumber on a number of occasions. Of course, no one figured it out. How would we? We had no reason to suspect shapeshifters, and gliders were a known and heavily studied species. Are there other enti out there?"

Liam shook his head, the very human gesture odd on the enormous glider. "I departed before the humans put all of their security precautions in place. And most enti are happy here. Why venture out into the unknown?"

"But not you. It's fortunate my father met you and not some other enti that day."

Liam gave me a knowing look.

I stopped and turned to face him. "You engineered the meeting?"

He cocked his head. "I've always been curious about the stars. When I discovered aliens had landed on my planet, I went in search of them. That's why we were in Perista where your father discovered us."

Before I could ask any more questions, a sea of enti swarmed out of the city. Beings of every shape imaginable surrounded us, all jabbering and touching—not just Liam, but me as well. Several grabbed my hands and clothing, pulling me gently toward the structure. As they swept us into the building, I lost sight of my friend.

CHAPTER TWELVE

I PEERED THROUGH A LARGE, rounded opening in the concave wall. The windows in this room, each of them asymmetrical and unique, had no glass, and the wall was ten to fifteen centimeters thick. I leaned on the smooth edge and watched the festivities below.

My room looked onto an interior courtyard and across at hundreds of other windows, none of them exactly the same. A few enti watched from the balconies, but most of the residents had gathered below.

From my perch, I could see the entire massive oblong, packed with enti. Occasionally I caught sight of Liam's blue and white stripes, but he was difficult to pick out in the mass. Most Darenti chose bodies in the blue and green shades—perhaps due to the profusion of such colors in the local foliage—but a sprinkling wore other colors ranging from grayish to brilliant pink and orange.

They appeared to be celebrating, but whether it was Liam's return or something else, I couldn't tell. I'd put in a brief appearance early on, but when I started yawning, Gara brought me to this room. She'd made it clear I was welcome to stay at the party, but I was grateful for the respite.

A room on the outside of the city might have been better. Here, the noise of the party would likely make sleep impossible, although they had provided me with several small pads pushed together to create a thick mattress. I considered returning to the courtyard, or exploring the massive building, but the low ceilings made both options unattractive. After crawling through the tunnel to get here, the idea of crawling back down seven levels made my hands hurt. In a pinch I could exit through the window and use my grav belt to get down, but my power reserves were low.

Which was going to be a problem unless the cavern's light source could charge my gear. I checked the levels in my jacket—thirty two percent. I hung the garment on the window ledge to see if the perpetual twilight would do any good. I hadn't thought to check when I left the surface—for all I knew, my gear could have been charging as I crawled.

The cavern around the city was covered in the fuzzy luminescent growth. I couldn't tell if it was a plant, a fungus, or a mineral. More glowed on the exterior walls of the bottom three levels in the courtyard. The stuff provided enough light to keep the space from being too dark, but according to my holo-ring chrono, the glows on the cavern walls and upper stories had dimmed in time with the sunset.

Leaving the jacket in the opening, I crawled across the room to a tray on a low platform. Soon after Gara brought me to the room, a band of enti had arrived with food and drink. These were different from the items Verdat had served on the boat and equally delicious. If nothing else, humanity should consider hiring the Darenti as chefs across the galaxy.

When I'd finished eating, I rolled onto the thick mattresses. The rough-looking covers felt like slubbed silk. In the dim light, the vivid fabric lost its vibrant color.

Why had it gotten darker? I sat up in surprise, and the glows on my wall brightened. I sat still for several minutes, but the light didn't change. As soon as I lay down, the glows dimmed. Motion detectors or something else? I tried several more times, with the same effect—the light decreased when I was prone.

I lay back, watching the glows fade from bright to dim and finally out. I closed my eyes and let the murmur of the party lull me to sleep.

My vibrating holo-ring woke me, its faint glow bright in the night-black room. The sounds of the party had died at some point, and when I peered out the window, the courtyard was bathed in darkness. Here and there, light glowed at a window, but most of the city slumbered.

I stretched as well as I could—the low ceiling prevented me from standing. My jacket hung over the window ledge where I'd left it, and the interface showed forty-two percent charged. The glowy stuff worked, but not quickly. I shrugged into the jacket and connected the charger to my grav belt, since my stunner was fully charged.

The building had no stairs—or at least Gara hadn't used any when she showed me to my room. We'd crawled through the halls, winding up a gentle incline until she pointed out my room. Thanks to my tracking app, I could find my way again, should I need to, but I'd lost my sense of direction before we reached the second level. I flicked my grav belt on and climbed through the window, rising above the building and over the undulating roof. In a few minutes, I reached the ground and turned the belt off.

I started around the city, heading away from our entrance. As I walked, the glows on the outer walls flickered to life, fading away behind me. This side of the building was dark except for a single lighted window in the twelfth level. The cavern wall on my right was rougher than the tunnel we'd entered through—like a naturally occurring cave. High overhead, a multitude of narrow slits glowed dimly. By the time I got a few degrees around the building, it was daylight outside. Or at least what passed for daylight on Darenti.

A scrabbling sound brought me around, sending me into a defensive crouch. Something—some*one*—climbed down the outside of the building—one of the preferred methods of accessing the city, it seemed. When I caught sight of Liam's bright fur, I relaxed and stood upright. "Good morning. How was the party?"

Liam morphed into his humanoid Lei-hawm shape and smiled. "Most welcoming. But it wasn't a party. That was a typical evening in the city. Darenti are very communal."

"That must have been hard for you—all those years alone in the human world."

He shrugged. "One of the reasons I chose to be a sair-glider. They are also communal animals. They are not mentally stimulating, but their company kept me from being lonely. Human companionship helped a great deal. Shall we?" He gestured, and we started walking again.

"Tell me about that. Have you—well, I guess 'belonged to' is not an appropriate phrase, now that I know what you really are. Who did you live with?"

"I traveled to Grissom on your father's ship. It was easy to blend in with the other gliders on that crew. No one noticed an extra member of the glider coterie. I joined several Phase 2 teams the same way—blending in with the crowd. I visited many planets during that time—I was with the Phase 2 team to Sarvo Six."

"You've been to Sarvo Six before?" My Academy team had done a training exercise there—one of the many times Liam had saved our lives.

"Yes." A tinge of sadness colored his voice. "In the years since I left Darenti, I 'belonged to' two other explorers. I was with Salina Govertz for twenty years and Robert Pascque for twenty-four. They were both very good to me, and it was hard to leave them. But gliders don't live very long, so I couldn't stay."

"How did you…?"

"Gliders often disappear when they're sick. It's natural for them to protect the herd by not becoming a liability. When they live with humans, they tend to live longer, since you provide medical care. But they still go missing as they age, and people accept that as the end."

"And how did you deal with medical care?" Glider vets had tons of diagnostic equipment. "Surely your internal organs don't look like a glider's?"

"I don't really have internal organs, so no. I used my mental powers to convince the technicians they'd done the work. It took some skill and some 'lost records' on occasion." As we talked, we continued walking around the building.

Lei-hawm pointed at a tunnel in the cavern wall. "There's the exit we'll take later today."

"We're leaving already?"

He smiled. "The sooner we can find the Stone of Avora, the sooner we can return to our team."

I stopped in surprise. "*Our* team? Do you intend to come back to the CEC?"

Lei-hawm's face wrinkled, and his shoulders rolled in a very alien-looking shrug. "I would like to stay with you. I enjoy exploring. But I have missed being able to speak to others."

"Yeah, being a glider for a hundred years must have gotten old."

He did the shrug thing again. "Once I transitioned to that form, it felt natural—almost as if I had become a glider. But now I realize I've missed being with my own kind. Despite your company." He smiled a little sadly, then shook his head in a very Liam-like way.

We walked in silence for a while, continuing around the building. The glows grew brighter, and a few enti emerged from the city but did not approach us.

"Do you believe in this Avora business?"

"It doesn't matter what I believe. It's what they believe." He swept his arm in an arc that encompassed not just the city but all of Darenti. "And they believe possessing the Stone will undermine V'Ov's control. If enough of them believe that, it becomes fact."

"I suppose. How do we find this thing?"

"That's a very good question. There are prophecies, of course."

I rolled my eyes. "Of course. I'd rather have a map."

GARA AND VERDAT, wearing their humanoid shapes, met us in a long, wide room on the ground floor. I shuffled through the door at a crouch, my hair brushing the ceiling, then sat against the wall. Lei-hawm stood beside me, his blue and white head well below my shoulder. Several other enti walked, crawled, or rolled into the room, depending on their form.

Unlike a human gathering, as the crowd grew, the chattering *decreased*. Perhaps they were switching to their internal communications. The occasional cheep or whistle continued to break the silence.

Gara approached me, her outstretched hands holding a metal circle.

Small metal disks etched with leaves and vines hung from either side. She lifted it toward my head. "To make wearing the protection easier."

I took the circlet. It had an opening at the back that would allow me to wear it like a headband, positioning the metal disks in the same location as the ones currently woven into my hair. "This is beautiful. Who made it?"

"Parento Encorcelos. You would call him a metalsmith. All of us can form things—as you saw at the beach. But some are more adept than others. Parento excels at metalwork."

"Thank you." I slid the circlet over my hair, leaving the other pieces in place, since removing them would require unraveling my braids.

A large green leaf with curly edges bounced up to us, hopping upright on its stem. It waved in a kind of bow, then turned to face the crowd, and they quieted. The leaf spoke in cheerful chirps and chatter for some minutes. From behind, I couldn't see how it was producing sounds—did it have a mouth? When it paused, Lei-hawm translated for me. "Iotentia Korvalo speaks for the enti of this city. She thanks you for coming, Lieutenant Serenity Kassis. We welcome you to Spire City and express appreciation for your willingness to help us locate the Stone of Avora."

I raised an eyebrow at Liam. "I wasn't aware I had a choice. They kind of kidnapped me."

He opened his mouth, but I shook my head. "No, don't say that. I'll try to help. But I need to communicate with my team—to let them know I'm alive. Someone has been blocking satellite access since we left the base."

Lei-hawm ducked his head. "That was you."

"What do you mean?" I glowered at him.

"You shut off your communications. In the settings." He tapped my holo-ring.

"I did not! Why would I do that?" I flicked my ring on and swiped through the screens to the communications portal. Sure enough, my comms were switched off. "Why is there even a switch to do that? Protocol requires us to stay in communication at all times. We shouldn't be able to switch it off. And I'd certainly never do that—I've learned the hard way to follow that rule." I looked up from my device.

Liam refused to meet my eyes.

Disbelief and anger coursed through me like fire and ice. "Are you telling me you used your mind tricks on me? That you convinced me to turn off my comms, then forget I'd done it? How many other times have you influenced me?"

I thought back over the last eight years since I'd "found" him on the *Return in Glory*. Some of the things I'd done had been risky—dangerous. Had it been the stupidity of youth, or did Liam talk me into them? What would he have had to gain? "Were you trying to get rid of me?"

"What? No!"

Lei-hawm put his hand on my arm, but I shook him off. "Don't touch me. That's how you do it—and I've let you ride on my shoulder—right next to my brain! It would be so easy to manipulate me! I thought we were friends!"

"Please, Siti, can we discuss this later?" He jerked his head at the enti.

They were so uncharacteristically quiet, I'd almost forgotten they were there. A sea of eyes stared at me—human orbs rather disconcerting in some of the faces and non-faces. Three bright blue eyes blinked from under the curly top of Iotentia Korvalo's leaf.

I repressed a shudder and rolled a hand at the leaf to continue. "Sorry."

A curved line appeared beneath the three eyes and parted to reveal several rows of sharp teeth in a menacing smile. Then the features closed and melted into the structure of the leaf, leaving its blank, green underside facing us.

I swallowed, hard. *Not creepy at all.*

Lei-hawm's lips twitched as if he'd heard my thought, and he continued translating. "Iotentia Korvalo is reminding the group of the prophecy—that a bright stranger will lead us to the Stone. It's much more complicated, of course, but that's the important part."

"Bright?" I looked at my dark CEC uniform and tan skin. "I'm not sure you've got the right gal."

"Your... aura, for lack of a better word, is bright. This is how we identify each other since physical appearance is not static." He waved a hand around his head and upper body. "This is how my people recognized me. In my glider form, part of my aura is missing, but once I transitioned back to this size, it is clear." He held his palm toward me and made a circular motion. "Human auras are all very similar, but some are darker than others. Yours is quite radiant."

"Thanks, I guess."

"The brilliance is no indication of character—at least not that I have seen. Former Cadet LeBlanc has a bright aura, too, although his was more angular, with red stripes, and yours is a lavender-blue swirl. Joss has a very dark aura. Aneh is between. And there are other aspects I can see but not describe. But none of them correlate to personality or psychology. Think of it this way—evil humans are not universally ugly."

"Sure, but their personalities are ugly, so I would expect that to be visible in an aura."

"What I described as an aura is not the same as the human concept. Maybe we should call it their enti face instead?"

"Aura is easier."

The leaf had stopped speaking. Now it waved at us again, but this time, I got the distinct impression it was impatient.

"Sorry. Please continue." I ducked my lavender-blue swirled aura.

The leaf glared, then the eyes disappeared again. The gathered enti stared at it in rapt silence, their humanoid eyes unblinking. This time, the leaf didn't make any noise, but it vibrated, its curly edges ruffling in an unseen wind.

I leaned closer to Lei-hawm and lowered my voice. "What's going on?"

"Iotentia Korvalo is reviewing the prophecy. Most of it is impossible to translate to human speech—it's more emotion and *therentia*." His eyes darted to my face. "I can't explain *therentia*, either. Call it feelings or faith if you wish a poor analogy."

"Do they believe this prophecy?" I nodded at the assembled enti.

"Most of them do but at a deep *therentia* level. We are educated, so we take it with a grain of salt, as you say."

"I don't think I've ever said that, but I get the point. Does the prophecy say anything useful? Like directions to the Stone?"

He held up a hand. I relaxed against the wall and let the silence wash over me.

"Siti, wake up."

I blinked my bleary eyes, and Liam's oversized blue and white face came into view, surrounded by a crowd of enti. Liam's whiskers twitched, and he turned to shoo them away. "You fell asleep."

"Sorry. I didn't sleep well last night, and it was so peaceful…"

"That's the prophecy. The *therentia* is calming. But now we must depart."

"A calming prophecy—that's a new one." I swallowed a groan as I rolled to my hands and knees and crawled out in the wake of the Darenti tide. "Do we have some kind of directions?"

Liam turned to face me, somehow switching the direction of his legs so he continued to move backward. "We have a starting point and some general pointers."

I focused on his face—the movement of his limbs was too disconcerting. "Why hasn't someone looked for this thing before?" I crawled into the central courtyard and gratefully straightened to my full height. The enti followed me into the open space, then swarmed up the wall.

"The prophecy is new." Liam climbed the building until he was on a level with my eyes.

"Uh, that's not how these things usually work. There's always an ancient prophecy."

He chuckled. "In the human world, perhaps. But here, we have new prophecies all the time."

"How?" I threw up my arms in confusion. "You have a prophet?"

He grinned. "You're looking at him."

I slapped a hand over my face in disbelief. "Oh, come on! You're the prophet? Why would anyone believe some random story you throw out?"

Liam brushed his facial hair back with a paw. "Darenti can't lie, remember? And this is a real prophecy. The information came to me in a dream when we were on Grissom. Over and over. That's when I knew I had to bring you to Darenti." He turned and scrambled up the wall, leaping from balcony to ledge as if up a ladder.

I flicked my grav belt to keep pace with him. "You got me added to the mission? I thought I was here because of my dad."

"That might have been the justification, but the initial idea came from me." He reached the top of the city, with a half-dozen enti swarming up behind him.

I lifted over the rooftops and followed him between the spires and domes, around many other courtyards, and to the outer wall. The sheer size of the structure amazed me. I had seen only a small portion of it. Then we dropped to the ground near the exit Lei-hawm had shown me earlier, with the enti moving almost as fast as my grav belt.

When he reached the ground, the big glider shifted to his Lei-hawm form. The change sparked an upwelling of sorrow in me, as if Liam were leaving me forever. "Were you going to come to Darenti without me if they didn't add me to the mission?"

His shoulders dropped as he gazed up at me. "I had to come. But I would have tried to return to you. I didn't want to disappear, like I've done in the past. We haven't been together that long."

"Eight years."

"Sair-gliders live for twenty or twenty-five years. We should have more time." He turned to face the building. Five other enti ranged behind him—Verdat and Gara, plus Iotentia Korvalo and two others I didn't know. They stared past me for a few seconds, then Liam dropped to all fours and took off, heading toward the tunnel he'd pointed out earlier. The other five raced after him, and the city seemed to erupt behind us.

I turned to see every balcony and window filled with Darenti. They cheeped, cheered, clapped, and waved, the cacophony deafening. I raised a hand in farewell, set my grav belt to "charging" and crawled into the tunnel.

G'lacTechNews

This is Starling Cross, reporting to you live from the Commonwealth embassy on Darenti.

You've seen drone footage of the locals, but I have to tell you—in person, they're so cute! Tiny people only a meter high!

I've met ambassador V'Ovidia Demokritos and several other Darenti, and they were delightful. I'll be posting the full interviews over the next few days.

The official talks haven't begun yet—we're in a getting-to-know-you phase, and I have to say it's going wonderfully well.

I mentioned in my last post that Lieutenant Kassis was missing. It now appears Major James, aide to Ambassador Slovenska, was correct. Kassis is performing normal duties as assigned. I don't have any current videos but will upload them—if she does anything interesting.

The Earth representatives have been spotted recently around the base, in the company of Lieutenant "Caveman" Torres. Lucky ladies!

CHAPTER THIRTEEN

WE CAME over the crest of a stony hill and stopped in a hollow just below the top. Lush blue-green jungle surrounded our rocky aerie like an ocean. Our depression held a small spring that cascaded over rocks to the cliff and a few smaller plants along the sides. Liam, now in his giant glider shape, stretched upright and raised his front paws. The small group of Darenti stopped around him. "This is a good place to camp. Let's set up shelter. Gara, you'll take first watch."

The enti scattered, most of them heading for the stream. They plunged parts of their bodies into the water—presumably to drink—then began pulling leaves from the small trees.

I followed Liam to the cliff edge and pulled out my water pac. "Why do we need a watch? Is V'Ov going to try to stop us?"

"She would undoubtedly try, if she knew what we're doing. But there are creatures on this planet who would like to eat you. They come out at night." He gazed over the jungle, the light from the sunset painting his white stripes pink.

I stooped to refill my water pac, then thought better of it. I'd wait until the Darenti were done drinking. My filter could handle anything they might leave behind, but the idea of drinking downstream from the strange conglomeration of beings gave me a pause. "Only me? They won't eat you?"

He shook back his furry blue and white fur. "They know we are not tasty. We are not meat. You are."

I poked his shoulder. "You feel like meat."

"Hazard of the shape I am wearing. To blend in with other gliders, I must move in the same way. That requires the appearance of muscles and bone structure. It's easier to configure myself that way than to imitate. But if a *portanth* bites into me, it will be disappointed." He shifted into his humanoid shape. "This one is less meaty." When he flexed his arm in one of Joss's favorite body-builder poses, the movement looked mechanical.

"You don't taste like chicken?"

"No, I taste like mud." He made a face as he turned away from the cliff edge. As we walked upstream, he left one damp footprint in his wake. Had he been drinking through his foot?

I suppressed a shudder. This shape-shifting thing was taking some getting used to.

Lei-hawm chirped and whistled to the enti. They gathered around the small pool where an amorphous blob and a stick-creature were still partially submerged. "We need some carbon to make food. It would be best not to strip the leaves from the sparse growth here." He turned to me. "Would you mind using your grav belt to collect some leaves from the jungle below?"

I checked my charge and nodded. "You know, if you'd asked me to join this trip instead of kidnapping me, I could have brought equipment. Grav belts, force shields, more team members."

The entire team froze, looking at me.

"What did I say?"

Lei-hawm paused, and I got the sense he was communicating with the rest of the team. Then he turned back to me. "We don't want humans on this continent."

"Are you saying no one from the embassy has been over here?"

He nodded. "That is exactly what I'm saying. Your father's team started their exploration in Perista. You know how it works—the Phase 1 team scans from orbit, then sends teams to a few select locations—places that show promise or potential danger. If those pass, the Phase 2 team comes in for a more global review."

I made a get-on-with-it motion. "I'm aware of the process."

Lei-hawm's lips twitched in a very human looking smirk. "Here on Darenti, they started with the east. And ran into us before they expanded to the sites they'd identified here." He pointed at the ground. "Once we established communications, they agreed to leave us alone. When they agreed to this meeting, they built the embassy where V'Ov requested and have stayed in that area."

"That does not sound like the CEC I know. They've been here a hundred years and haven't sent teams to explore the rest of the planet? They could have landed a small shuttle, and you might not have noticed."

He tapped his temple. "But you forget our abilities. V'Ov doesn't want humans over here. She makes sure no one thinks to do that."

I crossed my arms. "I'm not buying it. Don't get me wrong, I've seen firsthand how effective your mind tricks can be. But you can't influence the folks back at headquarters." I stared at him. "You can't, can you? Influence people on Grissom?"

He shook his head. "Of course not. Our reach extends only to those in close proximity. There've been a couple of times when humans have landed in other locations. V'Ov submitted a formal protest, and they withdrew. For the most part, humans respect our sovereignty. And we remind them that if we can't go out there, it isn't right for them to come down here."

I wrinkled my nose. "Still sounds very unlike the CEC leadership to allow it. But this is first contact. I guess they're being careful." I turned to face the others. "How many leaves do you need?"

The enti conversed silently for a moment. When I paid attention, I could tell they were talking—their bodies went very still, although they still emitted noises from time to time. After a brief conversation, Gara stretched her arms into a circle—a circle much larger than she should have been able to reach. "About so much? We will gather, too, so you needn't get all of it."

I gave her a sloppy salute and moved toward the cliff-edge. My jacket had brought my belt charge up to ninety percent, but with the sun going down, I didn't want to waste any power.

"Let me come with you. To keep the *portanth* away." Lei-hawm melted into a puddle again, then reformed in his sair-glider size and shape.

I debated saying no—I wasn't sure I wanted *any* Darenti riding on my shoulder. But Liam was… Liam. My doubts faded away—we'd been partners for too many years. Was that more mind tricks? Maybe, but he'd saved my life many times. Maybe that was part of a very long game plan, but if so, I had no hope of foiling it.

I reached down and let him jump into my hand, then transferred him to my shoulder. "They can smell your muddy scent and stay away?"

He chittered, which I took as an affirmative.

The sheer cliff presented no easy descent, so I used the belt to drop into the trees. My sample cutter—part of the standard CEC equipment on my belt—sliced through the leaves like butter. They were large—at least a meter in length, and curly around the edges, like Iotentia Korvalo.

My stomach lurched. In the early years of the CEC, a Phase 1 team had landed on Ferantino Two. Not realizing the plants were sentient, they'd taken samples. When the plants counter-attacked, the CEC realized their error. Several explorers had been killed, and since the locals were sentient but not intelligent, the CEC withdrew. Protocols had been enacted to prevent a similar disaster in the future. "How do I know I'm not cutting an enti?"

Liam made noises at me and put his hand under the metal woven into my braid. An image of Iotentia Korvalo appeared in my mind, along with the idea that she was not attached to anything.

"You're saying she imitates a leaf but isn't one? And these leaves are clearly part of the plant, so it's safe?"

He chirped once, an obvious affirmative.

Maybe this mind-to-mind thing wasn't so bad.

I took my bounty back to the clearing, and Liam glided from my shoulder to the ground. As he landed, he unfurled into his full size, then morphed into his humanoid shape. Gara and the others took the leaves and scurried away. In the deepening darkness, I couldn't see what they did, but several minutes later, they returned with food laid out on a few of the smaller leaves.

I took the leaf from Gara. "Aren't you eating?"

She shook her head. "We have eaten the foliage—we don't require" — she waved her hands at the food— "transformation of the material."

"Thanks for not making me eat leaves." I popped one of the familiar squares into my mouth.

She smirked. "You're still eating leaves."

"For humans, the shape and texture are important."

Lei-hawm took a morsel. "I have found this to be true. This is why enti wear humanoid shapes at the embassy." He chewed and swallowed. "Well, that and V'Ov didn't want the humans to know our capabilities."

I finished my meal and handed the leaf to Lei-hawm who pressed it to his chest and seemed to absorb it.

Darkness settled over the aerie. I flicked my holo-ring to life, creating a tiny pool of light. After a brief search, I found a place to sleep with warm stone at my back and pulled a ground cloth from the small pack the Darenti had provided.

Verdat appeared beside me. "Do you require a bed, Siti? We can create one."

"Not necessary. My clothing will keep me warm, and I can sleep on the ground."

"We can make a hammock." Lei-hawm swung his arms in an arc.

"There's nowhere to hang it. I'm fine. Did you schedule me into the watch rotation?"

The enti all shook their heads.

"We require less sleep than you—we will watch." Lei-hawm patted my shoulder, and they melted away, leaving me alone in my pool of light.

I reached to turn off the holo-ring, then paused. I had forgotten something. I scrolled through the menus on my ring until I came across the communications center. It was still turned off. How had I forgotten to check in? My team must be worried sick and scouring the area around the embassy to find me.

I glanced into the darkness, wondering if I should do it. I was safe enough with Liam—even with the lingering doubt about his ulterior motives, I was convinced he meant me no harm. No, more than that—that he cared about me and wouldn't allow me to be hurt. If I reported back to the embassy, they'd want to send a team. And that would make Liam and the other Darenti very unhappy.

Or maybe they wouldn't allow it to happen at all? There must be other enti in the embassy who could influence the humans, keeping them from exploring beyond the carefully cleared edges of the compound.

Before I could change my mind, I flicked the communication button and called Joss. A hologram of his head and upper body appeared in my palm. His dark braids were pulled back, and a sheen of sweat covered his bare shoulders and chest. The sounds of weights clinked in the background.

"Siti! Where are you? Why's it so dark?"

"I'm with Li—Lei-hawm. He's the Darenti my father met—"

"That guy is still alive? But where are you?"

"Darenti live for millennia, so yeah, he's still alive. I can't tell you where I am—it's a confidential, need-to-know kind of thing. But I'm safe, and I'll be back in a few days." Would we return that soon? I had no concrete understanding of where the fabled Stone of Avora might be found.

"Need-to-know? I need to know. We're teammates."

"Yeah, you've obviously been worried sick about me—you're at the gym."

He rubbed his eyes, and I noticed the dark circles under them. "I—why would I be worried? I just saw you—" He trailed off as if he wasn't sure how long it had been.

"I've been gone for two days." I squinted past the holo into the darkness. Gara's team had covered my departure.

"No. I just saw you…"

"Joss, I'm sorry. I can't tell you anything else." I shouldn't have called. They hadn't noticed my absence. I scrambled for a story to cover my error. "My dad sent me on this mission, and I'll report back when I can."

"Is that why he's coming?"

I sat upright. "My dad is coming to Darenti?"

Joss rolled his eyes, then guzzled some water, making me wait. He closed the water pac and wiped his mouth on the back of his hand. "If he sent you on this mission, you should know that."

"Look, get a message to him. Tell him I'm with Lei-hawm, and I'll call him when he arrives. When is that?"

"I'll have him call you."

I shook my head. "No. I'm going to turn off my comms again. I can't have anyone tracking me. I'll call again tomorrow night. Please, Joss, help me out. The Darenti need me."

His eyes narrowed, and his lips pressed together. "I'll get the message to your dad. Then I'm coming to get you."

"No. I told you, I'm turning off my tracking. I'm fine. Thanks." I flicked the ring before he could respond. He'd try to track me—I needed to get off the grid before he could get the request through to the comm center. I flicked the comms off, then sat in the dark.

Something rustled and I spun, hand on my stunner. Two eyes glinted in the darkness, almost seeming to produce light from within. "Who's there?"

"It's me." Lei-hawm's smooth voice calmed my pounding heart. "You spoke with Joss?"

"Were you spying on me?" I grumped.

"No. But humans speak loudly. And I figured you'd call back to base. Thank you for honoring our sovereignty."

"I'm definitely in breach of protocol, so I expect you to explain to my father why it was necessary. And my commanding officer. I doubt Major Featherstoke will be as understanding as Dad."

"If we succeed, I will happily explain."

"And if we don't?" I squinted at him in the darkness.

"If we don't, V'Ov will get off world. And then—well, you tell me. What happens when an amoral shape-shifting, mind-controlling enti gets loose among the humans?"

I flicked my ring so I could see him. "You're already loose among us."

"I am. Or I was. But V'Ov has no moral compass. She'll do whatever she wants."

CHAPTER FOURTEEN

Liam's whiskers tickled my cheek. I put up a hand to push him away. "Leave me alone. I'm sleeping."

"It's time to get up. We have another long day ahead."

The unexpected voice brought me upright in a single swift motion. I clutched a hand to my pounding chest. "Don't do that!"

The supersized Liam stood beside my little sleeping area. "Do what?" The sun had risen, hidden as always behind the thick cloud cover, but today, the clouds pressed in from all sides, leaving us in the center of a misty bowl. I'd need to watch my step—the cliff edge was impossible to see from here.

Around the camp, the other Darenti scurried about, doing whatever Darenti do in the morning.

"Don't wake me with your whiskers, then speak." I rubbed my cheek. "My sleeping brain doesn't remember you're talking now, and it freaked me out. I can't reconcile your multiple—" I waved my hands incoherently.

He nodded. "Noted. Humans are not accustomed to shifting physicality. I know this, but I forget you aren't comfortable with all aspects of me. I will not do that again." He froze for a second, then relaxed. "Verdat will bring you food."

"Thanks." I removed the circlet Gara had given me and unbraided my hair, then pulled a comb from my belt pouch.

"And your friends will be here soon."

"What? Who?" I froze, comb in hand.

"I assume Joss and perhaps others. Didn't you expect them?"

"I didn't tell them where we are."

Lei-hawm glanced toward the top of the hill. "Io saw a shuttle land—about five klicks that way at dawn—it's the closest area suitable for shuttle landing. They'll be here before you finish eating."

I closed my eyes. I thought I hadn't given Joss time to track me. "I'm sorry." My fingers flew as I plaited my hair into a single braid and put on the circlet. I tucked the metal pieces away in my belt.

"There is nothing to be sorry for. I suspected they would come. I could have insisted we move to a new location after your call."

"But it was dark."

"We can travel in the darkness. It is you who would have had trouble. But don't worry about giving away our mission or position. I sent a message, and the proper people have responded." He moved aside as Verdat approached with another leaf full of small morsels.

"What does that mean?" I took the food with a grateful nod.

The other enti left, and Liam sat beside me. "There will be no official record of that shuttle making this excursion. It will be conveniently forgotten. And the whereabouts of you and anyone on that shuttle have been amended."

"I'm *really* not buying this 'Darenti are honest' schtick anymore. How would you hide that kind of meddling from V'Ov?" I shoveled a couple of the cubes into my mouth. After a steady diet for the last few days, I was getting tired of the selection. Maybe I should get Verdat a cookbook. Surely, he could make something different?

"We're honest because it's easy for others to see when we aren't." The glider winked. "We learned subterfuge from you." His face sobered. "Not that I blame humanity for our failings, but it's true this is a new skill learned since humans have landed here. We saw that misdirection was not just common but almost required in human interactions."

I dropped the leaf into my lap and put my hands on my hips. "That's not true!"

"But it is. Humans rarely say what they really mean. They lie about appearance, activities, desires. Often by omission. For example, you are tired of this food. Yet, you pretend to enjoy it."

I clapped my hands to the headband. "You aren't supposed to be able to read my mind."

He held up both paws. "I can't. But I know you well—you ate those like you eat meal pac rations after a week in the field." His eyes twinkled. "And there's your proof—both of the efficacy of the headband and the lack of transparency in humans. If Verdat could 'hear' that you are getting tired of the food, he would happily provide something different. But you accept it gratefully, and he has no way of knowing you'd prefer something else."

I rubbed my forehead. "You're making my brain hurt. Or this headband is."

"Hey!" The shout came from above. Four figures descended through the clouds, the parting mist swirling around them like special effects in a music video.

I jumped to my feet, the remains of my breakfast tumbling to the ground, and raised a hand. "Over here." I glanced at Liam who had moved behind me. "Do you want them to know about the whole shape-shifting thing?"

He morphed into his Lei-hawm shape. "I think we will keep that to ourselves for a while longer."

The quartet landed around us, exclaiming and hugging: Joss, Zina, Tiah, and... Derek Lee?

I pointed at Lee. "What is he doing here?"

"He saw us sneaking out." Zina rolled her eyes.

"Not to mention you needed a ship. And a second pilot." Lee crossed his arms. "On an unexplored planet, that's standard protocol."

"Siti's a pilot." Joss glared at Lee.

"She wasn't there."

I shook my head. "And aren't they going to notice that the two remaining Earth reps are missing? Not to mention the shuttle."

"That's what I said!" Joss tapped his chest with his thumb. "I'm just one of many CEC lieutenants. You two are key personnel."

"There aren't any meetings for a couple more days. And we're supposed to be casually interacting with the locals." Zina stepped to the side so she could see Lei-hawm better. "Hi, I'm Zina, from Earth."

"Pleased to meet you, Zina from Earth. I am Lei-hawm." He spread his arms wide. "Welcome to Rovantu."

"Lei-hawm? The Lei-hawm?" Tiah limped closer. "I've read about you—you were the one who initiated contact with Admiral Kassis. Then you disappeared. No one—no humans have seen you in decades. Or are you his offspring?"

"I am that Lei-hawm. I've been… busy." He glanced up at me.

I introduced the two men to Lei-hawm, hiding a smile at the thought that they'd known him almost as long as I had. "Why are you guys here? I told you I'd be back in a few days. And more importantly, how did you find me?"

"Are you kidding? I started tracking your ring as soon as I answered the call." Joss smirked. "You've been missing for two days. We were worried."

"No, you weren't." Tiah's voice came out loud and flat. "No one was worried. Except me. You—all of you—kept blowing me off. 'She's fine. She's getting to know the Darenti.' No one seemed to think it was odd that you were gone." She turned to me. "And now, when you called, suddenly they're freaking out and tracking you."

I bit my lip and looked at Lei-hawm. "You wanna explain that?"

He nodded gravely and explained about Darenti's ability to implant suggestions. When he finished, he stared at Tiah. "I'm wondering why our suggestions didn't work on you? We have several Rovantu enti in the compound, and they were instructed to cover Siti's absence. How did they miss you?"

The small woman shrugged. "I haven't been hiding."

Joss pointed at my head. "What's up with the non-regulation hat?"

I put a hand to the metal circlet. "This is supposed to protect me from those influences. They wanted to make me a tinfoil hat, but they didn't have enough metal."

"And that stops them from reading your mind?" Joss reached toward me. "I need one of those."

"Hands off!" With a chuckle, I fended him off. "Get your own headband. Actually, I have some pieces in my belt." I opened my belt pouch. "You need some way to keep them on your head, though."

"We've got duct tape back at the shuttle." Lee smirked and pointed. "That would look great."

"We can get more metal, too, unless there's something special about this?" Tiah took the pieces from my hand.

"How do you know it even works? They gave it to you, right?" Lee gave Lei-hawm a narrow-eyed look.

I explained about the food. "Now that there are several of us, we can test it. We just have to think things and see if they respond when we're wearing the metal."

Tiah handed the pieces back to me. "Except they'll see who's wearing it."

"Perhaps you can experiment as we journey." Lei-hawm gestured at the other Darenti who had gathered around. "We must bring the Perista Darenti to our side before the humans agree to V'Ov's demands."

"Where are we going?" Joss asked. "Wherever it is, we can get there faster in the shuttle."

Lei-hawm called the other Darenti over and introduced them. Each of them had transformed to humanoid form, but they look oddly similar—as if they were siblings. After a moment, I realized why—Io, Valo, and Yentar had taken on a mix of Gara and Verdat's features. Only Lei-hawm looked different, with Liam's pointy nose and wide mouth.

"The prophecy says we should travel across the land," Gara protested.

Joss jutted a thumb in the direction they'd come. "The shuttle travels across the land, just at altitude."

The enti all turned to look at Lei-hawm. As the leader of the expedition, not to mention the origin of the prophecy, he would decide. "We can fly."

"Cool." Joss lifted off the ground.

Zina yanked on Joss's pantleg as he rose. "Wait, the Darenti don't have grav belts!"

"I'm gonna get the shuttle. We'll hover over this site, and we can use a transport pad to lift them up." Joss jerked his head at Lee. "Come on, co-pilot."

Lee fiddled with his belt and rose, too. "It's my shuttle—you're the co-pilot, Caveman." Their bickering faded as they swooshed away into the clouds.

CHAPTER FIFTEEN

THE SHIP WAS SMALLER than the Naval troop-hauler we'd taken to the surface. It was the admiral's gig that every large Navy ship carried and similar to the craft which had stranded me and Lee on Saha in our Academy years. Four could sit in the front, with room for many more in the rear. Joss suggested flipping a coin for the left pilot seat, but Lee insisted it was his right as the only Navy officer. The Darenti, Zina, Tiah, and I rode in the cargo area which was configured with plush seats for twenty. A ladder led to a door above the cockpit, which housed the small VIP sleeping quarters.

"As representatives of Earth, it's at our disposal." Zina smugly pointed at herself and Tiah. "Since Arya went back to the *Verity*." At my raised brow, she continued. "They found the real Arya tied up in a closet. He said a member of the human ambassador's staff had attacked him."

I glanced at Lei-hawm. "At the instigation of V'Ov?"

"Quite likely."

I bit my lip. "Maybe instead of taking this crazy rock-hunting trip, we should fly back to the embassy and explain the whole mind-control thing?"

"V'Ov would never allow us anywhere near the human delegation. And once she recognized me, she wouldn't allow you to speak with them, either."

I lowered my voice so the women wouldn't hear. "She didn't recognize you in your, uh, other form."

"I told you—enough of me is missing in that form to make recognition impossible. You saw that on the boat."

"I'm just saying *I* could talk to Ambassador Slovenska." I gestured at Tiah and Zina. "Or they could. Have the metal shop gen up some more of these." I fingered my headband. The other humans now wore similar items that we'd built from materials in the ship. We looked like a bunch of poorly dressed cosplayers.

"We'll have a better chance of turning her followers against her if we have the Stone." The capitalization was clear in his voice. As was the finality of that decision.

I could tell Joss to take us back to the base—and test the efficacy of the metal bands in the process. Or I could trust Lei-hawm. As a glider, he'd always seemed to have my best interests at heart, but now that we were on his home planet, his priorities had changed.

I was a CEC officer. My job—my mission—was exploration. But I'd been detailed to a diplomatic delegation. Did exploring take precedence over whatever we were supposed to be doing on Darenti?

I unlatched my seat restraint. "I need to talk to Joss."

Zina reached for her own belt, but I waved her off. "This is explorer stuff." I avoided Lei-hawm's gaze and made my way to the front of the ship. A short hallway between the sanitation station and a small cubby housing the loadmaster's station led to a closed hatch.

The two men sat in seats facing the large front windows. We skimmed above the jungle canopy, well below the heavy cloud cover. After carefully closing the door behind me, I dropped into the comfy admiral's chair.

"This is pretty cushy." I bounced on the seat.

Joss glanced over his shoulder with a grin. "Yeah. Don't get too used to it."

"What do you want?" Lee swung the left seat—the pilot's seat—around to glower at me.

"I need to talk to Joss."

Joss swiped an icon to Lee's side of the cabin, then spun his chair around. "We're on auto pilot. Nibs, you have the conn."

"I wish you'd stop calling me that. My callsign is Zen."

"You don't seem very calm—is that why they gave it to you? You get worked up over nothing?" Joss laughed loudly. "You'll always be Nibs to us."

I grabbed Joss's arm to shut him up. "What are we supposed to be doing here?"

"I'm supposed to be flying. You're supposed to be lazing around like a typical passenger."

"I don't mean on this ship, although that brings up another question. No, what are we, as junior CEC officers, really supposed to be doing on Darenti? They hadn't given us any actual mission when I, uh, left. We're explorers. We should be exploring."

Joss's brows drew down. "Now that you mention it, they still hadn't given us any real instructions as of this morning. I guess we're supposed to be interacting with the locals, like Tiah and Zina."

"Doesn't that strike you as weird? Why would they send CEC officers to hang out?"

"Everything about Darenti is weird." Joss pulled the plain black tie from his hair, then rebundled his many small braids into a regulation tail at his nape. "But we've never had first contact before, so I guess they're making it up as they go?"

"They've had a hundred years of 'first contact.' You'd think they'd have figured it out by now." I glanced back at the closed cockpit door. "How much of this is being controlled by V'Ov?"

"Good question."

Lee pinched his lips together. "A better question might be 'what, if anything, does V'Ov have to gain by three squadrons of CEC personnel on her planet?' What's that old saying you guys quote?"

"Never trust a Sicilian when death is on the line?" Joss and I said together.

Lee rolled his eyes. "No. 'Follow the money.' Who gains from this set-up?"

"V'Ov retains power by keeping Lei-hawm away from the humans. But she doesn't know he's here." I leaned forward. "She could gain access to the rest of the galaxy if these talks go well."

"I wonder why she's waited a hundred years?" Joss fiddled with one of his braids. "She's had plenty of time to use her brain magic to talk the ambassador into this."

"Darenti live a long time. Maybe this is fast for her?" I rubbed my eyes. "Or maybe Gara and Verdat have managed to keep her in check until now."

Lee smirked again. "Or maybe every time the Darenti have forwarded an official request for transport, supported by the ambassador, the folks back at HQ have said 'heck no.' Didn't you guys study up on Darenti before you came?"

I exchanged a look with Joss. "I read everything I could find in the CEC archives. There isn't much."

"That's your problem—when your dad discovered the locals, control of the planet was turned over to the Interplanetary Relations Department. They formed a new division specifically for Darenti."

"Yeah, we read that." Joss crooked his fingers in a "gimme more" motion.

Lee shrugged. "The CEC kept a few scientists at the base in orbit to study the local ecology and stuff, but since humans weren't going to colonize the place, the CEC leadership kind of lost interest in the planet. The Navy, however, has continued to monitor the situation. You know, potential threats." He thumped his chest proudly.

Joss cackled. "Yeah, those little dudes without ships are pretty dangerous."

"You mean those little dudes with mind-control?" Lee flicked a status report and swiped it away. The ship pretty much flew itself, but all Navy craft required human pilots to monitor the system. If he or Joss didn't respond, the ship would automatically return to the base.

"Good point." Joss swung his chair back and forth. "So, what info does the Navy have that we didn't?"

Lee waited a few seconds before answering—probably just to annoy Joss. Finally, his smirk dropped. "While there has been only one Darenti ambassador since we made contact, there have been—wait for it—fifty-eight human ambassadors."

"Fifty-eight! That's less than two years per appointment!" I flicked my holo-ring. How had that information not been part of our briefing packet? Planetary ambassadors were normally appointed for four-year terms.

"The first twenty years were particularly bad—thirty-seven appointments. According to the reports I read, something about Darenti seemed to cause a decline in mental stability." Lee raised his eyebrows as he tapped the metal circle around his head. "Those first thirty-six ambassadors would show up here, then immediately start demanding the government allow the Darenti access to the rest of the galaxy."

"The first thirty-six—what about the thirty-seventh?"

Lee gave Joss a grudging nod. "The thirty-seventh didn't request anything untoward. Served a completely uneventful four-year term on station, interacting with V'Ov and company at the pre-approved intervals, then returned to service in the Commonwealth."

I leaned forward. "You think V'Ov decided to be more subtle?"

"That's exactly what I think happened. Now that I know about this." Lee tapped the metal circle again. "Every ambassador after that filled out their term as expected, with one or two going a few months longer. After about fifty years, they started recommending *consideration* for inclusion in the Commonwealth. Until Ambassador Slovenska, who's been here seven years."

"And she suggested actually doing it?" I asked.

"Yeah. Only after she'd been retained for a second term." Lee swiped another status alert off the board. "That's unusual, but she was supposedly close to getting Darenti to give us access to the western continent, so they re-appointed her. To continue the 'good relationship.' That was probably all engineered by V'Ov."

A red icon flashed in the ship's interface, growing larger. Lee swiped through it, acknowledging the alert, and it slid aside. He pointed through the front window. "That's the landing site."

From altitude, the meadow looked too small to land in, but both pilots claimed it would be easy. "For someone with my skills." Joss flicked a few icons and regained control of the ship. "I have the conn."

Lee threw up his hands. "Whatever." He turned to me. "Don't let him fool you—that meadow is bigger than it looks. You could land there." His tone said "even you."

"Gee, thanks." I tightened my seat restraints.

We descended, the meadow growing larger as we approached. The ship passed through a low-lying cloud, the tendrils of mist splitting and whirling away from our bow. Joss and Lee swiped through screens, muttering status updates to each other. Despite their animosity toward each other—much of which was feigned—they worked together like a well-oiled machine.

The ship settled to the ground, but no one moved. A surprisingly uniform wall of jungle plants edged the clearing, as if it had been cut. Joss flicked an audio switch so we could hear outside. Silence stretched heavy and thick, then a single low whistle sounded. A few seconds later, another answered, followed by an almost deafening blast of hoots and tweets, underscored by other, more ominous sounds.

"Sorry." Joss swiped a control, and the sound diminished. "I had it overamped. It's not really that loud."

"Good, because that chewing noise definitely gave me second thoughts about leaving the ship." Lee glared through the screen at the blank wall of fronds and vines. "In fact, maybe I should stay here. You know—so we have an escape plan."

"Fine with me." Joss surged to his feet. "If you're scared of a few bugs, you can stay here."

I got up, blocking Joss's access to the hatch. "Be nice. Besides, we don't know what's out there—the CEC never got to this continent, remember? Lei-hawm says there are things that would eat humans, but we're safe as long as we're with the Darenti."

Joss gave me a knowing look. "*Lei-hawm says*. And probably reinforced, before you put on your crown of brain safety." He flicked the metal leaf over my temple. "Why do you trust anything that guy says? He's admitted to using his brainwaves on us."

I looked away. If I told him who Lei-hawm really was, he'd probably trust him, too. Liam had saved his skin several times as well. But Lei-hawm didn't want me to say anything.

I turned around and stepped through the hatch, thinking hard. When I first found him, I had considered Liam a pet. When I joined the CEC, he became a partner, but a subservient one—a trained animal who could make an explorer's life easier. Official regulations stipulated gliders were expendable, although no glider-owner I'd ever met would have abandoned one.

And Joss was my teammate. My Corps brother. Either of us would quite literally die for the other. So, why would I take the side of an alien who had been impersonating a pet over my brother? I should tell Joss who Lei-hawm was. It would help to have another person to bounce ideas off.

I stopped suddenly, and Joss bumped into me from behind. I swung around and came face-to-face with Lee.

"Oh. I thought you were Joss." My cheeks went warm.

Lee jerked his head toward the cockpit. "He's running the shutdown checklist. I think he's having second thoughts about the chewing."

I started to push past him. "I need to talk to him—"

"I know who that is."

Lee's words stopped me in my tracks. "What do you mean?" I kept my eyes on the hatch behind him and faked a laugh. "I know who Joss is, too."

His hand closed around my arm. "No, the Darenti. I know who Lei-hawm is."

I took a deep breath, making my face as neutral as possible, then glanced up at him. From this close angle, I could see only the tense line of his jaw and his cheek. "He's the enti my father met."

His head turned, and his eyes narrowed, staring down at me. "He's Liam."

How could he have figured that out? I feigned surprise, then chuckled. "What a stupid thing to say. How could he be Liam?" I held up my hands, demonstrating the glider's tiny size.

"Where is Liam?" Lee's hand tightened on my arm. "I've read the original data from the Darenti exploration. Your dad reported shape-shifters. His team agreed that their features were 'fluid.' But no one else saw anything like that, and the original reports were buried. They didn't want to tarnish the reputation of the Hero. Mental illness still bears a stigma."

"My dad said the Darenti were shape-shifters? That's ridiculous. I grew up on the stories of his mission to Darenti. He never mentioned anything like it. And why would he? Shape-shifting is a fairy tale." The words sounded weak and uncertain. "And how did you get access to the original files?"

His face went pink, and he turned away. "The Navy has—"

"Don't tell me the Navy has exclusive access to the CEC's sealed files. The early Darenti reports were carefully redacted—the Commonwealth government was worried revelation of a sapient alien race would cause a panic. None of those files have been released."

"That's where you're wrong. Some of the files have been leaked. But as I said, I gained access to the originals. I can't tell you how." He released my arm. "But Lei-hawm has been masquerading as your glider since the Academy. No doubt gaining information to forward his faction's goals."

I turned to lean against the bulkhead, staring up at him. Had Lee grown taller since the Academy? "His goal is to keep V'Ov from exploiting the Commonwealth government."

"Are you sure? Maybe his goal is to make us think that, so we help him overthrow V'Ov and take control of the planet. Maybe even the galaxy. Can you imagine what mind readers could do in the Commonwealth Senate?"

A cold finger of doubt slid down my back. Darenti lived a long time. Lei-hawm spoke of spending a few years—or even a century—as a glider as if it were a brief adventure. Could he have ulterior motives? Was he using me, all that time?

I shook my head. "No. If he had attached himself to a senator, or the Commonwealth prime minister, that might be believable. But there's no benefit to being the pet of a random teenaged girl or an Academy cadet. Or even a junior officer." I waved a hand at my rank.

Lee echoed words I'd heard too many times in my life. "You aren't a 'random' girl. You're the daughter of the Hero. And now, apparently, the defender of the Darenti. Just make sure your loyalty is to the right cause." He pushed past me, heading for the cargo hold.

G'lacTechNews

This is Starling Cross, reporting to you live from the Commonwealth embassy on Darenti.

Did you catch my interview with Ricmond of the Western Seas? Wasn't his story a tear-jerker? The Darenti have so much in common with humanity —it's hard to believe we've kept them isolated all these years. It's time to reach out to your planetary representatives and recommend they approve Darenti's entry into the Commonwealth at once!

In other news, the hot lieutenants, AKA Lee and Torres, headed back to the Verity *this morning. My drones caught their departure on vid. Come back soon, boys!*

CHAPTER SIXTEEN

Lei-hawm stood in the open external hatch, still and silent. The other Darenti stood around him, staring into the thick foliage near the ship.

"What's—"

Zina raised a finger to her lips.

Lei-hawm turned, his eyes lighting as they reached me. "Are we ready to go? Other enti are out there, but I do not think they will be a problem."

"Why would other enti be a problem? Can't you just tell them what we're doing?" I tapped my temple, then wiggled my fingers. "Or are they V'Ov supporters?"

"We can communicate with them, of course. But the Darenti are not a single community. Some groups prefer to stay isolated. When we have discussed the fate of the planet in relation to the humans, most enti from this area—the Gothod region—declined to participate. And I have no idea how they'll react to humans."

"Gothod?" Tiah's voice was sharp. "That's what V'Ov said about the enti who impersonated Mr. Arya. That he was a Gothodi."

Lei-hawm nodded. "The Gothodi make excellent scapegoats. They keep to themselves, which makes them easy to 'other.'"

Lee rested one hand on his sidearm and waved the other at Zina and

Tiah. "You're taking us into a potentially hostile environment with civilians?"

Zina poked a finger at Lee. "Who you calling a civilian? I've been defending my community since I was five." She looked around the ship. "But I would like a weapon if we're going into an unknown situation."

"Good call." I started to activate my comms, then thought better of it and pushed past Lee to the cockpit hall. "Joss, you got a munitions locker up there? Bring something for Zina."

"Already on it." Joss ducked through the hatch, weapons in each hand carefully pointed at the deck. "This one is for you." He handed the blaster to Zina, then turned to Tiah. "I know you aren't as well-trained—"

Lee put out a hand to intercept the blaster. "You can't give a weapon to an untrained—"

"I said 'not as well trained,' not untrained. She's had basic weapons' safety. We require it of everyone who spends more than a night or two in New Lake."

Tiah took a jerky step back. "I don't want a weapon. In fact, I think I'll stay here. The terrain looks kinda rough." She lifted her leg, bringing our attention to the extra-thick sole that evened out her unbalanced gait.

"You can use a grav belt." I turned to the workstation across from the lav. A narrow cupboard filled the space between the cubby and the cockpit bulkhead. I unlatched the door. "They're recharged." I pulled out a couple of belts and handed them over my shoulder.

"What about them?" Tiah pointed at the Darenti who still milled by the open hatch.

"They don't need grav belts." My eyes flew to Lei-hawm as I remembered he didn't want to reveal their shape-shifting abilities. Although based on my discussion with Lee, it was too late for that.

"No, we don't." Lei-hawm didn't say anything, but the little crowd of Darenti suddenly burst into motion, as if they'd been given a signal. A mental one, perhaps. Valo and Yentar stretched their arms like telescoping front legs and stepped out of the vehicle, contracting to their normal size as they hit the ground. Then Io shifted into her leaf form and bounced out the door, fluttering to the ground on a draft.

Joss, Zina, and Tiah gasped, staring at the remaining enti. Lee looked unsurprised but a little green.

"Wha—" Zina pointed at the departing enti. "How?"

Lee recovered quickly. "shape-shifters." His cold eyes fell on me. "She knew."

The other three human heads snapped in my direction, like magnets to iron. "You knew?" Tiah whispered.

I glared at Lee. "I found out yesterday. No, the day before. When we hit the beach. They demonstrated their abilities."

"Why didn't you say something?" Zina stomped to me, getting in my face.

"Oh, you mean like, hey, these people are shape-shifters. Because they didn't care to demonstrate their abilities, and you wouldn't have believed me without that. In fact," I glanced at Lee, "you probably would have taken me back to the base for a mental health check."

Tiah shuffled a few steps closer to Verdat, peering closely at the small being. "You don't really look like that, do you?" She glanced at us. "They're wearing human form to look familiar to us, right?"

"How'd you know?" I asked.

She shrugged. "I read a lot of fiction. And come on, what are the odds that the first sapient race we encounter would look so much like us?"

Verdat smiled, the expression not quite right in his human face. "But I like this form. Except for long distance traveling. Then four legs are better than two." With that, his arms lengthened, and his hands shifted into thick pads. He extended and retracted a wicked looking set of claws, then dropped to all fours and did the stretch and retract thing to reach the ground a meter below. Gara and Lei-hawm followed, their humanoid legs elongating one at a time.

Lee stepped back and gestured to the doorway. He waited for Joss to lift off the deck and glide past him. "After you, ladies."

Joss ignored him. "Running a perimeter check. Drones are active."

I blinked. I should have thought to send out the drones. Maybe Lee was right—I'd let Lei-hawm cloud my judgment. I flicked my holo-ring and reactivated my comms. I couldn't be an effective part of this team if I couldn't communicate.

My audio pinged. Lee. I glanced at him, standing a few meters away, as Tiah and Zina lifted from the deck and followed the others to the ground. "What?"

His rough voice came through my audio. "Finally come to your senses?"

I checked my stunner and took the blaster he handed me, carefully avoiding eye contact. "I'm trying to remain objective. And you might be right that I've allowed past relationships to affect my decision-making process in the last few days."

"Don't feel bad—it's normal." He chuckled, but it was surprisingly gentle. "Okay, finding out your glider is really a shape-shifting alien isn't normal, but distancing yourself from someone you trusted is hard." He looked away, his eyes sad.

Lee's mother had been an admiral in the CEC until she'd been convicted of larceny, embezzlement, conspiracy, and behavior unbecoming an officer. I hadn't really thought about her in years, but she must never be far from his mind.

As cadets, Joss and I had thought Lee was a spoiled troublemaker. Influenced by his mom, he'd gotten in with a bad group at the Academy. Although he'd redeemed himself later, the initial distrust seemed to linger. That was part of the reason he'd transferred to the Navy—to start fresh.

I touched his arm. "Thanks."

He jerked his head at the hatch, and his voice hardened again. "Get moving. Let's get this thing done."

I bit back a retort and lifted off the deck. As I exited the ship, Joss used his holo-ring to close and lock the hatch.

Lee muttered something under his breath and surged away before the closing door clipped his heels. Joss snickered.

The five humans dropped to the ground near the six Darenti. "Which way are we going?" Joss's hands flicked through holo-screens, guiding his drones.

"Hey—how did you get away from the news drones?" I asked.

"Easy." Joss's gaze flicked toward the overcast sky. "We launched as if we were going back to the station, did an orbit, then landed here. The news drones are suborbital, so we left them behind."

"And no one caught you leaving?"

"They probably assumed we were headed back to the ship." We both shuddered. Getting send back to the ship was an explorer's worst nightmare. It meant the commander determined you weren't explorer material.

Lei-hawm pointed into the jungle. The meter-high opening in the wall of foliage looked like a tunnel cut into a wall—very similar to the tunnels into the city. "The entrance to the local enti's dwelling is that way—about a klick, by your measurements."

A drone zipped past and dove into the tunnel, its faint buzz vibrating in my jaw.

"Looks clear. Anyone want to chicken out?" Joss circled his arm and dropped his hand.

"Hell, no!" I jumped when Lee's voice echoed mine in the traditional CEC exchange.

"Siti, you're on point." Joss nudged his sister and Tiah into a line. Then you two. Then me, Lee in the rear."

Lei-hawm held up a hand. "Verdat will take point. It is best if another enti is the first contact with the locals."

Joss nodded. "Your planet, your rules."

"Who put you in charge anyway?" I punched Joss's shoulder as I passed.

"We did." Zina pointed at Tiah, then swung her finger to indicate herself. "As Earth delegates to Darenti, we outrank all of you. And no offense, Siti, but I've seen Joss in action on Earth. He says you're good, and the commendation reports I've seen concur, but if I have to pick one of you, I'm going with the known quantity." She nodded at her brother.

I shrugged. "I'm okay with that. I don't have to be in charge all the time. Just wanted to make sure we knew what the pecking order was. You know, so we know who to blame." I winked at Joss and followed the Darenti into the jungle.

The low clearance meant walking crouched or floating in our grav belts. Maintaining a horizontal position for any length of time required abs of steel but traveling hunched over grew tiresome even faster. I crossed my legs under me and reset my belt to provide a little support under them. Then I pretended I was riding my magic carpet.

The path we followed appeared to be a natural animal trail, beaten down to bare dirt, but the brush overhead had been cut cleanly, as if they'd taken a laser hedge trimmer to it only a few days before. As Lei-hawm had predicted, we reached a crossroad in less than a klick.

"This way." Verdat had paused to wait for us to catch up but now started along the side path. Before long, it ended in a little dell. The foliage had been cut back almost two meters overhead, forming a green dome over a three-meter-wide circle. In the center of the circle, a carefully built grotto of stones arched over a round opening in the ground.

I crouched to look inside, but the dim light under the jungle canopy didn't penetrate more than a meter, leaving the bottom in darkness. "This looks familiar."

Joss raised his brows at me. "It does?"

I nodded. "Spire City—Lei-hawm's city—has entrances like this but without the fancy stone arch." I turned to the little Darenti. "Does your city have a name?"

"Not really. Since most of our communication is silent, we don't assign words to places. We identify them by the image and the *therentia*, so Spire City works."

Lee cleared his throat. Beads of sweat had formed on his temples. "No one said anything about going underground."

"Are you afraid?" Joss jeered.

Zina punched her brother, hard. "Cut the trash talk, little brother. Or I'll tell him about—"

Joss threw up both hands and interrupted her. "No ridicule here! It's perfectly normal to have phobias."

Lee scooted closer to Zina and put on his most charming smile. "Tell me more about Joss's phobias."

"You think I'm giving up my leverage? Forget it, fly-boy." Zina turned her back to the Navy pilot. "How deep does it go, and who's going first?"

Lei-hawm gestured to the hole, and Verdat and Yentar slunk in, disappearing into the darkness. "They will check for us, then we follow."

"Is the Stone down there?" I waved at the surrounding jungle. "Obviously, it's easier for you to travel underground, but maybe we can fly over and meet you wherever you're coming out? Those cramped tunnels are hard on taller folk."

"The Stone is down there."

CHAPTER SEVENTEEN

Lee peered into the hole as our Darenti escort disappeared into the inky darkness. "The fabled Pebble of Avon couldn't be somewhere easy to access, like an open air museum or a jewelry store."

"It wouldn't be much of a quest if it was easy to get." Joss flicked his grav belt controls and descended into the opening. This one appeared to be deeper than the entrance to Lei-hawm's Spire City. Joss's head disappeared into the darkness. Then a light flickered on—his holo-ring. The faint glow grew smaller and smaller, then disappeared completely.

"Torres, report." Despite the sheen of sweat on his upper lip, Lee's tone remained crisp and authoritative.

After a long pause—undoubtedly Joss trying to rattle Lee—he replied, "Looks good. There's a long tunnel—tall enough that Tiah shouldn't have to duck. We're waiting."

Lee, Tiah, Zina, and I exchanged a look. With a heavy sigh, Lee waved toward the hole. "Let's get this over with."

As Zina slowly dropped into the hole, I raised an eyebrow at Tiah. "Do you need help with the grav belt? I can tether yours to mine."

She rubbed her forehead. "I've been practicing at home."

"Are you okay?"

"I've had a headache since I got to Darenti. Maybe I'm allergic to something here." She descended into the dark entry. "See you at the bottom."

I turned to Lee. His pale face looked green, although that might have been reflected by the foliage overhead. I didn't suffer from claustrophobia, but I knew it could be debilitating. I touched his arm. "Are you okay with this? You can go back to the shuttle. I'll tell them I sent you—to relay communications or something."

He sucked in a deep breath, then his eyes hardened. "Don't try to do me any favors, Kassis. I'm fine." He brushed past me. "I'm not letting you and your boyfriend ridicule me."

"My boyfriend? Joss?" I laughed. "Please. Have you seen him around women? He's like a kid in a candy store. I'm not interested in a guy who can't make up his mind." Just to goad him a little, I added, "He is pretty hot, though."

Lee swung around, hovering over the lip of the entrance, scowling. "Why do women always look for 'hot'?" He started down, flicking his holo-ring to life.

"Same reason men do." I smirked until he disappeared into the shaft. I certainly wasn't going to tell him I thought he was hotter than Joss. *Yeesh, when had that happened?* As I waited, I gave myself a stern lecture. I didn't need to develop a crush in the middle of a mission—especially not on Derek Lee. Time to focus on the Stone.

When his light grew dim, I followed into the darkness. The glow of my ring illuminated the sides of the tunnel as I dropped. Like the path through the jungle, the sides were smooth as if they had been carved by a single sharp cutter. Near the surface, cleanly cut roots showed as pale circles and ovals against the deep brown of the dirt. Farther down, the roots disappeared, leaving a uniform curve of soil. I looked down, but the light from my ring prevented me from seeing anything outside its feeble glow. The altitude indicator from my grav belt showed negative twenty meters and dropping. At negative twenty-seven, my feet touched down.

I looked up at the circle of light over my head. How had the Darenti descended that smooth well? Turning slowly, I examined the walls. Behind me, a series of uniform horizontal slots led up the side in what must have been a Darenti ladder. Beside the lowest holes, a meter-high opening led onward.

I ducked into the tunnel. The floor sloped downward at a steep angle, while the ceiling stayed level. The others waited for me at the bottom. Joss and Lee had to flex their knees and duck their heads, but the overhead here cleared Zina's curls by a few centimeters. Tiah, being quite short, floated a handspan above the floor with plenty of room to go higher.

"The city is this way." Lei-hawm pointed down the tunnel, as if we had another choice. The rest of the enti clustered around him, chittering and cheeping softly. It sounded less cheerful than usual.

"Is something wrong?" I darted my eyes at the other enti.

"Something is... different." Lei-hawm gestured to Verdat and Io. "We aren't sure what, exactly. But the presence we sense ahead is not—" He did a very human looking shrug. "I have never been to this city before. But these enti feel...."

"Is it safe?" Joss asked. "Will they think we're invading? I don't want to provoke an attack."

Tiah looked at the enti—none of them much more than a meter high. "They don't look very dangerous."

"Don't let their size deceive you," Zina said. "If they think we're attacking their home, who knows what they're capable of? You don't look very formidable, either, but you wouldn't let invaders into the Dome, would you?"

A shadow of distress darkened Tiah's face, then disappeared. "Good point."

"I believe you will be safe." Lei-hawm turned decisively. "We will not let them hurt you."

Lee reached out to grab the little Darenti's shoulder. "They can hear you coming, right? Telepathically. They'll know you're here to steal that Stone. That's going to make them cranky."

"The Stone is not a problem." Lei-hawm slid out of Lee's grasp. "That is the least of our worries." He disappeared into the inky darkness.

"What is that supposed to mean?" Lee straightened, knocking his head on the top of the tunnel. "Ow!" A small shower of dirt sifted onto him. He rubbed his head, then brushed the dirt from his shoulders.

Zina shrugged. "I guess we'll find out." She squared her shoulders and followed the enti. The rest of us trailed behind, leaving Lee to bring up the rear.

Although the tunnel had the same clean-cut appearance as the entrance, it changed sizes as we walked. In some places, we had to bend almost double to get through, but it opened up after a few paces. Why had they dug some places so large and others so narrow?

"Boulder." As we walked, Lei-hawm had slowed until he and I walked side-by-side. "The lower places are due to rocks that couldn't be sheared."

"How did you know what I was thinking?" I touched the metal band on my head. I knew it was still there—constant pressure had given me a slight headache. I fingered the flat leaves soldered to the band. All intact.

"I've learned to read your face." Lei-hawm's bright eyes twinkled in the dim cavern, almost seeming to have a light of their own. His voice dropped to a faint whisper I could barely hear over the thudding of boots and the shushing of enti feet, pods, and Io's bouncing leaf stem. "As Liam, I was able to feel your emotions but couldn't read your thoughts."

I nodded absently. Liam had always seemed to know my mood. And while he had learned many commands and signals, he'd never responded in a way that made me think he could read my mind. "How did they make these tunnels?"

"Creating a tunnel is simply a reforming of the dirt. But stone is dense. You saw how much effort it took to withdraw and shape the metal from the pebbles. Those rocks were small. Trying to change the form of a large rock? It's easier to go under or around." He nodded at the curve ahead of us. "We're almost there."

We rounded the corner—the shape of the boulder more obvious now that I understood—and stopped. The tunnel stretched wider, into a large cavern. Brighter light silhouetted a vast army of moving shapes. None of them resembled humans, although I picked out several two-legged forms. Our dim holo-ring glow wasn't strong enough to pick out features. They stood in a ragged group, blocking the exit from the tunnel.

Lei-hawm tugged my hand. I leaned down so he could whisper in my ear. "Verdat is speaking with them."

The enti stood silent, gazing at each other. Occasionally, a murmur of sound washed through the group, sometimes sounding friendly, other times menacing. Individuals moved slightly, and one of the opposing enti reformed into a vaguely humanoid appearance.

My comm pinged, and Lee's voice came through, along with a notification that I had been connected to a multi-channel call. "What's going on?"

"They're talking." I tipped my head at Verdat. "I imagine they're discussing who we are and what we want, but I don't know."

"Ask him what's going on." Joss jerked his chin at Lei-hawm.

I shook my head a tiny bit. "No. Let them figure it out." I shifted from one foot to the other, rolling my shoulders as inconspicuously as I could. The tunnel here was high enough that even Joss didn't have to slouch, and he took advantage of that to follow my lead. Lee stood beside him, his blaster held across his body. When had he unslung it from his shoulder?

"No shooting," I told Lee.

"Do we even know what blaster fire would do to them? If they can shift their shape, maybe they can just reform after a blast."

I blinked. As far as I knew, no one had ever shot an enti—which was surprising, considering human history. Except now that we knew the humans had been under a form of mind control, maybe it made sense. "I'm not sure it's been tested. How would it be? And why? Until now, we thought Darenti were just flesh and blood."

Zina looked at the weapon in Lee's hands. "Maybe you should put that thing away." She mimed slinging it over her shoulder.

Lee didn't move. "I don't plan to shoot anyone, but I'm not ruling it out if they attack."

"Siti!" Lei-hawm's deep voice snapped my head around. "These enti, Tribe Gothodi, have granted us entrance to their city. They understand our mission and will allow us to search."

"Search?" Joss stepped forward. "You don't know where this Stone is?"

"What kind of quest would that be?" Lei-hawm produced a fair imitation of Joss's voice. "It's more fun this way."

Joss snorted a laugh.

"This isn't a game." Lee glared at the little creature. "We have jobs to do and playing hide and seek isn't one of them. Let's find this thing and get out of here."

Lei-hawm's smile faded, and he nodded regally. "You are correct. We will find the relic and take it to Perista. Before we enter, however, you must remove the inhibitors." He tapped his temple.

My hand went to the metal band. During the silent negotiations, the headache had intensified, and taking it off sounded like a great idea.

"No." Lee held up a hand. "Don't do it. We won't make ourselves vulnerable to an unknown threat. If that's a problem for them, we'll leave. You and your buddies can look for the Stone."

"I hate to say it, but Nibs is right." The sour expression on Joss's face made his distaste clear.

"They're asking as a sign of good faith." Lei-hawm held up both hands, palms open. "They can't read your intentions."

"You can vouch for us, but we aren't letting them control us, and I'm surprised you'd ask." Lee glared at Lei-hawm. "You know what V'Ov did to the ambassadors. Or is that your plan? To get us under their control?"

"Why would he have had his people create these if that was the plan?" I tapped the metal positioned over my temples.

"I'll take mine off." Tiah reached for her headband. She paused when the others protested, then held up a hand for silence. "There is some evidence that I am not susceptible to the Darenti mind control." She gestured at Lee, Joss, and Zina. "Unlike the rest of you, I was concerned that Siti had gone missing. I asked questions. Besides, if they do take control of my mind, the four of you are more than capable of overpowering me. I have no weapon, so I am not a danger to you."

I bit my lip. Her arguments seemed sound. "But if you aren't susceptible to the mind control, will they be able to read your intentions? Don't those two things go together?"

"We have one way to find out." She reached for the band tucked into her dark hair. "Three, two, one." She pulled the metal free.

The enti seemed to snap to attention, all of them zeroing in on Tiah like laser guided missiles. Even our companions swung around to look. Lee's hand moved to the grip of his blaster, and Joss's back straightened, his fingers quivering near his holster.

Tiah swallowed, loud in the stillness.

"Are you okay, Tiah?" I whispered.

Her shoulders twitched. "I think so? I can almost feel them inside my mind. It's crowded in here."

"Can they hear what you're thinking?" Zina asked.

"I don't—not quite? It's... difficult to describe."

As one, the enti moved away, leaving us alone in the tunnel.

"Tiah!" Zina lurched forward to catch the smaller woman as she wavered, then slumped. The grav belt kept her from hitting the ground, but her body went limp. Zina lowered her to the dirt and pressed her fingers against the girl's neck. "Her pulse is solid. Do you have a med-scan, Joss?"

"I'm fine." Tiah tried to sit up. "Just got a bit woozy."

Zina nudged the smaller woman back down. She took the medical device from her brother and pressed it against Tiah's arm. The screen lit, and data flowed across it. "Nothing wrong with her, except her blood pressure dropped, but it's coming back up. What happened?"

"Good question." I grabbed Lei-hawm's arm. "What did they do to her?"

"She was overwhelmed by the number of enti trying to interact with her. Her mind is different from the rest of you—not that they would know that, since they can't see yours, but we saw it." He gestured at the rest of our escort and himself.

"Different how?" Tiah sat up.

"Maybe you shouldn't—"

Tiah brushed Zina off. "I'm fine. You can take the scanner thing off me. I had a full physical before I came."

Zina tapped the screen again and pulled the device away from the other woman's arm. "It says you're fine, too."

"Told you." Tiah turned to Lei-hawm. "Different how?"

His nose twitched, reminding me of Liam. "I can't explain exactly, but you're difficult to read and impossible to influence. I can't believe I didn't notice it before."

"Before?" Joss looked up from stowing the med-scan in the large pouch he carried around his waist. "You mean when we arrived this morning? We got the new metal things put together pretty quickly."

Lei-hawm looked at me for a long moment, then turned back to Joss. "I should have seen it before you put them on."

"We really need to come up with a better name for those things." Joss closed the pack and slid it around to the small of his back. His eyes twinkled. "Brain wave suppressor? Mind protector? Non-infiltrator?"

"Like those are better than headband." Lee scowled.

"Headband it is." Zina stood and offered Tiah a hand.

The smaller woman waved off the assistance and hit the controls of her grav belt, rising above the ground. "I told you, I'm fine. Let's go find the Stone."

"You think they'll let us in?" I asked Lei-hawm as we moved to the mouth of the tunnel.

"Oh, yes, they said they need our help."

CHAPTER EIGHTEEN

LIKE SPIRE CITY, this settlement was built as a single edifice but on a much smaller scale and a completely different architecture. The familiar fuzzy glows illuminated the high, blank walls, giving the fortress-like structure a mottled appearance. Lei-hawm translated the Gothodi's instructions, directing us to lift over the building and drop into the single central courtyard. All of the enti, including our own escort, disappeared through the single door, which shut behind them with a solid thunk.

I set my grav belt to a slow lift. "Looks like they're prepared for a siege."

Joss zipped past me, then slowed his ascent to match mine. "That's what I was thinking. This looks a lot like the walls we built back home, except stone instead of wood. I thought you said the Darenti weren't afraid of the local wildlife?"

"That's what Liam—I mean Lei-hawm—said."

Joss's brows drew down. "Where is Liam? He came dirtside with us, but I haven't seen him since we got here. Did he get left back at the base? That isn't like him."

I raised my eyebrows, trying to look surprised. "No, he's here. Somewhere. He enjoys leaping through the jungle, so he might have stayed on the surface. You know Liam—I'm not worried about him."

Joss leaned back, studying my face. "The locals are obviously worried about something." He gestured to the wall as it slid by. "Anything that might eat an enti could finish off a glider in one bite."

I frowned, assuming a concerned voice. "Good point. I hope he's smart enough to come down here. He always finds me."

"Yeah, he does." Lee moved up beside us, and he gave me a pointed look. "I'm sure he'll be fine."

"What's going on?" Joss's gaze darted back and forth between me and Lee. "You two are up to something."

Lee and I exchanged a look. I shook my head. "Nope. Nothing. Oh, look, there's Liam!" I pointed behind Joss.

He spun around, and I made a face at Lee. He held up both hands, as if to say he wasn't playing my game, and put on a burst of speed to lift away from us.

Joss turned back. "I didn't see him."

I waved past him, toward the top of the structure. "He just went over the top. We'll find him inside." I increased my lift and followed Lee over the high wall.

Inside, the structure looked more like Spire City, with wide, irregular windows, sinuously curved walls, and a dozen levels of balconies. We skimmed over the gently arched roof and dropped into the central courtyard, which boasted a profusion of blue-green plants and a central fountain. As we approached the ground, the enti swarmed out of the lower windows, gathering at one end of the space.

Lei-hawm hurried to meet us, with Verdat, Io, and the rest of our escort on his heels. Although he was the smallest of the group, he moved faster than the others and reached me quickly.

I stooped to whisper, "Joss was asking about Liam."

Lei-hawm nodded. "We should tell him. But not now."

"Tell who what?" Lee stared down at us with his arms crossed.

"Nobody. Nothing." I stood. "Why are you here? You could have stayed in the shuttle."

His lips pressed together, and his shoulders tensed, but he didn't reply.

The other humans gathered around, and we watched the Gothodi mingle at a slight distance. Many of them now wore humanoid shapes. A little blue sphere grew four arms with three fingered hands on each, then retracted them. Other enti followed its example, cycling through different body parts as we waited.

The crowd settled, and their attention turned to us. I could almost feel the weight of their regard, even though many of them didn't have recognizable eyes. A green, three-legged being with multiple antennae standing out from its barrel-shaped body took a place next to Lei-hawm, towering over him.

Lei-hawm stood silent, then turned to look up at us. "Will you remove your headbands to receive information directly?"

"Nope." Lee's flat response prompted an indrawn breath from Joss, but none of us argued. Lee's military training might have made him more cautious than the rest of us, but in this instance, I was grateful for his vigilance.

Lei-hawm gave a tiny nod, as if he agreed with this wariness. "Very well, I will translate." After another moment of silence, he went on. "The Gothodi have lived in this valley for many generations. Hundreds of millennia, by human reckoning. Enti have no natural predators—as I told you before, we don't taste like chicken."

I hid a smile. Lee snorted softly. Joss's head jerked, and he stared at Lei-hawm, his eyes narrowing.

"However, in very recent times—perhaps five or six years—the Gothodi have experienced losses. Enti disappearing with no indication of where they went or what happened to them. They are feared deceased." His voice changed to an informational tone. "*Enti* disintegrate very quickly after death. Traditionally, when we reach the end of life, we take leave of the tribe and spend some time alone in the jungle. When the end comes, it is quick and painless, and not much is left."

He turned back to the barrel-shaped enti. "Ungala says these enti disappeared without notice—something that almost never happens. As you've seen, enti are social—they wouldn't leave without a farewell. In addition, many of them were far too young for a final departure."

Zina cleared her throat. "Five or six years—they must have some idea what is happening."

"Yes, they do. There has been activity in the next valley—human activity. Ungala says the humans are killing the Gothodi."

We all spoke at once.

"There are no humans in—"

"That doesn't—"

"Who would do such a thing?"

Sticking my fingers in my mouth, I whistled, cutting through the babble. The enti—except Lei-hawm—all shrank back, but whether it was fear, distaste, or discomfort, I couldn't tell. "Yes, there shouldn't be humans on Rovantu. But this is a big planet. Let's hear what they have to say."

"Thank you, Siti." Lei-hawm turned back to Ungala, then began his narrative again. "The humans are digging a deep tunnel—much deeper than enti go, through stone, which is difficult for enti to shape. They are removing something from the ground."

"Mining?" Lee scratched his chin, his fingernails rasping through the beginnings of stubble. "Did the CEC do a mineral assay on the planet before they met the locals?"

Zina nodded. "Yes. That's one of the reasons they wanted to explore this planet—in addition to its location in the goldilocks zone, initial scans indicated potential for large deposits of promethium and smaller amounts of senidium. But once they discovered sapient life, the planet was quarantined until the local population was deemed prepared for integration."

Joss snorted and put on a mechanical voice. "Prepare to be assimilated."

Zina gave him a stern look, but humor threaded through her tone. "Integration is the approved terminology."

"You think we're dealing with pirates?" I raised an eyebrow at Zina.

"If humans are mining here, they're pirates, even if they're sanctioned by our government." She rubbed the back of her neck. "We should probably call in the big dogs."

"Who would that be?" I turned to Lei-hawm. "Do you think V'Ov knows about this?"

Tiah raised her hand. "Speaking of her, why didn't the Gothodi just do the mind control thing like V'Ov?"

"Trying to influence another's thoughts is extremely difficult with other enti." Lei-hawm gestured to the enti gathered around us. "The Gothodi have remained isolated from the humans—they chose to stay apart. And they shun contact with any who might interact with the humans. As a result, they were unaware of what has transpired in Perista. They believed V'Ov must have approved the human facility."

"But why didn't they complain?" I asked. "Surely even V'Ov wouldn't stand by while humans killed enti?"

"V'Ov is entirely focused on getting off-world. She sees that as her best opportunity to maintain power. She may have allowed these humans access to the planet, and if so, it is to further that goal. I think it is more likely she is unaware of these predations and her meddling has allowed them to slip through the safety net your government has put around our planet."

Lei-hawm stared silently at Ungala again, then turned to us. "The Gothodi ask you to help them get rid of the humans."

"Maybe now that they know what V'Ov is up to, they can just—" Joss wiggled his fingers near his head, then extended his arms toward Lei-hawm "—use their freaky mind waves to send them away?"

Lei-hawm cocked his head at Ungala, and a little smirk crossed his lips. "Desperate times call for desperate measures. They *have* tried to control the humans—several times, but with no success. In fact, until we arrived, they believed humans were not susceptible to such persuasion. That's why they wanted to see into your minds. I assured them you were trustworthy, but after their recent experience..." He looked at Tiah. "And why they overwhelmed you—they all tried to control you at once, in a desperate bid to learn to protect themselves. Ungala offers his sincere apologies for that invasion."

"Based on what we've seen in the history of Darenti, every ambassador—and their staff, apparently—have been immediately overcome by V'Ov. Of course, this is pure speculation." Lee pointed at Tiah. "But she's the only person *we know of* who can withstand them. She's from an isolated gene-pool—maybe it's genetic."

Tiah jumped to her feet, fists on her hips. "Are you saying you think those pirates are from the Dome?"

Zina held up a hand. "No, he's not saying that. Are you?" She glared at Lee.

The Navy pilot shrugged. "I said she's the only one we know. There could be other people with the same genes."

"None of her relatives willingly leave the bunker." Zina turned back to Tiah. "But there could be others in the galaxy with the same ability."

Joss had been leaning against the wall, but at this, he peeled away and stood upright. "And they just happened to be the ones who came to Darenti to steal minerals? That's a crazy idea, Zina. No one but the Darenti knew about V'Ov's mind control, so the idea that a special group of humans were selected for this mission is ludicrous."

Zina waved a hand. "Granted. Obviously, it's something else. Or someone knows way more than we think."

We all stared at each other, until Tiah finally voiced the thought. "Could the Commonwealth government know about the Darenti's abilities?"

CHAPTER NINETEEN

LEE CLEARED THIS THROAT, cutting through our arguments. "I haven't seen anything to indicate the Commonwealth government knows about the Darenti's mind control. If they did, the embassy would have taken precautions." He tapped his headband.

"You're just a lieutenant." Joss ran a hand over his head, the gesture an unconscious imitation of his father. If his hair hadn't been tightly braided, he would have shoved his fingers through it. "You hardly have access to all classified information."

"I was assigned to the Darenti mission. I was given access to all information about the planet in support of the embassy." Lee's lips pressed together.

"You saw exactly what V'Ov allowed you to see." Lei-hawm pointed at each of us in turn. "She controls all information that leaves this world. We need to investigate and bring in an outside entity."

Lee's eyes narrowed as he stared down at the tiny enti. "You don't give the orders around here. You're *asking* for our help, not commanding it."

The two stared at each other for a few seconds, then Lei-hawm held up both hands. "Agreed. On behalf of our hosts, I request you investigate the mining that is occurring. If we help them stop the humans, they will give us the Stone."

"Why didn't you say so?" Zina jumped to her feet. "Let's stop lollygagging around and get to investigating so we can get that rock and kick V'Ov's butt."

We all snickered. Tiah, sitting on the fountain's low stone wall, held up a hand. "How do you propose investigating?"

Joss smirked and gestured at me and Lee. "We got pretty good at snooping in the Academy. Leave it to us."

Zina put her hands on her hips. "You aren't leaving me behind."

"Or me." Lei-hawm stepped forward.

"Oh, are you part of the team, Lei-hawm?" Lee affected a surprised air. "I thought you were some random Darenti we'd stumbled on in the wilds."

"What is going on?" Zina looked from Lee to the little enti. "Why are you so hostile, Lee?"

"He's always hostile." Joss rolled his eyes, then focused on Lee. "But there's something else this time."

Lee raised an eyebrow at me. "Do you want to tell them, Siti, or shall I?"

"Tell us what?" Tiah struggled up from her seat.

I turned to Lei-hawm. The Gothodi had disappeared, melting away into their fortress while we bickered. Only our escort remained. "You said you were going to tell them."

"I'll show them." Lei-hawm went still, then did his melting thing, leaving Liam in his place.

"Holy—" Joss clapped a hand over his mouth in shock.

The two women stared at Liam in disbelief. Lee looked a little green but unsurprised.

After a long moment, Zina turned her eyes on me. "Did you know?"

"I found out when I arrived here—in Rovantu. I didn't have any idea before that."

"How did he get off Darenti?" Joss asked.

I shrugged and turned to look at Liam. "He can't speak in this form—he said something about part of his essence being stored in an alternate dimension when he's in this shape. But he said he snuck aboard the original CEC ship—the one my dad was on."

The little glider morphed back into Lei-hawm. "Siti is correct. I accompanied her father when he left Darenti, although he didn't know it. And I have been seeing the galaxy with various CEC members since then. But when I heard the Darenti were petitioning again for the opportunity to leave the planet—and that the Commonwealth was considering their plea, I—" He broke off, looking guilty.

Lee pointed at Lei-hawm. "You did your mind control thing to make sure Siti was assigned to this mission. Admit it."

"I do admit it." Lei-hawm held out both hands, palms up, and bowed low. "I didn't like doing it, but I wanted to come home, and I didn't wish to leave Siti without explanation. It's hard to fake your own death."

Zina nodded. "It's hard to lose a pet—and I assume that's what he considers you."

Lee snickered.

I stared at Zina in amazement. "I'm *his* pet?" I looked at Lei-hawm. "Is that how you feel? I'm a cute little—big—creature you take care of? I'm not sure I like being an alien's pet. Especially since I have to find my own food!"

"No, I don't consider you a pet. I hope we are friends. But I did influence people around you to ensure you were assigned to this mission, and I apologize for that."

"Can we just get on with the investigating?" Tiah rubbed her leg. Even with the grav belt, the rough travel appeared to be taking a toll on her. "I would like to get back to the embassy where I can have a hot shower." She smirked in response to our surprised looks. "Sure, it wasn't something we had in the Dome, but I've gotten used to the luxury."

I LAY on my belly in the mud just below the top of a hill. The thick foliage provided excellent cover—obviously, the pirates weren't concerned about a surprise attack. Or they considered the risk worth the cover provided from overhead satellites.

Lee and Zina held positions on my left, with Joss a few meters ahead, peering over the top. Liam, in his sair-glider form, had scrambled off into the jungle as soon as we reached the hill. I assumed he was investigating the camp on his own.

"I think I figured out why the Gothodi can't control these miners." Joss's voice came through our audio implants. "They're wearing helmets."

"Helmets? All the time?" Lee sounded disbelieving.

"There's a building in the center of the compound. Everyone who comes out of that building has a helmet on. Their protocol must require helmets when outside. Maybe they don't believe the atmosphere is safe."

"They're mining," Zina said. "They probably don't want rocks falling on their heads."

"They have a shuttle, but it's under cover. Looks like they've built it from the naturally available material, maybe to hide the craft from satellites."

"That might also be why they wear the helmets." As he continued to speak subvocally, Joss gave us the hand signal to advance. "Camouflage. Not just visual, but if they've worked out a way to hide life-signs from the satellites…"

I belly crawled to the top of the hill. "That's brilliant. Not something we'd ever employ because the CEC wants to be able to find our people." Squinting through the thick foliage, I picked out a rectangular structure. It looked similar to the portable buildings we deployed during exploration, but the sides had been painted with a greenish-blue camouflage. The unnaturally square corners were the only reason I had been able to pick it out.

"That's one advantage pirates have." Lee came up to my side and pulled a piece of gear out of his belt pouch. "They don't care if they lose personnel."

"What is that?" I tapped the case of his device as he swiped through screens on his holo-ring.

The corner of his mouth turned up. "This is classified Navy tech." He lifted the device and pointed one end at the boxy building. "I can't tell you what it does." With a wink, he adjusted the hologram so I could see better. It displayed a semi-transparent, three-dimensional model of the building below. Two human-shaped blobs moved inside the building. One raised its arms as if to put on a hat and disappeared from the screen.

In real life, the door to the building opened, and a helmeted individual came out.

"That's pretty cool." I poked a finger at the hologram, rotating the view. "Those helmets really hide them!"

"Yes and no." Lee adjusted something, and a ghostly figure appeared in the holo, exactly where the real human now stood. It looked around the tiny clearing, then headed toward the hills where we suspected the mine entrance would be. "At short distance and high power, I can detect them. But it's a serious drain on the device." A power indicator flashed yellow in a corner of the screen. He flipped a few icons, and the ghost disappeared.

"Navy ships have enough power to detect these folks from orbit, but none of them are in system." Lee turned the device off and returned it to his pouch.

I stared at him. "Zina said Ambassador Slovenska was agitating for a military presence at Darenti. Could she be fighting the mind control in some way?"

He raised his eyebrows in a "who knows" kind of shrug. He leaned close to whisper instead of using the audio implant. "Have you experienced it? The mind control."

It was my turn to shrug. "Would I know if I had?" A foggy memory of my meeting with Gara and Verdat came back to me. "Actually, yes, I have. You can tell you're doing something you wouldn't normally do, but it's foggy. Like a memory from a party where you drank too much Yager Hula."

"Now what?" Joss didn't turn to look at us. "We know they're down there and why the Gothodi can't control them. What do we do?"

Zina started ticking options off on her fingers. "We could call in the Navy and get them to do a scan. The enti could go inside the building and take them over when they don't have their helmets on."

Joss slid backward down the hill to stop beside us. "We could grab one of those guys, wrestle his helmet off, and let Lei-hawm do his mind control thing."

I raised an eyebrow at Joss. "I expected you to say we could take over the camp."

"You know I love my action-hero opportunities, but we don't exactly have superior numbers."

"Are you kidding?" Lee waved a hand behind us. "We have a gazillion Darenti with vengeance on their minds. We could totally take over the camp."

"If the Darenti had vengeance on their minds, they would have taken these guys out by now. Three of them could stand on each other's shoulders and pretend to be a human, then walk right in." Joss used his fingers to mime the scenario. "They're leaving this to us. And if we want to get that Stone, we need to do it for them."

Below us, the door opened again, and the last human came out. Something small and brown scuttled out from under the building and slipped inside.

"That was Liam, wasn't it?" I asked.

No one answered.

G'lacTechNews

Welcome to G'lacTechNews. This is Aella Phoenix with Odysseus Helliesen in the studio. Starling Cross is reporting live from Darenti Four where preparations for the treaty talks are underway. Starling, what's the situation there?

Starling Cross:

Hi, Aella and Odysseus! The talks are progressing. You can see in this vid, the representatives chatting with the Darenti. Aren't they cute? And this place is amazing! I hope they open the planet to the general public because everyone should have the chance to travel here and see the sights.

Aella Phoenix:

I see a lot of jungle and some Explorer Corps living modules. Are there some local sites you can show us? And you haven't sent any vid of Siti Kassis or the Earth contingent lately.

Starling Cross (looking confused):

Uh, sure, I'll get some vid tomorrow. Back to you, Aella.

CHAPTER TWENTY

"How much longer are we going to wait?" Zina stood a few meters down the hill, where she wouldn't be seen from the other side, stretching and twisting. "Liam is in, probably transformed back to his weird, brain-melting self, waiting for people to come back. They just left, so I'm going to assume they're working an eight- to twelve-hour shift. Maybe someone will come back for lunch. It will be hours before that happens."

My audio implant pinged with an unknown ID. I frowned. My system hadn't connected to the satellites—I didn't want anyone back at base finding me. Therefore this must be a local call, which meant it was one of the three humans with me, or Tiah, back at the Gothodi city. But those IDs were all registered. "Who is this?"

"It's Lei-hawm."

I held up a hand and the conversation around me cut off. "It's Lei-hawm. How are you calling me?"

"Put it through to the rest of us!" Lee hissed.

I shook my head as Lei-hawm replied. "I'm in the pirates' base. I'm using their comm system. Come down and help me with the evidence."

"He wants us to go in." I rubbed the back of my neck. "Is this our best option? As Joss pointed out, we hardly have superior numbers."

"We don't need superior numbers." Lei-hawm's voice was firm. "You can pull evidence of their crimes from the equipment here and turn it over to the proper authorities. I can control anyone who comes inside."

I relayed Lei-hawm's idea to the others.

"Let's do it." Joss jumped to his feet and checked his weapons.

"I'm not sure…" I checked my stunner. Lee reached down to help me, but I shook him off and rolled slowly up.

Lee pulled his stunner from its holster. "It's easier and safer than trying to jump someone."

"More fun than sitting in the mud." Zina pulled out her own weapon.

I followed my friends down the hill. The plan seemed rash—could it have been influenced by Darenti mind control? Maybe Lei-hawm had figured out a way to use my audio implant against me. That didn't explain why the others were so eager to jump on board, and I was the holdout.

The idea of mind control had me doubting everything. Would I ever trust my own thoughts again?

We moved slowly, pausing often to watch and listen for the miners. Luckily, they had no idea we were here and didn't seem to have posted a guard. They clearly didn't know about the Gothodi—or didn't consider them a threat.

At the bottom of the hill, the others stood beside a familiar blue bollard. Lee waved an arm at the shimmering force shield. "This is standard Commonwealth tech—where did they get it?"

Zina pressed her hand against the blue force shield. "Explains why they aren't worried about the Darenti—or the local wildlife—because they've got a defense field up."

Joss shrugged. "Liam can get through those, remember?"

"Yeah, but we can't. And I don't think the average Darenti can, either." I turned to follow the wall of blue static through the thick foliage. "This is a pretty sophisticated shield. We usually clear a circle or rectangle. They had to plant bollards much closer together to weave around the trees."

Lee followed. "It must only be a wall—if it was a full dome, it would be visible from space."

"Good point. Can we go over?" Zina asked through the audio.

"We don't have to." I pointed. The next two bollards were only a few meters apart—they'd been placed that way to go around a thick multi-trunked tree. I flicked to the other call. "Lei-hawm, can you turn off the shield between Echo-247 and -248?"

"You'll have to talk me through it—I've never done it."

"You figured out how to use the comm pretty fast." Had he done *that* before? I walked him through the sequence, and the blue fizz dissolved. I turned to Zina, Joss, and Lee. "After you."

Once we got inside, Lei-hawm brought the field back online. "You won't have an easy escape route if something happens."

I smirked. Lei-hawm wasn't infallible after all. "If something goes wrong, we use the grav belts to jump out. Easy, peasy, since there's no force dome over this facility." I flicked to the group call. "Activate the emergency jump sequence on your belts. If we have to exit, we'll need to do it fast."

The others nodded. Joss and Lee flicked through the screens as fast as I did, but Zina—the civilian—needed assistance. When we finished, we moved carefully toward the building.

Joss's voice broke the silence. "Bogie at eleven o'clock." We froze, watching the human.

"Lei-hawm, someone's coming in. Hide!" I grabbed Zina's arm and yanked her behind a large tree.

The connection went dead. Zina and I crouched in the shadow of the tree, holding our breath. From the corner of my eye, I could see Lee braced against another tree, his weapon and eyes glued to the scene.

"Where's Joss?" Zina's voice came through softly.

"Here," Joss replied. "I have eyes on the door. He's inside."

We held our breath. Nothing moved, except the breeze rustling in the curly fronds of the trees. Lee's hand slowly moved toward his belt, probably to pull out his black box.

Then Liam scampered around a tree and stopped at my feet. I bit back a cry of relief. The little glider stood on his back legs, then took off the way we'd come in. We followed him to the force shield and activated our grav belts to rise over the twenty-meter fence, staying in the shadow of a tree until we reached the top of the field. Then we zipped away.

"I THOUGHT you said you could control the humans?" Lee paced across the clearing below our hillside. "Why'd we bug out?"

"There are too many. I am strong, but not that capable. And they return to the base too irregularly. If we knew their schedule, we could come up with a better plan. I wonder if they've figured out the helmets protect them?"

"I guess we watch and wait." I spread a drop cloth on the damp earth.

"Any idea who they are?" Lee glared at Lei-hawm.

"He wasn't wearing a nametag or company logo, if that's what you're asking." Lei-hawm grinned at Lee's dumbfounded look.

"I keep forgetting you've been living with Siti for eight years. Then you say something like that." Lee scratched his chin again. "That building was definitely Commonwealth design."

"Agreed. It looked like every CEC living module everywhere. Including the ones back at the base. I wonder if any went missing." Joss pulled some protein cubes from his pack and handed them out.

"If they did, no one appears to be looking for them."

Zina paused in unwrapping her food. "Could V'Ov have covered that up, too?"

Lei-hawm grunted. "She could have, but why? What does she gain from allowing pirates to mine Darenti?"

We watched the camp all day, the four of us taking two-hour shifts in pairs. Lei-hawm went back to the Gothodi fortress to speak with the leaders and the other Spire City enti. As we watched, the pirates came and went, but nothing interesting happened.

I sighed and rolled onto my back, peering up at the leaves arching over our heads. "After all this dim, cloudy sky, I need some time on a beach."

Zina chuckled. "You and me both, sister."

At nightfall, the four of us withdrew to a spot a few klicks away.

"Should we go back to Fort Gothod?" I glanced behind me. "Gara and Verdat said there are things out here that might find humans tasty. And we don't have a force shield."

"We can go to the shuttle." Lee pointed vaguely in the direction we'd come from. "It's within lifting distance if we go direct."

We agreed. As we flew to the shuttle, I called Tiah to tell her our plan.

"Do you want us to come get you? Are you okay spending the night in Fort Gothod?"

"Fort Gothod." She chuckled dryly. "That's appropriate. I'm fine. In fact, the room they've given me is probably way more comfortable than sleeping in a shuttle bunk."

"You haven't seen the VIP quarters. It's pretty cushy. Of course, there are only two bunks, so the four of us will have to arm wrestle or play poker to decide who sleeps where."

By the time we arrived, it was full dark. Lee opened the hatch, and we went inside. "I'm taking a hammock in the cockpit." Lee didn't wait for us to reply before stomping away.

"We should probably set a watch." I grimaced at the twins. "Why don't you two take the bunks, and I'll wake one of you in a couple of hours." My brain was still swirling with everything we'd learned that day. My chances of sleeping were small.

"Ace." Zina gave a thumbs-up and started climbing the ladder to the VIP bunks above the cockpit. "But let Lee do the second watch."

Joss snickered and activated his grav belt, beating his sister to the top. They argued good-naturedly as they turned in, then silence settled over the shuttle.

I flicked my holo-ring, but I hadn't slaved the surveillance system to it yet. I'd have to go to the cockpit to do that. With a soft tap on the open hatch, I went in.

A hammock swung gently above the two pilots' chairs. The forward viewscreen was dark, but the indicator lights from the active systems gave the scene a cozy glow. I crept forward and crouched near the co-pilot's seat.

"I'm still awake." The hammock swung over my head as Lee leaned out. "What are you doing?"

"Surveillance." I flicked the controls and brought up the correct screens. "Didn't want to wake you later, so I'm sending the signal to my holo-ring."

"I shoulda thought to do that before I turned in. I already have it on mine, so I can monitor the ship while we're out and about." He watched me work, then settled back into his hammock. "Are we doing the right thing?"

I turned, straightening so my head was on a level with his. Shadowed by the sides of the opaque hammock, his features were impossible to make out. "By helping Lei-hawm? Or what?"

The hammock swung as if he'd shrugged. "Any of it. Maybe we should go back to the embassy and give a report. This whole situation is way above our paygrade. My first Navy boss always told me to make her a culprit."

"What does that mean?"

"That if I kept her in the loop, she'd stop me from doing anything stupid. And take the blame if it went wrong."

I chuckled. "It's good advice for an *ensign*. But it won't work this time. Everyone on Darenti is subject to V'Ov's control and monitoring. When we bring in the big guns, it will need to be someone off-planet. Like my dad. Or Joss and Zina's."

A derisive snort answered that. "Must be nice to have the big players on speed-dial."

"It can be helpful. It can also hurt." I slumped into the co-pilot's chair. "No one believes I got to this point on my own—everything I do is attributed to being my father's daughter. It gets old."

"Yeah, I guess I see that. I took full advantage of being the admiral's son before..." He trailed off. His mother's fall from grace during our cadet years had been my fault.

Well, not really my fault—she committed the crimes. I was the one who caught her. The stigma was the main reason he'd left the CEC to take a Navy commission. They knew about his mother, too, of course, but only through hearsay. In the CEC, we'd lived it. Surprisingly, he didn't seem to hold it against me. I wasn't sure I could have been so magnanimous if our positions had been reversed.

I slapped the chair arms and pushed myself to my feet. "I'm going to leave you to get some sleep. I'll wake you in two hours."

"Roger."

CHAPTER TWENTY-ONE

"Last night, I put together a message for my dad." I took the meal pac Zina handed me and pulled the seal open. "You two should probably draft one for your dad, too. We'll see if we can figure out how to send it off planet without V'Ov or the ambassador stopping us."

"That's going to be tough." Lee ripped open a Chewy Nuggets packet and poured a few into his palm.

"Where'd you get those?" Joss dumped his meal pac into his lap and sorted through the smaller envelopes. "Mine only has Snacky Sticks." He held up the offending orange packet by one corner. "Any takers?"

Lee tried to look innocent. "Just lucky, I guess."

The rest of us rolled our eyes. He probably hid the good meal pacs.

"We need Chymm," Joss said. "He could help us get information out."

"Chymm is in a lab on Grissom." I finished my protein pac and shoved my snacks into my belt pouches. "But that's a great idea. We can send the messages to Chymm, with that encrypted pic thing he built. I still have it on my holo-ring." When we were cadets, Chymm's inventive engineering had gotten us out of a lot of trouble.

Joss slapped his forehead. "I knew I should have kept that thing. I deleted it when my storage got too full."

I pulled up the app and imported my message. Then the four of us posed for a selfie that would hide the data underneath. "Do I need to tell him to look for the datapacket?"

"How often do you send selfies to this guy?" Lee's voice sounded kind of aggressive... almost jealous? That was ridiculous.

"Uh, rarely."

"Then if he's smart enough to develop this encryption, he's smart enough to look for the packet." Lee got up and tossed his empty Chewy Nuggets packet into the recycler.

"Maybe I should send one, too." Joss flicked his holo-ring.

Zina lifted a hand. "I think one is enough—anyone watching our outgoing messages is going to be suspicious if you both start sending stuff to this Chymm guy. Speaking of which—Siti, you're off the grid. You can't send selfies to friends."

"Ugh." I swiped the file to Joss. "You send it."

"We chat all the time. He's not going to be looking for secret files in my stuff."

"I'll send it." Lee made a "gimme" motion with his fingers. "No one here has any idea if I am in contact with him, and he'll be one thousand percent suspicious of anything I send. When he sees you two in the pic, he'll go over it with a fine-toothed comb."

"That's a great idea." I flipped the files to him, then sent the contact information. "And with that picture as the cover, he'll know the message is really from us." I gestured to Joss.

Lee heaved a sigh. "Done. Listen, I think I should head back to base."

Joss's eyes narrowed. "Why?"

"The CEC may be okay with you all going on a walkabout, but my squadron commander is going to notice if my sit reps come through from this location. And he's expecting one in a couple of hours. Plus, I can snoop around the embassy and see who knows what."

"How are you going to hide your headband from V'Ov?" I ask.

He snorts. "You think V'Ov pays any attention to random lieutenants? She only knows about you two because of your connections." He held up a hand at my instinctive denial. "I'm not saying you only got where you are because of your dad, but in this particular case, it's very much true. You're the daughter of the Hero of Darenti Four." He said the words in a vid-announcer voice. "Everyone here knows who you are. Maybe you should come back, too—they're bound to notice you're missing."

Zina shook her head. "Except they didn't, remember? Lei-hawm's people covered it up. They probably don't remember she exists."

"Either way, I'm covered." He held up his flight cap and grinned. When no one responded, he waved the cap, then slid it onto his head. "In the Navy, we call them covers."

The rest of us groaned.

We took the extra grav belts from the shuttle and a crate of meal pacs. Lee pulled a small survival cube from the cargo area. "This is supposed to be for emergencies, but you might need it." The float panel held a meter long cube with netting on the sides to store other items. We tucked the meal pacs and belts into the webbing and activated the lifter. Joss towed the cube from the ship, with Zina on his heels.

I turned to follow them, but Lee grabbed my arm. "Be careful."

I frowned. "Of course. You, too."

"No, I mean be extra vigilant. Liam claims to be your friend, but I'm sure he has his own species' best interests at heart." He tapped the metal tucked into his hair. "And don't ever take that thing off."

I tried not to roll my eyes, but my voice came out on the far side of sarcastic. "I'm touched by your concern, but Liam has saved me more times than I can count."

"When you were off planet, he was alone. Out seeing the galaxy, and his only responsibilities were to himself. But here he has a whole world that's probably more important than his human pet." He nods emphatically. "Think about that. Would you sacrifice humanity's best interests for a sair-glider? I'm not sure he would for you."

Anger burned in me, but a cold drop of doubt trickled through the flames. What would I sacrifice for Liam? Even asking the question made me angry again. I wrenched my arm away. "Thanks, I can take care of myself."

We watched the shuttle take off, then lifted toward the mining camp. Lei-hawm waited for us on our hill. "I've been watching—the last of the humans left the building a few minutes ago."

Leaving the survival cube hidden under the foliage on our hilltop, we crept to the force shield. Joss, Zina, and I lifted over, keeping to the shadows of the largest plants. Lei-hawm transitioned to Liam and walked through the blue field. I'd seen him do it before, but it was still as unbelievable as seeing someone walk through a wall.

When we landed beside him, he'd already transitioned back.

"Can't you do that in this form?" I waved at the force screen, then at him.

Lei-hawm interlaced his fingers. "As Liam, I just… push a bit more of myself to that other space, then I weave the rest of myself through."

Joss set a drone to watch the building. It scanned for life-signs, but found none, so we crept to the door. Finding it unlocked, we slipped inside.

"Why lock it?" Zina mused. "They think they're the only ones here."

The interior was trashed. Dirty clothing lay draped over chairs and hung out of hammocks strung near the far wall. Food scraps cluttered stacks of dishes on the table and counter. The scents of sweat and rotting food caught in my throat, making my eyes water.

Almost hidden in the chaos, a small office space took up one tiny corner of the room. Whoever worked here kept the corner obsessively tidy. The only thing marring the pristine surface was a slip of paper with two strings of letters and numbers: a login credential.

"Operational security is clearly not a priority." I logged into the communication system and pulled up the logs. "They're in contact with a ship in a very high orbit on a daily basis. How could the station not notice this?"

Joss leaned over my shoulder and pointed. "It's a low-power transmission, sent once or twice a day. The station is in geosynchronous orbit over the embassy. Any transmission from here would only be intercepted via satellite relay. I'm betting the pirates have tampered with the system—or put in a dampener that runs only during the transmission times. Or maybe intermittently, to imitate a random glitch. The kind of thing techs discount because they can't replicate the problem."

"When did you learn so much about comm systems?" Zina asked in surprise.

He shrugged. "Gotta do something when I'm waiting around to fly people. You know I've always been interested in comm stuff."

I poked his well-muscled chest. "I thought you spent all your free time in the gym."

"I thought he wasted it on comic books." Zina closed the cupboard she'd looked through, then went on to the next. "Hey, there are some helmets in here." She pulled one out and pushed it over her head. "Does this stop you from reading me, Lei-hawm?"

The little enti glanced up from the comm panel. "I can't tell—you're already "off" because of the headband."

She pulled the helmet off and reached for her temple. "I'll take it off—"

"No!" The word popped out of my mouth before I thought about it. The others stared at me in surprise. "Call me crazy but running a test during an active mission is usually frowned on." I couldn't look at Lei-hawm. Lee's words had gotten to me—could we trust the enti to have our backs?

Joss nodded. "Good call. It's not a risk we should take here. How many of those helmets do they have? Do you think they'd notice if we stole one?"

Zina swung the door wide, revealing a closet full of helmets. "Probably not. There are a few to choose from."

"Check it for trackers. We don't want them following us." Joss turned back to the comm system.

I flicked further through the comm logs. "I thought we decided our mission was to get evidence of this illegal activity, then send it to our dads. Taking their equipment might alert them."

Joss joined me and flicked a few commands, and a recorded conversation popped up. "Holy crap on a cracker!"

CHAPTER TWENTY-TWO

I STARED AT THE SCREEN. "That's Micah LeBlanc."

"The guy who got kicked out of the Academy? Isn't his dad a big deal?" Zina moved closer. "He's kinda cute."

"If you like psychopaths." Joss glared at his twin before turning back to the console. "He went through some kind of rehab, but if you believe he's reformed, I can sell you some oceanfront property in Nebraska."

"Isn't he a friend of Derek's?" She went back to the cupboard she'd abandoned.

Joss's head came up with a jerk. "They were friends in the beginning. You don't think they still are, do you?"

I shook my head. "No. Definitely not. Lee cut ties with LeBlanc."

"Doesn't it seem odd they're both involved in Darenti?" She closed the door and moved on to the last cabinet. "Just an Autokich'n."

"I'm sure it's a coincidence. What's he saying, Joss?"

Joss turned up the volume. "—expect the next shipment to be on time and complete. I'm not paying you for that last delivery."

"We need that credit to buy supplies. Sneaking food in from off-planet ain't easy or cheap. My support team needs credits." The second speaker wasn't visible.

Joss hit pause. "Looks like someone down here was collecting evidence of LeBlanc's involvement—probably for blackmail. His video is not included, and the voice has been run through a neutralizer."

"You can tell that?" Zina gave her brother a surprised but admiring look. "Not bad, little brother."

"How did you find this?" I asked.

"I was scrolling through the recordings, and this one was labeled LeBlanc." A sly smile flickered across his face. "How could I ignore that?"

"Can you tell if it's genuine?"

He flicked a few more commands. "The meta data shows his location—he's on Elliot's World, and we can check the exact coordinates later. The video could be a deep fake—those are cheap and easy to produce. But the voice print is harder to fake. Law enforcement can run it through their systems and determine if it's him."

"But what if he used a neutralizer like our local guy?" I waved at the console.

Joss scoffed. "Those might obscure someone's identity from an amateur like me, but the pros can still read them. This is the smoking gun." He swiped through the commands, copying the file and saving it to his own ring. "I'm going to send it to Chymm."

Zina put a hand on his arm. "Is that a wise idea?"

"Chymm and I have been chatting pretty frequently lately." At my raised eyebrows, he went on. "He's having a girl problem."

"And he thought you would offer good advice?" Zina shook her head. "Poor deluded soul."

Joss ignored his sister. "I'll encrypt this under a pic like we did the last one. After that one from Nibs, I'll bet he'll check for encrypted messages from me." He flicked his ring. "And it's off."

The door opened, bringing all four of us around. A man and a woman entered the room, arguing over something. They saw us and stopped in surprise.

"Who are you?" The woman's hand went to her hip, as if for a weapon, but came up empty. She spit out an expletive.

Joss whipped his blaster off his shoulder and pointed it at the pair. "Doesn't matter who we are. You're mining this planet illegally. In fact, just standing here is illegal for a human. If you give us your statement now, we might be able to plead leniency for you."

While Zina stared at her twin, I pulled out my own weapon. "Get down on your knees, hands behind your head." I'd watched enough crime vids to sound legitimate. I hoped.

The man swaggered forward. "You two are CEC, not Commonwealth cops." He froze when Joss raised his blaster a little higher to point at the man's head. "You won't shoot me."

"You're right." I slung my blaster on my shoulder and pulled out my stunner. "But I will." I fired.

The man collapsed in a pile. His companion gasped.

"Siti!" Zina dropped to her knees beside the man and pulled out the med kit Lee had removed from the shuttle. "BP is low but rising. CL is depressed. Heart rate is nominal."

"Exactly what you'd expect from a stun." A tiny tremor shook Joss's voice—only someone who knew him would notice—and he gave me a wild-eyed look. Then he turned to the woman. "Suppose you tell us what we want to know?"

The woman raised both hands, and her words came out fast and garbled. "What do you want to know? My name is Garenta DuBois. I'm from Sarvo Six. We were hired to mine here. I don't know anything about illegal activity—I took a contract. I do my work, I don't ask questions, and I get my credits." She glanced at the man still lying at her feet and her face hardened. "I'd better get my credits."

"Is he the boss?" I jerked my chin at the man. "Zina, secure his hands and move away from him."

"I can't believe you stunned him, Siti." Zina pulled a slip-tie from a belt pouch and bound the man's hands.

Joss frowned at his sister. "You sound proud, not surprised."

Zina shrugged. "It's something I would have done, but I didn't think Siti would."

"Sometimes a show of force is the best argument. And we are in a hurry." I pointed at a chair. "DuBois, have a seat. Zina, restrain her, too."

When Zina finished tying the woman's hands and feet to a chair, I holstered my stunner. Joss and I wrestled the groggy man into another chair and secured him as well.

Zina put the remaining slip-ties back into her belt pouch. "What are we going to do with them?"

"You're the politician. Why don't you see if you can find out who's running this show—if they know. Joss, finish your magic." I wiggled my fingers as if manipulating a holo-interface. "I'm going to step outside and make sure we aren't disturbed again."

I opened the door and sucked in a deep breath of clear air, pushing the stench of unwashed socks out. Flicking the controls on Joss's drone, I sent it skimming along the path to the mine. Residual heat showed only two pairs of footprints coming this direction—everyone else was still at the mine. I hovered the drone near the entrance. As I finished, Lei-hawm materialized beside me. "Where did you go?"

"You were handing the situation, so I decided not to muddy the waters." He tried an unconvincing shrug.

"You disappeared the moment the door opened." I crossed my arms. "You had no idea how we were going to handle it. Were you going to hang us out to dry?"

"You know I'd never leave you in trouble." Lei-hawm put a hand on mine, but I jerked away.

"We both know your priorities have changed." I flicked the drone interface, set an audio ping for motion, then swept it away. "You have your planet's welfare to consider now. For all I know, you might decide leaving me to pirates is in the Darenti's best interest."

Lei-hawm stroked his blue and white hair, the action an uncanny imitation of the little glider grooming himself. "It's true I have more to consider now. But I would never leave you to fend for yourself. We may be different species, but we are friends. I value the loyalty of friends, as I know you do. Besides, you are an extremely capable officer, as is Joss. I had no doubt you would triumph in that confrontation. But if you hadn't, remaining free to assist you seemed a prudent course."

"You've been talking to Derek Lee. That sounds like his policy."

"*You've* been talking to Derek Lee—he's given you reason to doubt my loyalty."

I looked away. "He's right, though. You have to put the Darenti first. If it comes down to a conflict of interest, I'm going to lose."

The little enti stroked his hair again. "Now we're even."

My eyes snapped back to him. "What do you mean?"

He shrugged. "You've always put the mission over personal ties—now I'm doing the same."

"I've never left you—" I broke off. I had *frequently* left Liam to fend for himself—but only because I knew he could. *Just like he did.* But he'd come to my aid time and again. Maybe I really was his pet rather than the other way around. "Fair enough. I guess we have to agree to work together as long as our missions align." The statement felt final, like the end of our friendship.

Or maybe just a new phase. As equal partners.

"We both believe in the same ideals. I think our missions will continue to align." Lei-hawm pointed. "A shuttle. It doesn't seem like the right direction to be the pirates."

I squinted into the overcast sky, searching for the craft. When my eyes finally locked on, it was much closer than I expected. "No, that's a Navy shuttle. Lee is back." I raised my hand to flick my holo-ring, then swung around and knocked on the door instead. Without waiting for an answer, I pulled it open. "Lee is inbound. You got the evidence?"

Joss threw a thumbs-up in my direction. "Almost done. Zina?"

His sister shrugged. "I think I've gotten everything Ms. DuBois knows. The gentleman has been less helpful."

The man strained at his bond. "You gotta let me go. I'll clear out the entire team. It will be like we was never here."

"Why would we let you go?" Zina asked. "You're a criminal."

"No, I'm not! I didn't know mining here was illegal!" He swung his shoulders left and right, trying to pull his arms free from the slip ties.

"Tell us who hired you. We've got all the evidence we need." Joss flicked a finger at the comm console.

"Then you know who hired us. And if you know anything about him, you know I'd be safer in a Commonwealth prison with my mouth shut than ratting on him and going free." He pressed his lips together, as if refusing to say anything else.

DuBois's eyes had grown wider as the man spoke. "Who's he talking about?"

"Micah LeBlanc." I threw the name out as if it meant nothing, just to see how she reacted.

Her eyes squeezed shut and her lips trembled. She sucked in a few panicked breaths, then a deeper one before opening her eyes again. "I didn't know. I didn't tell you anything."

"Why is everyone so afraid of him?" I leaned back to peer toward the shuttle as it settled to the ground in the one clear spot.

"He's a psychopath, remember?" Joss closed down the comm system and turned to face us. "But he's on Elliot's World—"

"You two really don't know nothin', do you?" The words burst out of the man as if he couldn't stop himself. "He has money, power, and an incredible network. He can reach anyone, anywhere, and thanks to his daddy, he's untouchable." He clamped his mouth shut again.

Joss and I exchanged a look. We knew about LeBlanc's father—when the younger LeBlanc had been expelled from the Academy for attacking other students, the father had gotten him sent to a "treatment facility" rather than prison. The senior LeBlanc had diplomatic connections and a desire to keep his deranged son from negatively impacting his political career. Micah—no one really knew what Micah wanted, except probably revenge. And, apparently, promethium from Darenti.

"They're here." Lei-hawm's soft voice brought me around. As I turned, he melted and transformed back into Liam. I looked down the path, wondering who might have prompted that response.

Derek Lee rounded the corner, with a dozen humans and a handful of Darenti on his heels.

Darenti shaped like humans.

"They got him!" I spun back to the half-open door. "V'Ov is with them!"

G'lacTechNews

Welcome to G'lacTechNews. This is Aella Phoenix with Odysseus Helliesen in the studio.

First, the financial news. Promethium prices are up, raising costs for interstellar space craft and AutoKich'n production. LeBlanc Corporation claims technical problems at the mines on Elliot's World are influencing galactic supply.

Also, LeBlanc Corporation reported record profits this quarter. Does that sound like a coincidence to you, Odysseus?

CHAPTER TWENTY-THREE

Joss, Zina, Derek, and I sat in the last row of seats in the Navy shuttle. V'Ov, Ricmond, and Glaucia Ivengard sat with Ambassador Slovenska and her staff in the front row as a pair of Navy pilots returned us to the base.

The miners had been secured in their own facility with four CEC explorers standing guard. Slovenska had submitted a request to headquarters for an extraction. From there, they would be returned to Grissom for investigation and trial. Apparently, V'Ov agreed the pirates should be prosecuted. Either she hadn't known about them, or she'd decided to cut her losses and thought they wouldn't be tracked back to her.

Zina leaned forward, ducking down so the high seat back would hide her from the others. "Why do I feel like we're in trouble?"

"Because we are?" Lee glared at her.

"What happened?"

"They caught me landing. Grabbed the location data before I could purge it from the shuttle's system. Then demanded to know where I'd been and why. What was I going to do? Refuse to take them? They're way better situated to deal with pirates than we are."

"Good point." I reached a casual hand up to tap my metal headband. "But they didn't read you, did they?"

"No, I got lucky. I had my flight cap on when Maj James grabbed me, so he didn't see mine. V'Ov probably knew, since she couldn't read me, but she couldn't say anything to James without tipping her hand. I was afraid she was going to make him take off the band, but maybe there were too many humans around? With the negotiations, the enti must be concentrating their influence on the top brass." He nodded toward the front of the shuttle. "You can bet V'Ov is going to figure out a way to get us under her thumb. If she had a thumb. Where's Lei-hawm?"

I flinched at his sardonic question. "He's here, somewhere. He's not going to abandon us."

"Are you sure? He got what he wanted. Slovenska is taking care of the pirates. The Gothodi will give him the Stone, and he'll overthrow V'Ov." Lee leaned back in his seat, as if daring me to contradict him.

"And? Once V'Ov is gone, we'll be fine. It's a win-win," Zina said.

"Until V'Ov gets them to remove our headbands. And we give up Lei-hawm's plan, and she's ready for him when he gets back." Joss ran a hand over his braids, carefully avoiding the metal disks woven into them.

"Tiah is our get out of jail free card," Zina said. "She'll come back with Lei-hawm and vouch for us."

"They can't really do anything to you, anyway." I nudged Zina with my elbow. "You're a planetary representative. Neither Slovenska nor V'Ov have any authority over you."

The shuttle landed, and we released our restraints. Major James waited by the hatch when we exited. A swarm of news drones buzzed behind him, filming the encounter. "You'll come with me." He didn't wait for us to answer, just turned and marched toward the ambassador's office. The drones buzzed expectantly.

Joss gestured for his sister to precede him. She raised a finger in a "let me take care of this" gesture. "Major James, these officers were assisting me. I need to debrief them." Three of the drones moved in to get a better view of Zina's face.

James spoke over his shoulder as he walked. "You can do that in the security office, Ms. Torres. That's where we're going."

"I'll speak with them in the junior officers' lounge." She angled across the grass, but a pair of enlisted explorers closed in on either side of her, forcing her back onto the path. "Excuse me. I'm going that way."

James stopped and turned. "No, you aren't. You're coming with us." Six more explorers joined us, forming an escort we couldn't hope to escape. The buzz of the news drones seemed to change pitch, as if they were snickering.

"I protest! I am a representative from Earth! You have no right to treat me like this! I intend to lodge a formal complaint with the ambassador!"

James turned away. "Who do you think ordered this?" Ignoring Zina's continued objections, he led us to the back of the embassy building.

The security office occupied the end of the building. The sergeant at the desk looked up as we entered but asked no questions. Most of the news drones paused at the threshold. One blundered straight toward the door, then sparked when it hit an invisible shield. The damaged drone limped away.

At James's nod, the sergeant flicked a holo-interface to life and swiped an icon. A door on his left clicked open.

James's escort herded us inside a small room—a cell. Two narrow bunks hung from a side wall, with a small closet-like bathroom in the corner. The door clanged shut, and the electronic locks engaged.

Zina banged on the door. "Hey! I am a planetary representative from Earth! You can't lock me up!"

"Too late, sis. They already did." Joss dropped onto the bottom bunk, then looked up at me. "This would be a good time for Liam to show up."

I put a finger to my lips and activated my internal audio to call the other three. "Our local comms are still working, and they didn't take our holo-rings. What does that mean? And ix-nay on the iam-lay talk. We don't want to put them on alert."

Joss rolled his eyes. "Everyone in the CEC knows about Liam. I'll bet Sergeant Desk Job out there was warned to watch for him."

"Good thing he can imitate other creatures." I slumped beside him.

Lee leaned his shoulders against the wall across from the bunks and slid down to the floor. He stared over my head while he spoke subvocally through the comm link. "I just tried to send a message to my squadron commander up on the *Sentry*—this cell must be shielded. Makes sense. On a regular mission, they put drunks in here to dry out. You don't want to bother taking their holo-ring, but you don't want them to drunk dial the commander."

I snorted a laugh. "Sounds like the voice of experience. How many times have you drunk dialed the commander?"

"Zero. But I've stood night watch enough times to know what happens at three a.m. And it's pretty universal to the human condition. People on boring missions get drunk if given the chance. And then they make stupid calls."

Joss grunted. "He's right—we've seen it, too."

I nodded. "The question is, can we use that to our advantage? Can they monitor us while the block is on? Do they have any way to hijack this call?"

"No," Joss and Lee said together. Lee gestured for Joss to continue. "Nibs is right, this cell would have been set up as a drunk tank. Although we know the faux Arya was held here for a while. But it's doubtful they would have had the time or reason to change the electronics of the system. They can watch through the window." He gestured to the mirrored surface next to the door, then flicked his holo-ring. "My scan isn't picking up any active cams."

"You have an app for that?" I leaned closer to look at Joss's holo.

He pointed to the signal and flicked through the screens for me. "Thanks to Chymm."

"That means if they're watching, it's real-time through that glass." I tipped my head at the window. "And they could be listening, but they can't hear us if we only communicate on point-to-point calls. Perfect. What's our plan?" I looked at the other three in turn.

Zina shrugged, then climbed up the end of the bedframe to the top bunk. "I guess we wait. Unless your friend gave you some kind of universal unlock code." She peeked over the side at us, her curly ponytail hanging down in front of Joss's face. "No? Then I'm taking a nap." Her head disappeared.

"Sounds like a good plan." Joss pulled his legs up and rolled behind me to stretch out on the mattress. "You can snuggle in here, Siti." He patted the mattress. "I promise not to get fresh."

"Fresh? Were you born five hundred years ago?" I stood.

"Nope, only two-fifty. Plenty of room if you change your mind." He rolled over to face the wall, leaving very little space for anyone else.

I slid down the wall next to Lee and flicked to a private call. "I don't want to just sit and wait, do you?"

"You got a better plan?" He crossed his arms over his chest and shifted away from me a fraction.

"You really don't like me, do you?"

"That's your biggest failing, Siti. You think everyone has to like you. Sometimes people don't."

The statement bit like a viper, but I tried to deny it. "I don't need everyone to like me. But I thought we'd gotten past the—the past. That we could be friends, now."

His eyes snapped to mine, and our gazes held for a second. Annoyance, regret, and something warmer flicked across his face so fast I couldn't read the emotion. Then he looked away. "I don't know if we can ever be friends."

My heart contracted, and my hand clapped to my chest as if real pain throbbed there. My eyes stung. Maybe he was right. Why should I care if he didn't like me? "Whatever." I rolled to my feet.

A flicker of shadow crossed the window and the door clicked.

"Doesn't matter, I think our reckoning has arrived."

The door opened, and my father stood in the doorway, his broad shoulders blocking the narrow space. He wore his black utility uniform, but instead of stars, he wore lieutenant's rank on his collar. A flight cap covered his head, even though he was indoors. His tired eyes roved over me. "Lieutenant."

"Dad!" I fought the urge to throw myself at him, instead pulling my shoulders back and stiffening my spine. "Admiral."

Lee jumped to his feet, bracing at attention. Joss rolled over. His eyes went wide, and he struggled off the bunk. "Sir!"

Zina sat up and yawned. "Oh, hey, Admiral Kassis. How are ya?"

A grin twitched across Dad's lips, then disappeared. "Doing better than you, it would appear." His eyes traveled over Joss and Lee, then settled on me. "The three of you have been reassigned to me. Zina, you've been replaced."

She scrambled down. "Replaced? By who? The only one who can replace me is—"

"Me." Zane Torres appeared at my father's shoulder. He wore a matching uniform, and his thick, dark hair stuck up in a messy style that had been popular five years ago, and a dark shadow covered his chin. "Let's go."

"Dad!" Zina lurched forward, but the two older men turned and walked away, leaving the door open. The four of us followed behind, like naughty children.

I avoided the desk sergeant's gaze—he undoubtedly got a kick out of watching three junior officers and a "planetary representative" being led away by their parents.

A swarm of news drones met us at the door, forming and reforming around Zane and the admiral as they paced down the hall.

Joss pushed past me to reach his dad. "How's Mom?" Lee and I moved aside for Zina to join them.

Zane flicked a glance at the drones, then at his son. "She's fine. Better than you."

Joss grinned and pointed at my dad. "You two rehearsed that, didn't you?"

We crossed the plascrete courtyard toward the embassy headquarters. A white-garbed man stepped out of the rear of the support building—the server who had fawned over Zina on the first day. He raised a hand. My father nodded at him without changing directions.

I stretched my legs to catch up to my dad. "Who's that?"

He glanced at the drone escort. "You don't need to know."

That meant he was more than just a server in the mess.

"You sent a spy."

He coughed loudly over my last word. "Sorry. The Darenti mist always does this to me." He coughed again, a little more convincingly this time. "It just takes a little bit to get accustomed to it again."

"Always?" I rolled my eyes. To my knowledge, this was his second visit. "All the times you've been here."

"Yes, always." His firm tone indicated an end to the discussion.

I sucked in some of that Darenti mist. It did tickle the back of my throat. "What brings you to Darenti, Dad?"

His lips pressed together, and he gave the barest headshake before turning to Lee. "Lieutenant Lee, I believe you have access to the admiral's gig. I need you to take me to the first contact site."

G'lacTechNews

Welcome to G'lacTechNews. This is Aella Phoenix travelling aboard a CSS courier ship to Darenti Four where recent footage has shown some very odd events.

Two CEC officers, a Naval lieutenant, and a planetary representative were detained today. The ambassador's office declined to comment, and Starling Cross is indisposed. Rumors report the officers went AWOL, but we have no further information. I hope to get to the bottom of it when I arrive on site. Until then, back to you, Odysseus.

CHAPTER TWENTY-FOUR

My father and Derek Lee took the pilot seats, starting the check list as Joss, Zina, and I filed into the passenger area. Zane hovered in the doorway for a moment, then went into the cockpit. Joss closed his eyes and leaned his chair back, faking relaxation. He hated riding in the back. Zina bounced in her seat, clearly eager to find out what was going on.

The cloud of news drones buzzed around the interior of the ship like a swarm of insects, swooping in for closeups, then zipping away. By the time we launched, most of them had dropped to a perch. The two that remained airborne hit the deck with a crack when the shuttle's artificial gravity kicked in late.

"They did that on purpose," Joss muttered without opening his eyes.

After a twenty-minute flight that felt like hours, the shuttle settled to the ground. The three of us unlatched our restraints and stood. Zane and the admiral came out of the cockpit a few minutes later.

"What's going on?" Joss asked.

My father held up a hand. "We're going to see the site where I first encountered the Darenti. You three don't seem to understand the importance of your mission here. First contact with a sapient alien race—" As he spoke, he exited the shuttle. His voice floated back to us, unintelligible under the squawking of some local animal.

"Us three?" Joss followed me to the airlock. "Nibs is above reproach?"

"I wish Liam was here." The whisper slipped out before I could stop it. I missed my little blue and white friend, even though our relationship had changed forever.

We moved out of the shuttle, pausing on the ramp above a wide, slick-looking slope. Thick jungle grew on either side, creating the appearance of a long, straight road. In the center, a hole disappeared into the ground.

"The mudslide has some strange effects on electronics." My father squelched across the shiny mud flow, leaving footprints that filled in behind him, disappearing into the slick, brown surface. He stopped and tapped his grav belt, lifting a few centimeters above the mud. The rest of us activated our own belts, hovering above the sticky ground, as the drones spiraled around my father.

Dad nodded. Inside the shuttle airlock, barely visible in the shadows, Zane swiped something in his holo-interface, and every drone plummeted to the ground. The weird mud seemed to pull the tiny electronic devices in, forming again over them and leaving no trace.

Dad skimmed forward, pausing over the shuttle's step. "Check the hold."

Zane nodded and disappeared deeper into the shuttle.

"What's—" I swallowed the question when Dad flung up a hand. We waited in silence.

Zane poked his head out of the shuttle. "Clear."

"Good. Back into the ship. We have a ways to go, and even though we seem to have eliminated our nosy friends…" He gestured at the muddy slide behind him. "We won't speak until we arrive at a secure destination. I recommend a nap." He disappeared into the cockpit with Zane on his heels.

The three of us exchanged a silent look.

My audio implant tinged with a three-way call initiated by Zina. "He knows we can do the audio thing, right?"

"Maybe he has reason to not trust it." My voice was not convincing, even in my own ears.

Joss dropped into a seat and reclined it all the way. "I'm going to take his advice. Three things I always take advantage of when the option arises: toilet, nap, and food."

"Don't forget the gym." Zina disconnected the call before he could reply.

Hours later, I woke when the shuttle's engine changed tone. Thanks to the excellent shielding, we couldn't hear the engines, but they emanated a constant vibration that became background noise after a while. When it changed, you could feel it.

The ship landed. We disconnected our power chargers, unbuckled our restraints, and waited for the cockpit to open. Finally, Dad, Zane, and Lee came out.

"I had Derek bring us back to your previous location on Rovantu. Gear up—we might be here a while. Lee, get the comfort cube ready to go."

"Actually, it's already here, sir." Joss waved at the hatch. "We deployed before and didn't get to bring it back when they picked us up."

Dad gave Joss a sour look. "That's poor resource management, but I understand you didn't have a choice."

After donning grav belts and putting every available meal pac into our bags, we headed out. We followed the now familiar flight path to our little hilltop. The camp below was deserted. The building had been air-lifted out, along with the remaining ore, leaving only a scar.

Lee pulled out his little box. "No sign of humans down there, but they've left a web of alert lines. If anyone wanders into the area, whoever's monitoring will know."

Zane clapped a hand on Lee's shoulder. "Perfect. We don't want to go down there anyway. We just wanted to get away from anyone who might be monitoring us. Scan your gear, too."

Lee pointed his box at the survival cube and ran it over each of us in turn. Then Dad took the device and checked Lee. "All clear—we're as sure as we can be. Now, let's get comfortable."

We moved to a small glade about a klick away from the hilltop observation post. Lee scanned the clearing and came up empty. I unlocked the cube, and we folded the sides out to create a three-sided shelter. The fourth wall we left open, with a force shield to keep the weather and fauna out. Joss set a drone to patrol overhead.

Dad handed out meal pacs and made a circling motion with his hand. "Circle up and spill."

We dragged the folding camp stools into a rough circle and dropped onto them. For a moment, we all stared at each other, then Lee, Joss, Zina, and I all started talking at once.

Zane raised a hand. "Stop. One at a time." He pointed at me. "The rest of you, eat. First things first—where's Tiah?"

I explained about the Gothodi city. "I guess we should go get her, although she seems more comfortable with the enti than in a camp." I gestured to the temporary building around us.

Zane nodded at my father. "Over to you, Nate."

Dad swallowed his mouthful of food and took a gulp from his water pac. "I got an interesting message from a friend of yours—Lieutenant Leonardi di Zorytevsky."

"Chymm came through!" Joss pumped his fist. "I figured that had to be it."

"Lieutenant Leo—" Dad stumbled over the last name. "I'll just use his callsign. Diz told me a strange story about shape-shifters and mind readers." His eyes locked onto me. "The shape-shifters came as a surprise but only briefly. The mind reading, on the other hand... I guess it makes sense in retrospect."

"What do you mean?" Zina asked.

His mouth twisted into a grimace. "When I first met the Darenti, they didn't know Standard, of course. They seemed to learn it from me. Like that." He snapped his fingers. "Looking back, I guess I was so overwhelmed by their shape-shifting ability that the speed at which Lei-hawm learned to speak didn't really register. And no one else seemed to question it."

My new doubt of Lei-hawm's goals grew a little. I cleared my throat. "They can influence thoughts. It would have been easy for him to—" I waved my hand in a "these are not the droids you're looking for" way. "He could easily convince people not to question that."

"Diz said you've been in contact with Lei-hawm."

I bit my lip. "You have, too. Not recently, but... Lei-hawm is Liam."

I waited for the explosion, but it didn't come. Dad raised an eyebrow at me. "Where is he now?"

Lee pointed at my dad. "You don't seem very surprised, sir."

"I was, when I first found out."

"How long have you known?" The words burst out of me. Lei-hawm had said my father didn't know. Or at least implied it. I tried to remember his exact words. Verdat had said my father didn't know Lei-hawm snuck off the planet, but that didn't mean Lei-hawm hadn't contacted him since.

Dad's face turned a little pink. "Remember when you had to leave him with me when you started at the academy?" At my nod, he went on. "That's when I found out. He changed back to his—well, not his true form, because he doesn't have one—but to his humanoid shape. We had a long discussion about his motives, and eventually he convinced me he could protect you. I had heard there were some unsavory forces at play in the Academy, so I wanted you to have that protection." His jaw clenched. "Now I'm wondering how much he influenced that decision."

"Not at all." Lei-hawm stood just inside the blue force shield. "Well, I did nudge you a little, but I didn't coerce you."

"Lei-hawm!" I jumped up, tipping my camp stool over with the force of my movement.

The others exclaimed. My father surged to his feet, pointing at Lei-hawm. "I trusted you to watch over my daughter."

"You also trusted him at large in the galaxy," Zane said quietly. "The Commonwealth government interdicted the planet, but you discovered an enti outside the blockade and didn't do anything to stop him."

He was right. We all turned to stare at my father. The Hero of the CEC had broken protocol by allowing Lei-hawm to stay free.

Dad's jaw dropped. He glared at the small enti. "You! I would never—" He rubbed his hands over his face. "What have I done? What did you make me do?" He dropped into his chair.

"Hold on—why isn't Lei-hawm controlling you right now?" Lee asked.

Zane tapped his temple, his fingernail clicking against something hidden in his thick hair. "Your buddy Diz warned us. You didn't think I *chose* this hairstyle, did you?"

"I wouldn't try to control you." Lei-hawm moved closer to my father. "Not now. I admit I used unscrupulous means to remain free. And I might have *leaned* on you to trust me when I first revealed myself. I enjoyed exploring the galaxy with the CEC, and I value Siti's companionship. I hoped one day we could work together in the best interests of both humans and Darenti. I had no idea what V'Ov was up to until I returned here with Siti."

Zane offered Lei-hawm his seat, then sat again when the little enti declined. "Why did you decide to return to Darenti?"

"I heard about the mission—the potential change in the planet's status—and I wanted to be here for the occasion. To see what my people thought of this. And I was a bit homesick." His sad smile looked very human.

"As I explained to Siti, deceit is a foreign concept to our people—mainly because it's difficult to pull off. There have always been those who tried, but when you can read others' intentions…" He spread his hands. "Over the years I have been away, I learned to influence others—to use my 'mind tricks' to stay at liberty. I used them to help protect Siti and to influence her selection for this mission."

He faced me. "You were on the manifest—I just made sure your name was selected for the first drop. It wasn't really necessary—I could have snuck aboard on my own. But I wanted to share my planet with you—my friend."

He turned to my father. "When I discovered what V'Ov had done—and her intentions to, well, take over the galaxy—I knew I had to stop her. I want humans and Darenti to be partners, not master and slaves. So, I encouraged Gara and Verdat to bring Siti to Rovantu, to help me retrieve the Stone and end V'Ov's influence."

Zane shoved his hands through his hair, pulling them away with a groan when his fingers encountered the metal pieces. "You must see we can't let the Darenti be free to roam the galaxy if you can control others without their knowledge and consent. Earth will vote no."

Lei-hawm spread his hands. "Please, keep an open mind. I will not try to sway your decision except through my words." He chuckled. "Your technical friend has ensured that—not that I would try to use such tactics anymore."

"How do we know you're not?" Lee stood and paced around the circle of chairs. "This protection" —he tapped his temple— "is something you invented. Maybe it doesn't work at all."

Lei-hawm lifted his hands. "You must test it."

"How do you propose we do that? You can pretend to try to influence us and then claim it was unsuccessful." Lee crossed his arms, glaring.

"Tiah can tell." Zina leaned forward. "She can feel when they're trying to influence us, and she isn't affected."

"Then let's go see Tiah."

CHAPTER TWENTY-FIVE

After a long discussion, we decided to bring Tiah to the camp for the test. Zane and my father volunteered to go, since they wanted to see the Darenti city. Joss and Zina went along for support, with Lei-hawm to guide them, leaving Lee and me to mind the camp.

"We'll spend the night there." Dad buckled his grav belt around his waist. "It's getting dark, and Lei-hawm recommends we don't travel at night." He unplugged his stunner from the wall charger and put it into his belt. "I think we'd be fine, but this will give us time to see the local culture up close and personal. You sure you don't want to come?"

I bit my lip. "Zina and Joss want to spend some time with their dad. Lee wants to stay here—he really doesn't like going down there." I spread my hands. Explorer protocol prohibited leaving anyone solo unless absolutely necessary. "And frankly, I could use a break from all the togetherness. Lee and I are very good at ignoring each other."

He chuckled and pulled me in for a swift hug. "I'm proud of you."

"For ignoring Lee? It's not hard." I squeezed his ribs, then pulled back and poked a finger into his chest. "When this is over, you and I are going to have a discussion about boundaries, Dad. I'm an adult. I don't need a Darenti nanny."

His face went red. "It seemed like the right answer, back then." His jaw clenched. "Of course, we know why, now."

"You have to admit, Liam saved me on more than one occasion. And he didn't have to tell you. He could have struck off on his own. Or stowed away in my luggage. Or a million other things." I looked away for a second. "For what it's worth, I trust him. Maybe not as unconditionally as I did when he was just Liam, but I believe he's an honorable being. Unlike V'Ov. Did you speak with her when you arrived on Darenti?"

"No." He chuckled. "Zane and I came down incognito. That's why we're wearing these." He touched the lieutenant's rank on his collar. "None of the CEC personnel bought it, of course. We're too old to be lieutenants. And some of them probably recognized us. I'm sure as soon as V'Ov came across anyone on our flight, our deception would have been exposed. That's why we were in such a hurry to get out of there. We went straight to security when we landed, grabbed you four, and commandeered the shuttle."

"Ready?" Zane stood in the doorway of the little module.

"As ever." Dad gave me another hug. "Anyone want to chicken out?"

"Hell, no." I kissed his cheek. "See you tomorrow."

Zane flashed a thumbs-up and disappeared. Dad and I went out to join the others outside the structure. The tiny clearing was gloomy in the late afternoon. A thick drizzle came down, and the ground around our cube had turned to mud. Joss helped Zane activate his personal shield while Dad fitted a tethered grav belt around Lei-hawm's waist. The four humans and the tiny enti waved as they lifted off. Lee and I watched until they disappeared behind the treetops

"They're letting Lei-hawm use a grav belt?" I stepped inside the module and shook the rain from my head and jacket.

"It's tethered to your dad's, and Caveman made sure the controls were locked. Probably not optimal, but they didn't want to go through the jungle, and Lei-hawm is their guide."

"Do *you* think we can trust him?" I pulled a pair of hammocks from a side cabinet and tossed one of the small bags to Lee.

He caught it and shook it out, the lock hooks clanging softly against the plastek floor. "You're asking me? I don't trust anyone." He clipped the first hook into the wall ring.

I followed suit with my own hammock. The routine activity brought a sense of comfort and control. "You seem to trust me."

He snorted. "Yeah. Lucky you."

"Why?" I clicked the second lock hook onto another ring and faced him across the swag of fabric.

"Why do I trust you?" His gaze locked on me. "We've known each other eight years. And while you've done some sneaky things, in hindsight, I can see it was in response to other people being jerks." He poked a thumb at his chest. "You gave me the benefit of the doubt after that mess at the Academy."

"Hah! It took me *years* to get to that point. You might remember I wasn't particularly friendly when we got assigned to Qureshi or crashed on Saha."

"Yeah, but you could have been like Caveman. He still doesn't like me." He ducked under the two hammocks and joined me in the small open area near the force shield.

"You don't exactly make an effort to be friendly." I leaned against the wall, crossing my arms.

"I'm being friendly now." He smiled, transforming his face. Lee rarely smiled like this—usually it was a sardonic smirk or a dark grin at the misfortune of others.

I sucked in a deep breath. When he smiled, Derek Lee was hot. "You didn't answer my question. Do you think we can trust Lei-hawm?"

He sat on one of the camp stools to unfasten his boots. "Only as far as we can throw him."

"He's pretty little. That's a long way."

"And even farther when he's a glider." He put the boot down and went to work on the other one. "It's like I said before—we can trust him until his people's interests conflict with ours. I hope he'll do the courtesy of discussing that with us instead of just going rogue."

I chewed on my lip while I thought this over. "It's kind of like trusting someone in a different squadron at the Academy. When our missions align, it's all good. When they don't—"

He leaned over to put the boots by the wall under the end of his hammock. "Exactly. And right now, the Darenti want to get out into the galaxy. Humans want—or would want if they knew—to keep them sequestered."

"Maybe there's a third option. What if we can let them out but protect against their abilities?" I pulled the headband from my hair and twirled it.

"You think everyone in the human race wants to wear a headband for the rest of their lives?" He got up and headed for the tiny bathroom.

"Of course not." I contemplated the metal circlet for a few seconds, then slung it through a belt loop so I could unbraid my thick hair. The tight side braids kept it out of my face, but after a long shift, it was such a relief to let it loose. I massaged my scalp. Did I dare leave the circlet off tonight? With Lei-hawm gone, would we encounter any other enti?

Lee came out of the bathroom and stopped short. He wore shorts and a tight T-shirt, which showed off his broad shoulders and narrow waist. His uniform pants and jacket hung over one arm. "You look different with your hair down."

I pulled my fingers out of the thick mess. "You look different with your clothes off." My face went hot, and I looked away. "I mean, out of uniform."

His lips twitched, but his laugh came out kind of strangled. He dropped the clothing on a camp chair near his boots, then took a step closer to me. "You probably look different with your clothes off, too." His voice was deep and velvety, his breathing uneven.

My heart went into overdrive. I couldn't deny Derek Lee was a very attractive man. And over the last few days, our relationship had become less prickly. But did I want to get involved with him? And what did "involved" mean to him?

I stood and put up a hand. "I'm not a one-night fling girl. If you're looking for some quick 'tension relief,' you should find someone else."

His face went blank. "I thought that's why you stayed here. So we could spend some 'quality time' together." He spun away and ducked under the first hammock, putting his back to me.

"Is that what they call it in the Navy?" I stood and bundled my hair into a ponytail. "Sorry, that wasn't my intent. I was trying to be nice. I noticed how much you disliked going underground and didn't think you wanted to do it again."

He glanced over his shoulder at me, his eyes soft and vulnerable. Then his face tensed, and cold, sardonic Lee reappeared. "Don't do me any favors, Kassis." He grabbed the side of his hammock and swung into it with the ease of long practice. "You've got first watch."

I stared at the gently swinging hammock, my heart still galloping at double time. We had a drone monitoring the exterior of the camp and a force shield around the module. Nothing on Darenti—except Liam who was with my father—could disturb us without warning. More than one CEC explorer had used similar situations to get a little "quality time" with a willing partner.

But what I'd said was true. I didn't do casual flings. Then why was I disappointed he'd given up so easily? It didn't take much soul searching to figure out the answer. I'd developed feelings for Derek Lee. A complication I really didn't need—especially in the middle of a mission.

Focus on work. Following protocols would occupy my mind and stop it from wandering to the hot pilot in the tight T-shirt swinging in the hammock behind me. With a flick of my holo-ring, I set the lights to minimum, turned my campstool toward the screened end of the room, and started my watch.

CHAPTER TWENTY-SIX

D<small>EREK</small> and I barely spoke when I woke him for his watch. I gave him a few minutes to get a drink and use the facilities, then climbed into my hammock. As the night wore on, I watched the glow of his holo-ring over the edge of the bag, trying to ignore his movements around the small room. I finally fell into a fitful doze and woke at dawn.

As I emerged from the bathroom, Derek threw a meal pac at me. I caught it without conscious thought, my gaze snapping to his. "Thanks."

He grunted and turned his shoulder away, clearly not interested in talking. With a sigh, I dropped onto a stool and ripped the pac open. The contents dropped into my lap, including a green envelope marked Chewy Nuggets. I checked the label on the outer wrapper—he'd given me the most popular meal. "You didn't want these?"

He half-turned, his darkly shadowed eyes roving over the nuggets and my face. He shrugged. "I'm getting tired of 'em." He scooped some stew into his mouth from a steaming red pouch. "There's hot water if you need to warm anything up."

I followed his gaze to the pop-open pan sitting over a compact heater in the center of the room. Steam wafted from the pot. I sorted through my meal and dropped my red bag into the pot to warm. The stew was vile cold but not bad when heated.

We ate in silence, then he got up and began stowing the hammocks. I watched him as I finished my meal, trying to think of something to say that might put our relationship back into balance. Instead, I found myself admiring the movements of his back muscles under the snug shirt.

As if he felt my regard, he turned. "What?"

"Nothing. Thanks for putting my hammock away."

He grunted as he rolled the second one into its attached pocket.

"Look, I'm sorry about last night—"

He spun around. "Don't be sorry. You had every right to say no. I'm just—" He tossed the folded bags into the cupboard, then faced me and gave a smug grin. "I'm being a baby. I'm not used to getting turned down." The smile faltered, and he turned away.

A little thrill of triumph zinged through me. Look at me, turning away the irresistible Derek Lee. I almost said it but bit the words back. "Thanks for not pushing."

"No means no." He shrugged into his uniform jacket and gave me a once-over, his normal expression firmly in place. "Is the admiral going to warn us before he comes back?"

"Why would he—" My eyes widened as I realized what he was asking. "You think he expected—" I gestured wordlessly between us.

He leered. "You *offered* to stay here. With me." The expression faded. "I guess we were all wrong."

I covered my hot face. "Just what I want my dad thinking. Ugh. Another disadvantage to being the daughter of the admiral."

His jaw tightened. "Yeah, poor you." He flicked his holo-ring and initiated a call. "Caveman, what's your ETA?" He listened to the response, then barked out a harsh laugh. "Me and Kassis? Please. She wishes."

A spear of anger went through me. How dare he make this my doing? I resisted the urge to call Joss and tell him it was the other way around—that Lee wanted me and I said no. That would only make me look more desperate. Instead, I lifted my chin and turned away to call Tiah. "What's your ETA? I'm getting bored here."

A growl brought me around. Lee glared at me. "I'm going to check on the shuttle." He stomped to the door.

I smothered a bitter laugh as Tiah called out to someone else, and muffled replies sounded. "They say we'll be there in twenty minutes."

"Roger." I disconnected the call and followed Lee out of the shelter. He lifted off and disappeared over the treetops before I could say anything.

What would I say? He'd been a jerk, and I'd been a jerk right back. At least we were back to our normal relationship—strained distaste.

When the others arrived, we met in the shelter to run a few more tests. They'd done several rounds at Spire City, but Zane wanted to try a few with me and Lee as well.

Zane handed a headband back to his daughter. "I'd say that's as conclusive as we're going to get. Lei-hawm and the other Darenti are able to impact our thoughts when we aren't wearing the headbands. Some of them require touch, some just need to be within a few meters. Multiple Darenti in concert can do it from a farther distance or affect multiple humans. With the protective headbands in place, attempts are futile. Thank you for participating in the trial." He nodded to the six enti who had accompanied them back to our camp.

Two humanoids and a large sunflower garbled something and bounced out the door, disappearing into the jungle toward Fort Gothodi.

Dad turned to Lei-hawm. "You can walk through the force shield—Siti told me after Sarvo Six. Can the other enti do it?"

Lei-hawm shook his head. "It is something I learned over the years. My ability to transform into Liam—into a smaller physical size—is part of the ability. When leaving parts of myself in the alternate location, I am also leaving whatever prevents me from passing through. I can't do it in this form."

My dad's lips twisted. "Something else we should test. Later. We can return to Perista, now, correct?"

Lei-hawm put his hand out, displaying a dirty, gray rock. "We have the Stone of Avora. It is time to end V'Ov's tyranny."

"That's the Stone?" I reached for it, then pulled my hand back. "What does it do?"

"It sure is ordinary-looking." Tiah leaned closer, her hands gripped behind her back, as if she were afraid to touch it.

"It does nothing." Lei-hawm tossed it a few centimeters and caught it again. "And it *is* ordinary."

"You're going to take my suggestion and make a fake?" I touched a finger to the rock. Cold, damp, and inert. I rubbed the dirt from my fingertip. "You'll need to wash it if you want to paint it gold."

"No, this is the real Stone of Avora. A completely normal rock. Except for one thing." He squeezed the Stone between his hands for a few seconds, then released it to display—

A dirty, damp rock.

"No one can transform it. That is its unique power. If your scientists examined this, they would find nothing extraordinary—it is made up of the same elements as any other rock from that area. But while enti can reform—with great effort—those other stones, this one is immutable."

"And this rock is going to help us how?" Zane folded his arms.

"The Stone itself has no value. But the people of Perista know the prophecy—that the speaker of Darenti must possess the Stone." Lei-hawm tucked the rock away somewhere. "V'Ov has a stone she claims is the Stone of Avora, which is how she maintained her position. She never let anyone test it, of course, except her—what did you call them?" He turned to me.

"Minions?" I smirked.

He nodded. "Her minions. They have claimed it is the true Stone of Avora—"

"Hang on. If Darenti know when other enti are lying, why do they believe this story?"

"Enti have different abilities. Some, like Gara, are excellent 'messengers'—skilled at reading and influencing. Others excel at transforming materials." He gestured to Verdat, who bowed. "V'Ov's specialty is hiding her thoughts. She is a rarity, and it's the only reason she was able to accomplish what she has. She also discovered how the bits of metal can help others do the same." He tapped the metal bits embedded in Gara's head. "Her discovery is the reason we know how to do this—and how we've kept our existence secret from her. She uses it to lie to the enti.

Once we remove her from power, we can expose the others who have used this technology."

Dad frowned. "And we believed the Darenti couldn't lie because V'Ov wanted us to believe that. How persistent are the effects?"

Lee cleared his throat. "According to the reports I read, the first ambassadors to Darenti all had 'mental breakdowns' that led to their reassignment. Many of them later seemed surprised by what they had requested during their terms. And they all went on to other employment. That would lead me to believe the effects are short-lived."

"Remember I am operating on the limited data I have gathered since we arrived a few days ago." Lei-hawm turned to confer with Gara and Verdat. After a short exchange, he lifted both hands. "It appears Lieutenant Lee is correct. Long-term deception requires constant reinforcement. Or an appeal to logic in the initial suggestion."

"What do you mean?" Zane asked.

"If the idea implanted is based on logical-sounding arguments, some humans will continue to believe it forever."

Zina laughed. "That's just human nature. Why admit you were wrong when you can double down on claiming to be right?"

Lee glared at Zina until she stopped snickering, "The point is we can't just wave the Stone and tell everyone V'Ov is an imposter. We'll need to convince Ambassador Slovenska that V'Ov has been dishonest with her."

"That shouldn't be too hard." Joss pointed at me. "None of them seemed to notice Siti was missing. When she suddenly shows up with Lei-hawm and the Stone, they're going to know something was wrong."

"We can hope it's that easy." Dad dusted his hands together and stood.

Zane stood, too. "Five credits says she won't believe it."

Dad bumped his fist against Zane's "Done. I hope you're wrong. Let's get this show on the road."

G'lacTechNews

This is Aella Phoenix reporting live from Darenti Four. Some kind of local anomaly has damaged many of our news drones, but my support team has deployed new ones, and we'll continue to monitor the situation.

Ambassador Slovenska has agreed to a live interview tomorrow.

The Hero, Admiral Nathanier Kassis, is rumored to be on Darenti, but I haven't been able to locate him yet. My requests for information about the AWOL officers have been rebuffed. Major Featherstoke, the mission commander, claims all personnel actions are protected under Commonwealth privacy laws.

I haven't met any of the Darenti yet but hope to remedy that this afternoon. Back to you, Odysseus.

CHAPTER TWENTY-SEVEN

THE SHUTTLE TOUCHED down on the landing pad beside the ambassador's office. Ambassador Slovenska and her staff hurried out of the building, followed by the usual cloud of news drones. Before we'd left Rovantu, Dad had put a call through to Ambassador Slovenska, requesting she attend a secure briefing on the CEC ship *Verity*.

The hatch popped open, and Slovenska and Major James stepped inside. One of the drones attempted to follow but hit a wall of blue sparks and fell to the deck. James kicked it out of the shuttle. The two officers strode into the passenger area, but the ambassador stopped short when she spotted me and Zina in the back row of seats. "What are they doing here? They're supposed to be locked in security!"

"They're with me." Dad gestured for the little woman to take a seat in the front row. "I require their presence during the meeting."

"Look, Nate, I know the kid is your daughter, but they went AWOL. With a shuttle! I can't ignore that, even for a friend." Slovenska dropped into a seat. James took a spot a few seats away, to give his boss the illusion of privacy.

"I'm not asking you to ignore anything. I am asking you to stop ignoring a few things."

Slovenska looked up from buckling the restraints across her thick middle. "What's that supposed to mean?"

Dad held up both hands. "Nothing. But since what we're going to discuss is—or should be—classified, we'll wait until we reach the secure vault on the *Verity* to continue this discussion."

She twisted around to stare at us. "But how did they get out of Security?"

"I let them out when I arrived."

"You just got here."

"That is one of many things you have been misled about." He pointed to the cockpit door as Zane stepped out.

"Ambassador Torres? When did you arrive?" Slovenska jerked as if trying to stand but was held in place by the seat restraints.

"I came with Nate." Zane dropped into the seat on her other side. "Everyone strapped in?" He checked on Major James before fastening his own belts. "Joss, we're ready back here."

Slovenska's jaw clenched at the name, but she didn't say anything.

Joss's voice came through the speakers. "Shuttle is cleared to launch." The vehicle jerked once before the artificial gravity smoothed the ride. "Estimated rendezvous with the *Verity* is twenty minutes. Enjoy the ride."

THE SHUTTLE DOCKED in the same landing bay we'd departed from less than a week before. It seemed like months. The maintenance crew swarmed around the ship as we exited, connecting power and data cables to the external ports. The captain's aide escorted us through the wide hallways deep into the center of the ship.

"The captain's conference room is at your disposal, Ambassadors, Admiral." The aide swiped the door open, then stood at attention beside it. "If you require her attendance—"

"That won't be necessary, Ensign. Thanks for your help. I'll drop in on the captain before we depart." Dad swept in and took a seat at the end of the table. Zane, Slovenska, and James joined him, while the rest of us stood against the wall. The aide retreated, allowing the door to close with a whomp. The "secure" light glowed red above it.

Dad placed his hand on a discreet panel, and the edges of it glowed blue. The light flickered in time with the androgynous voice that issued from the speakers. "Welcome to the *ECS Verity*, Vice Admiral Nathanier Kassis. Identity confirmed. Access Alpha One confirmed. Please state the names of the meeting participants for the record."

"This meeting includes Slovenska, Amanda, Ambassador to Darenti. Torres, Zane, Earth Ambassador. Torres, Zina, Earth Representative. Ross, Tiah, Earth Representative. CEC Major James—" He raised an eyebrow at the man.

"Calyx."

Joss nudged my arm with his elbow and mouthed "Calyx?" at me. I ignored him.

Dad went on. "James, Calyx. CEC lieutenants Torres, Joshua, and Kassis, Serenity. Navy Lieutenant Lee, Derek. And Darenti representative Lei-hawm." On the last name, the light around his hand flickered to red.

Ambassador Slovenska's head snapped around so hard it looked like it hurt. "What? Where?"

Liam jumped from my shoulder, landing on the conference table. He raced to the far end and leaped, transforming into Lei-hawm before he landed on the deck.

Slovenska's eyes bugged out of her head. James gasped, his jaw hanging slack.

Lei-hawm bowed. "Ambassador Slovenska, it is good to make your acquaintance."

James pointed at Lei-hawm, then at me. "He...she..."

"Yes, my daughter's sair-glider is actually a Darenti. And not just any Darenti but the legendary Lei-hawm." Dad leaned back in his chair. "The Darenti *neglected* to tell us about their shape-shifting abilities."

Slovenska sat up straight. "Neglected to tell us? How is that possible? I thought they didn't lie?"

Dad raised an eyebrow at Zane. "You owe me five credits."

Zane sighed and swiped his holo-ring. "You could argue they didn't lie about it—they just didn't mention it."

"True." Slovenska's eyes narrowed. "But you don't believe that, and neither do I. Their claims of honesty have always *implied* honesty in all things. Complete honesty. Masquerading as a glider for eight years is not honest."

"A hundred and seven years," Lei-hawm said. "It's not that we can't lie—it's more that we know when another enti is not honest. We can read it. Therefore, most of us don't try it very often."

"Read it how?" Slovenska's eyes bored into Lei-hawm. "And who else can you read?" The woman was sharp.

"Exactly." Dad folded his hands together on the table. "The Darenti can read our thoughts to some extent—mainly surface thoughts. More importantly, they can influence them. I've experienced it firsthand—"

Major James lurched to his feet. Slovenska flung up a hand to stop James's outburst before he got the first word out. "Let the admiral continue."

Dad explained about the experiment we'd done. "After the fact, it's hard to recognize what happened—even when you're completely aware of what's going to be done. The primary indication is a kind of dream-like quality to certain memories—as if they aren't completely your own. And decisions you made that seemed right at the time are hard to dissect after the fact. There's a very real inclination to simply not think about the event." He gestured to the rest of us. "That was universal."

"You've all been influenced by this Darenti mind control?" James's eyes went wide, the whites clearly visible all around the irises. "You're under their control?" He swung around, pointing at Lei-hawm. "Is he trying to control us now?" He backed away toward the door.

"Relax!" Dad held out a pair of plain metal headbands. "Lieutenant Chymm Leonardi di Zorytevsky designed these, and we tested them. For the most part, the Darenti require direct contact. Even the strongest must be within about three meters to influence your thoughts."

Lei-hawm's face twitched into an apologetic smile. "A large number of Darenti can also create a kind of blanket. That's more about emotions than thoughts—we can convince a group of humans to feel a certain way, but for specific ideas, direct one-to-one physical contact is most effective."

James lunged forward and snatched the device from Dad's hand.

Halfway to his head, he stopped. "What if this is actually the mind control device?"

I rolled my eyes. "Check with Diz—Lieutenant Chymm Leonardi di Zorytevsky. He invented this one, and he hasn't been anywhere near Darenti. Sir."

"As far as you know," he muttered. His gaze flicked from the headband gripped tightly in his hands to Lei-hawm, then to the VIPs.

Slovenska looked down the long table, obviously measuring the distance. "Three meters? But he ran right down the center." She pointed at the smooth synth-wood surface.

"When he's in glider form, Lei-hawm finds it difficult to influence us. Based on our tests, it would take more than a few seconds from a meter away."

"You trust him on that?" Slovenska's eyes narrowed as if she was assessing Dad's motives.

"We have an ace in the hole." He gestured at Tiah. "For some reason, Tiah seems to be impervious to his control. In every test, she pinpointed exactly when he began his attempts and was able to correctly identify what the test had been."

"You're assuming he was trying to influence her. Maybe he left her free on purpose." The ambassador fingered the slender metal band. "Even if we assume Lei-hawm has been honest with us—on this—which I have to say, now that I know about the Liam thing, his track record is not impressive…" She slid the metal band over her hair and nodded at James, still dithering by the door. "This is a potential nightmare."

"We have a possible solution to that—Lieutenant Leonardi di Zorytevsky—" Dad broke off, chuckling ruefully. "Diz believes the audio implants can be tweaked to provide the same protections these bands do. He'll be here soon to start testing. If we push that out on the next update, it will protect at least eighty percent of the population without anyone even knowing."

Zane's lips pressed together.

Slovenska noticed the tiny movement. "Ambassador? This isn't a viable solution?"

"A good chunk of that remaining twenty percent resides on Earth.

Most citizens of Earth have no audio implants. Like Mr. Arya, they don't trust the technology. Or they just haven't had the chance to get one." Zane shoved his hand through his hair, stopping when his fingers encountered the headband. He yanked his hand away with a sigh. "Earth may have to be a Darenti-free zone for now."

Lei-hawm lifted both hands. "That's a shame—Earth is a lovely planet. And has great historical significance. But it's fair."

"What's to keep them from doing a sair-glider thing?" James pointed a finger at Lei-hawm. "Let's face it—we have no real way of knowing where these creatures have gone. They could be out there—already doing irreparable harm to humanity."

Slovenska threw a glare at her assistant, then turned it on the Darenti. "That's actually a good point. You were out there. How many others have already snuck aboard CEC ships? I assume that's how you got away a hundred years ago." Her angry gaze swiveled to my dad. "Unless you were in on it?"

Dad sat back in his seat, hands aloft. "I had no idea he'd come along. That's one of the things Lieutenant Diz will be working on, though—a Darenti detector. And Lei-hawm assures us most enti are not able to transform into something as small as a glider. We certainly haven't seen anyone else do it."

"To my knowledge, I alone have achieved this feat." Lei-hawm sounded both proud and humble. "The ability to leave part of oneself elsewhere is like ascending to a higher level on Earth. Something many have heard of but no one has really witnessed or achieved."

"Not no one, clearly." Slovenska drummed her fingers on the table. "This is going to be a huge headache. At least you have the most obvious questions answered. The sooner your tech wiz can get here and figure out the rest, the better. I'll ask headquarters to assign a research team. Let's try to keep it under wraps for now."

She beckoned James to her side. The major went around the far end of the table, staying as far from Lei-hawm as possible, with the headband still gripped in his fingers. She took the metal circle from the man. "What if Lei-hawm wears this? Will it neutralize his abilities?"

Dad cleared his throat. "We didn't test that. Lei-hawm, as a sign of good faith, would you be willing to try it?"

"Of course." Lei-hawm spread his hands. "We used something similar —to hide our operatives from V'Ov."

I nodded. "Gara wore pieces kind of embedded in her head when she was at the base, so the other enti wouldn't catch on that she wasn't a V'Ov supporter."

Tiah took the band from Slovenska and held it out to the little enti. "Your crown."

Lei-hawm's lips twitched in a very human smirk, and he lifted his hands. "Be my guest."

Tiah lowered the metal onto Lei-hawm's head.

CHAPTER TWENTY-EIGHT

A BUZZING I hadn't noticed stopped. Its absence echoed in my mind like an empty cavern. "Do you hear that?"

"I didn't know it was even there."

"How did we not notice that?"

Tiah rubbed her temples. "I've had a headache since we arrived. Now it's gone."

Dad rubbed his chin. "I guess there's some proof—unless Major James is going to claim Lei-hawm manufactured that, too."

"He could have!"

"Major James, perhaps it would be best if you retired from this meeting." Slovenska glared at the younger man. "And remember, please, that *everything* about this meeting is classified Alpha One. Discussion, participants, everything."

James stepped back. "I'm sorry, Ambassador. I'll try to control my—" He broke off, his head shaking wildly. "No. I can't. This is treason against the human race!" He lunged around the table, headed for the door.

Joss snapped forward, blocking the major, his fingers wrapping around the man's bicep when he tried to evade. At the same moment, Lee shifted until he stood in front of the door. James stopped, his head swiveling from Joss to Lei-hawm and back.

"He's not going anywhere." Dad waved at the touch pad by his hand. "Alpha One automatically locks the doors until I unlock them. Or the captain overrides." He turned to Slovenska. "We clearly can't let him leave until he's calmed down."

"Major James." Slovenska stood, her voice going softer instead of louder. "Calyx! Will you please sit down?"

James pulled his arm from Joss's grip. "Unhand me, Lieutenant!"

Zina whispered, "Unhand me!"

I smothered a nervous giggle.

James stalked around the table again, taking a seat against the back wall of the room, as far from the enti as he could possibly get.

Lei-hawn shifted, as if uncomfortable. "This is an unnerving sensation."

James made a growling noise, then subsided.

"Unnerving how?" Slovenska asked.

The little enti reached toward the metal encircling his head, then with a glance at James, his hands dropped. "Wearing this is like being in an empty room. I feel... muffled. When I am Liam, I don't 'hear' your thoughts. This is the same feeling, but since I have all my other abilities, it's—" He broke off. "It's unnerving."

"But it's working." Tiah pointed at Lei-hawm. "Try to influence someone." She swung around and pointed at me. "Try to get Siti to do something. Siti, take your headband off!"

A protest erupted from James, but at my father's raised hand, he cut it off. Lee jerked, as if restraining himself from responding. With a shrug, I pulled off my headband. "I still hear that emptiness."

Tiah reached out and took Lei-hawm's hand. Her eyes went to the ceiling as if she were listening for something. "He's definitely trying. I can feel it when I touch him."

I went closer, taking Lei-hawm's other hand. I felt a weird urge to leave the meeting, but I easily deflected the impulse. "It works. But we shouldn't be surprised—Gara wore something similar when she was at the base—so the other enti wouldn't know what she was thinking."

Lei-hawm nodded, then dropped our hands. "Now you have a way to —what was the word, Ambassador? Neutralize our capabilities."

"But it requires you to be willing." James's words were carefully clipped, as if it took great effort to speak civilly.

Lei-hawm nodded. "That is true."

Dad shifted in his seat. "This isn't really our fight anymore. We've alerted the authorities to the mind-control and shape-shifting abilities of the Darenti." He nodded at Slovenska. "The ambassador must decide how to continue."

Slovenska fiddled with her holo-ring. "This isn't something I can determine on my own. As Ambassador, I can recommend the conference be pushed back and all humans withdrawn from the planet until the Commonwealth government establishes a new policy."

James cleared his throat. "I recommend we institute new screening methods at the station. We need to make sure they don't get out. Again." He pointed at Lei-hawm, disgust and fear clear in his tone.

The ambassador raised a hand. "The admiral said his team will work on such a device. We can discuss these things in a more appropriate venue, Major James."

Dad's lips pressed together, and he exchanged a look with Zane. The Earth Ambassador leaned forward. "I would like to be a party to those discussions."

"You know how this works, Torres." Slovenska folded her hands on the table. "Someone at a higher pay grade than us will create a blue-ribbon committee and appoint participants. You and I may or may not be included in that group. Got any friends on Grissom?"

"I'll start reaching out." Zane grimaced. "In the meantime, will the government send in miners to strip the elements from the Gothodi region as a 'punitive' measure? It would be a convenient excuse."

"We'll do our best to make sure that doesn't happen. The Darenti must be treated fairly. Which may mean simply going away and leaving them on their planet in peace." Slovenska raised her brows at Lei-hawm. "That's probably a best-case scenario. I can't imagine they'll get approval to allow any Darenti off-world in the foreseeable future. Working with us is likely to make you very unpopular here, Lei-hawm."

Lei-hawm bowed. "I believe you are incorrect. Most enti have little interest in seeing the galaxy."

"Except you." Slovenska's lips pressed together.

"And V'Ov. Before you abandon my people to our world, will you help me depose her? I realize this is not your battle to fight, but I would welcome your assistance in this matter."

James started to speak, but my father overrode him. "I think it's the least we can do." Dad glared at the major until the younger man shut his mouth. "She hasn't acted in good faith. Lei-hawm has put our welfare above his own freedom." He beckoned me, Joss, and Lee to join the table. "You three are good at plotting—let's come up with a plan to 'neutralize' V'Ov."

FOR THE NEXT WEEK, Joss, Zina, Tiah, and I were kept away from the rest of our group—apparently, we didn't have a need to know what they were up to. We all went through extensive medical exams—to rule out any damage from our enti interactions. Our brain scans came back normal.

When we weren't in sickbay, I'd caught glimpses of Lei-hawm, Dad, Zane, and even Lee entering and leaving the conference room, but they told us nothing. I thought I saw Chymm at one point, but we didn't get a chance to say hello. Joss spent most of that time in the gym. Zina and Tiah played cards. I did a lot of reading.

Finally, we returned to the planet. Joss landed the shuttle in the central courtyard of the Darenti base. We were going for maximum impact, and landing in the middle of the compound instead of the designated pad would accomplish that. The location looked even more cramped than the tiny clearing Lee had used in Rovantu, but Joss executed the drop flawlessly.

I pulled up a feed from the G'lacTechNews drones buzzing outside the shuttle, throwing the video to the big screen in the front of the passenger cabin.

A stream of enti surged out of the building. I caught a glimpse of one transforming into his human form—if I hadn't known their capabilities, I would have dismissed it as a trick of the light. I hid a grin. Sloppy operational security. V'Ov was going down.

"Let's do this." Slovenska moved into the airlock, standing by the external hatch. Dad and Zane moved in behind. The rest of us, including Lei-hawm, hung back. Joss flicked the controls, and the hatch popped open. The buzz we hadn't noticed until it disappeared—when Lei-hawm donned the headband—started again, droning under the soft chittering of the Darenti. The landing ramp extended from the side of the shuttle but didn't fold to the ground. It hung a meter above the green turf like a stage.

Ricmond of the Western Seas stood on the plascrete steps of one building with a swarm of enti around him. "What do you think you're doing? You are not following the established protocol. This is not a landing zone for CEC shuttles. I will file a complaint with the ambassador!"

Slovenska walked onto the ramp, stopping at the end.

Ricmond went still for a moment, then he bowed, his head almost brushing his legs. He rose—the action looking more like a hinge unfolding than a person straightening. His voice took on a smooth, oily tone. "Welcome, Ambassador! I wasn't expecting this visit."

"That's our cue." Dad and Zane strode out. I flicked my holo-ring to record the G'lacTechNews feed, so we'd have an independent record of the event.

"Admiral Kassis?" Ricmond stopped short. "And Ambassador Torres? I wasn't informed you'd arrived."

Dad's eyebrows rose. "I've been busy. Where is V'Ov?"

"Dar Demokritos is inside the embassy." He gestured to the building behind him.

"We need to meet with her. Immediately." Dad jumped off the ramp. On the ground, he still towered over the diminutive Darenti.

Ricmond took a step back. The expression on his face didn't change, but I got the impression he was feeling intimidated and didn't like it. "She has a full schedule today. Can we set up a meeting for tomorrow?"

"No, now would be good." Slovenska stalked closer. Despite her short stature, she still towered over the Darenti. "This can't wait."

Ricmond held up both hands. "It can wait."

Beside me, Joss snickered. "These are not the droids you're looking for."

Slovenska blinked, then shook her head. "It really can't."

The enti froze again. His eyes flicked to the crowd of Darenti now surrounding the humans like floodwaters. Several of them reached toward the humans, stretching their arms to unnatural lengths so they could place their hands on the humans' legs.

Tiah tapped her grav belt and lifted above the tide with a shudder.

"Please ask your…" Slovenska paused for a second. "…minions to give us some space. Humans aren't generally comfortable with this much physical contact."

Again, Ricmond's expression didn't change, but he took a step back, waving to the others. "Move away from the humans." His eyes flickered toward the second-floor windows of V'Ov's office. "Dar Demokritos is coming."

"How did you call her?" Slovenska cocked her head. "You've never really explained your communications capabilities to us. Do you have some tech similar to our audio implants?"

Ricmond seemed to shrink a little. "Uh, no. I sent an envoy to request her presence." He tapped the enti standing closest to him. "Go investigate her continued absence."

As the enti turned toward the door, it opened. The golden litter V'Ov had ridden to the human compound on my first day appeared, with a team of stout enti bearing it into the courtyard. V'Ov rose, putting her eyes almost on a level with Dad's. She stared down at Slovenska. "Ambassador. What a pleasant surprise."

"Is it?" Slovenska crossed her arms. "I'd love to come in and chat." She waved at the news drones swarming around the scene. "I'd like a little privacy."

V'Ov turned to look at the drones, then stared at her people, her face blank.

"She's telling her people to send us away." Lei-hawm stood beside me, watching the feed.

"Can you hear it?" I asked.

"No." He tapped the metal circlet still around his temples. "Remember, V'Ov is not a strong sender. She's using physical signals to speak with them. I can also see her aura—there's confusion. She's wondering why the humans aren't following instructions."

Outside, V'Ov stood silent in her litter. Slovenska, Zane, and Dad watched, unmoving.

"Looks like a standoff." I grinned at Lei-hawm. "I guess it's showtime. Anyone want to chicken out?"

The little enti grinned and reached for his metal circlet. "Hell, no!"

CHAPTER TWENTY-NINE

UNNOTICED BY THE mob of enti, Joss and I moved out of the shuttle with Lei-hawm in our wake. We stopped near the end of the ramp. Lei-hawm stepped between us and removed his metal headband.

Every enti in the courtyard snapped in our direction like compasses encountering a magnet.

"Lei-hawm!" The name rang through the courtyard, muttered by dozens of enti.

"The traitor!" V'Ov pointed at Lei-hawm. "This enti has attempted to undermine human-enti relations! Seize him!"

The enti milled around, staring from Lei-hawm to V'Ov and back, as if unsure what to do.

Joss leaned down and pitched his voice low. "Are you talking to them?"

Lei-hawm lifted a finger.

Joss straightened. "Never been shushed by an alien before."

"Still haven't." I lifted a finger. "Shush. And now you have—we're the aliens here."

"I wish I could hear what he's saying." Joss gazed around the courtyard, then stared up into the sky. "And where's Nibs? Shouldn't he be here by now?"

As one, the crowd turned and focused solely on Lei-hawm.

"Keep an eye on V'Ov," Dad said through the audio implant. "It looks like the tide could turn here, and we don't want her disappearing. She has a lot to be held accountable for."

"Yes, sir." I locked my surveillance system on V'Ov and flew a stealth drone to land on her. The Navy had provided several of the devices, designed to look and behave like insects. The little drone transmitted for a few seconds, then went dead. I ran diagnostics. "She killed my bug." I launched a second one, this time programming it to hover over the enti.

Lei-hawm put out a hand. Joss reached into his pocket and deposited the dirty little Stone of Avora in the enti's palm. Lei-hawm grasped it with two fingers and his arm stretched, raising it high above his head.

Every enti eye followed the movement of the Stone, some of them shifting across the watchers' faces when they forgot to move their heads.

Joss shifted uneasily. "That is not creepy at all."

My audio pinged. "We're inbound. Arriving in two minutes."

"Roger." I jerked my head to the west. "Lee is coming."

"Right on schedule," Dad said.

"About time," Joss muttered at the same moment.

Lei-hawm's arm contracted, and he raised the other one. He spoke aloud, for our benefit. "Send forth from among your number enti to test the Stone."

The enti milled around the courtyard, their chirping and muttering amplified by the walls.

"Stop!" V'Ov's yell rang out, and the rumble cut off like a switch had been thrown. "That is not the Stone of Avora! I possess the Stone!"

"Then bring it forth for testing," Lei-hawm replied, his volume magnified to fill the space. "You claim to hold the Stone—prove it."

"Since when is proof needed among our people? You can read my intent." V'Ov spread her arms, as if inviting inspection.

I moved closer to Lei-hawm. "How can she call our bluff? They will know she's lying."

"Most of these enti are her creatures. She has layers of followers—only the closest know the truth about the Stone. They use protection" —he nodded at my head— "to hide their knowledge. Others believe what they are told, and they tell still more. The only way to prove the Stone is ours is to demonstrate its abilities."

Dad and Zane, with Slovenska between them, waded toward us. The sea of enti parted as they approached, then filled in behind like water. Dad stopped at the end of the shuttle ramp.

My audio pinged. "Lee is inbound." I rolled my eyes toward a growing speck in the sky.

The Navy shuttle flew low over the compound, hovering above us. The cargo ramp lowered slowly, and a mass of Gothodi swarmed out. They poured out of the open bay like syrup off a plate—a shifting blob of bright colors and eye-watering shapes dripping slowly from the end of the ramp. The mass grew as it approached the ground, and the enti filling the courtyard backed away.

The blob touched down, breaking free from the ship with a loud snap. The shuttle rebounded, swinging wildly into the sky. It settled at a higher altitude almost immediately, then flew to the landing pad.

"Don't tell Nibs I said so, but that was some first-class piloting." Joss stared after the shuttle in admiration. Then he ruined it. "Almost as good as I coulda done."

I slapped his arm and rolled my eyes.

The Gothodi mass separated into dozens of weird shapes. I spotted Iotentia Korvalo's ruffled leaf and a small blue ball. They mixed into the local enti, some of whom changed shape in their wake.

Still on the ramp, Lei-hawm held the rock aloft again. "Our Gothodi siblings have joined us. They will reveal to you the truth of my claims." He held the Stone out to Iotentia who extruded a smaller leaf-like appendage to take it.

"It's up to them, now." Lei-hawm stepped back from the edge of the ramp. "V'Ov will not remain in control."

"V'Ov! Crap!" How could I have forgotten it was my job to watch V'Ov? I swiped my drone controls open, but they showed V'Ov still in the litter. She stood still and silent, still pointing at the shuttle.

"That's not V'Ov. She's escaped!" Lei-hawm leapt into the sea of enti, transforming into Liam mid-jump. He bounced across their heads—or the tops of their bodies, whatever they happened to be—and into the litter. When he reached V'Ov, he landed on her shoulder, then leaped again, disappearing into the colorful crowd.

"How did she escape?" I swiped madly through screens, checking my settings. "The drone should have alerted me if she so much as breathed hard. Not that enti breathe."

"Got it." Joss flicked a few commands, and a swarm of the Navy surveillance drones scattered across the crowd.

"How are you going to find her? She can look like anything." I rubbed my eyes, then flicked my drone into action again. "Someone needs to grab that enti and make her talk." I pointed at the small imposter.

The enti holding the litter had dropped their burden and disappeared into the crowd. Without waiting for a reply, I tapped my grav belt and took off, launching directly for the lone enti who stood unmoving on the litter.

I landed beside her, but the fake V'Ov didn't acknowledge my existence. Reaching out, I pushed her shoulder, as if I were challenging her to a playground fight.

V'Ov toppled over, landing amid the dropped litter, still in the same pose. "It's a fake—not even a real enti." I poked the decoy with a finger. It was solid, with a little give—just like touching Lei-hawm. "I don't know what it's made of." I touched it again, and the whole thing dissolved into a pile of powder.

I jumped back. "That was just weird." Standing, I turned in a circle, trying to find Liam. Amid the riot of Gothodi color, the little glider was impossible to locate. I flicked my grav belt controls and rose above the crowd.

Iotentia stood in the middle, holding the Stone. Individual enti moved forward one at a time, then moved away, mingling with the crowd. I assumed they were each testing the Stone, then reporting to their neighbors, but it was impossible to tell.

I rose higher, above the low buildings. A flash of movement caught my eye, so I shifted directions, heading for the shuttle pad where Lee had landed the Naval craft. A streak of blue and white flickered amid the blue-green jungle below me, headed for the shuttle: Liam.

I streaked after him, pushing my grav belt to top speed. As I approached, the passenger hatch on the side slammed shut. I arrowed down, aimed directly for it. Lee rushed out of the undergrowth on the same trajectory. My feet hit the rough ground, and I stumbled forward, slamming into the Navy pilot. We smacked into the side of the shuttle with a resounding bang.

Lee grabbed my upper arms and pushed me away. "What the heck, Kassis? You trying to injure me?"

"V'Ov is trying to steal the shuttle!" I threw out a hand to catch my balance against the ship's still-extended ramp.

He smirked, dusting his hands together. "She's not going anywhere. I locked her in the air lock." He jerked a thumb at the hatch.

"What?" I lifted off the ground again to peer through the porthole set in the hatch. The long, narrow space—large enough for five or six humans—seemed to be filled with a mess of sticky strings. "Ew. It looks like a cobweb in there. Or chewing gum in someone's hair."

Lee rose beside me. "That's V'Ov."

I swallowed. "I think she's trying to get out. You don't suppose she can damage the shuttle, do you?"

Liam landed atop the shuttle with a thud. He scrambled down the side to perch on my shoulder as we all stared through the window. Some of the strings contracted and thickened while others stretched thinner. I swallowed again and dropped to the ground, feeling a little queasy.

Lee crouched beside me. He lifted a strand of my hair that had come loose from the braids. "You ever get gum stuck in here?"

I wiped the beads of sweat from my upper lip. "Yeah. Once. My dad had to cut it out."

Liam dropped beside me, transforming into his familiar humanoid shape. "She is contained?"

Lee nodded. "Diz's resonator seems to be working."

"Diz's what?"

Lee wrapped the strand of my hair around his finger, his eyes firmly focused on the action. "Your friend Diz built a device that keeps the

Darenti from transforming. We had it installed in the airlock of this shuttle."

"I knew I saw Chymm! Why didn't someone tell me?" I jerked my head and yanked my hair from Lee's hand.

"Ow!" we said together.

Lee rubbed his finger, still avoiding my eyes. "You didn't need to know. Keeping information close is even more important when the enemy can read your mind."

I tapped my headband. "They can't read my mind."

"They could have read his mind, when he took the headband off." Lee nodded at Lei-hawm. "And if you knew, you could have—"

Quick anger burned through me. I jumped to my feet and glared down at Lee. "You think I would have shared classified information with him?"

"No! But you might have removed your headband when he was nearby." Lee held up both hands. "You trust him."

The anger drained out of me. "I do. But I understand the importance of operational security, and I haven't removed this headband since—" I flushed when I remembered that night alone with Lee at the camp.

Zane and Dad angled down from the sky, followed by a familiar lieutenant. The three of them looked into the ship, then landed beside us.

"Chymm!" I flung my arms around the dark, pudgy man. "How long have you been here?"

He returned my squeeze and let me go. "The admiral brought me. After I got Lee's message—boy, that was a shock! I haven't seen him since the Academy, and why would he message me? I mean, after Sarvo Six… And I know he helped you on Saha, but I wasn't there— Of course, that was the point, right? I knew something was up right away. Then when I saw you and Joss in the pic—is he here?" He turned to look around the clearing.

"He's at the base." I motioned for him to continue.

"Anyway, I scanned the message and found data encrypted using my own algorithm. Obviously, that was from you or Joss since I only shared that version with Charlie Blue. Which reminds me, I have an update." He flicked his holo-ring.

I closed my hand over his, shutting down the interface. "Later."

He grinned sheepishly. "Right. When I decrypted the data, I sent a message to your dad at the Academy. I was lucky it got through to him—I imagine he has the AI screening out a lot of junk, but mine got through. Maybe he has your friends on a whitelist?" He raised his eyebrows, but I rolled my hand in a get-on-with-it motion. "Sorry. Anyway, he had orders cut for me to join the team. I came to the *Verity* to do some research. Then we came down here for the testing. Lei-hawm's friends helped us. They're fascinating!"

Lee lifted again to look inside the airlock. "She's back in one piece but a single brown blob."

Chymm nodded enthusiastically. "That's what happens with the disrupter. It doesn't allow them to maintain a conscious form. Did you know the Darenti have to think about what they want to look like, but after they get into that configuration, they don't have to do anything to maintain it? It's like flipping a switch. Knowing that, I created a device that triggers them to think of their form, which—"

I cut him off before he could gain speed on the technical details. "Does it hurt?"

"My test subjects said no." Chymm pulled up some specs on his holo-ring. "See—"

I held up a hand. "I'd love to hear the technical details later, but now what?" I turned to Dad.

Lee's lips twitched. He must have noticed my eyes glazing over when Chymm got on a roll. I flushed and looked away, focusing on my father.

"Now we turn her over to the Darenti to deal with. They are a sovereign race—we aren't going to impose justice on them. We are installing Diz's technology in the airlocks of the station." Dad pointed at the sky. "That will trigger any Darenti attempting to enter to revert to their non-conscious form. In addition, we'll increase the Naval presence around the planet to prevent any additional piracy and unauthorized transport off the planet. The reasons will not be broadcast for public consumption, of course—shape-shifters and mind-readers are terrifying, and that information is classified at the highest level. Ambassador Slovenska will meet with whomever the Darenti choose as V'Ov's successor, and they'll begin the negotiations again. This time with full disclosure."

I turned to Lei-hawm. "If they're installing the disrupter, you'll be stuck here."

He nodded. "That is true. But thanks to you—and other explorers before you—I had a very nice off-world vacation."

Zane choked. "A hundred-and-seven-year off-world vacation?"

"A century is not so long for someone my age. And I still have many more centuries before I am dust."

The words sparked a memory. "Lei-hawm, when V'Ov escaped, there was an enti who looked like her, in her place. But she—it turned out to be a thing—maybe a statue? And when I touched it, it disintegrated."

A shadow crossed Lei-hawm's face, and his expression darkened. He glared at the shuttle. "V'Ov has much to answer for. That sounds like an elderly enti. I told you that we generally return to nature before we pass and leave little behind. She found someone near the end and convinced them to stand in for her."

"That was—some*one*?" I looked at my hands. The urge to wipe them on my pants was overwhelming but felt so wrong.

Lei-hawm reached over and grasped my wrist. He pulled me to a crouch, gentle but inexorable, and placed my palm on the ground. "Return her to Darenti."

I rubbed both hands in the dirt, trying to wipe the creepiness from my mind. I had held a dying enti as she passed. Leaving her crumbling in the litter as I raced here seemed so callous in retrospect. My eyes pricked.

Lee crouched beside me, and his arm went around my shoulders. "You didn't know."

I collapsed against him, a strange grief overcoming my sense of self-preservation. Lee's solid bulk offering warmth and comfort without words. We huddled together in an irrational wallow of melancholy. Then the sadness dissipated in a flash, leaving me light and hopeful. I pulled away from Lee's arm and stared at Lei-hawm. "What was that?"

The little enti smiled. "Did you feel the joy? When one of us returns to the land, their joy is released to the universe. It is a happy thing, although your kind interpret it as sad."

"That—that's exactly what I felt. Joy returned to the universe." I looked at my dusty hands with new eyes. "Amazing."

Lee smiled—a true smile, not his usual sardonic grin. "I felt it, too."

"The end is a new beginning. But co-opting someone else's end for her own gain is wrong. This is perhaps the most heinous of V'Ov's crimes."

CHAPTER THIRTY

Lei-hawm looked around the little clearing. "Where is Nate Kassis?"

Lee pointed to the back of the shuttle. "They went inside, I think. Through the cargo lock."

As Lei-hawm bounded away, I turned to Lee. "How did you fly here alone? What about the Navy regulations requiring two pilots? Surely, you didn't break the rules."

"I didn't. Major D'metros is aboard." He grimaced. "He didn't know anything about this part of the plan. He helped with the airdrop."

"You're admitting you didn't do that spectacular flying on your own?" I widened my eyes.

He rolled his. "Paulus is an excellent pilot. One of the best in the corps. Definitely better than your boyfriend."

I rolled my eyes but didn't bother contradicting him. "How did you get V'Ov into the airlock?"

He considered me for a second, as if deciding what to tell me. Then he shrugged. "Your buddy Diz and I left Paulus in the ship and hid in the jungle. Liam chased V'Ov this way—a shuttle with an unprotected pilot was impossible to resist."

"What if she'd gotten Major D'metros under her control?"

He shook his head and leaned against the side of the ship. "That's why Chymm and I were here. Lei-hawm said V'Ov required direct contact to influence anyone on her own—remember, she used other enti to do her dirty work. Apparently, she could tell that he was inside and unprotected but couldn't read that the inner hatch was closed. And since Paulus didn't know about the disruptor, she didn't either."

"She didn't realize you were here?"

"Diz got his audio implant modification working. He included a way to make us essentially invisible to the Darenti. At least, it works when they're distracted. Based on our brief tests, it wouldn't fool any of them in an up-close-and-personal encounter. But V'Ov headed straight for Paulus, and we closed her in the airlock."

"Still seems pretty risky."

"Risky is all in a day's work for us Navy guys." He gave me a smug grin.

There was the Lee I recognized. "Major D'metros is CEC, not Navy."

"He knew this mission was risky—just not exactly how."

"Why did you get to be part of the fun, and the rest of us were kept in the dark?"

He shrugged. "I'm lower profile than the rest of you. I'd already 'helped' V'Ov catch you once, too. And using a Navy shuttle and Navy pilot made the operation less suspicious—the Darenti are used to the CEC, but the Navy is kind of off their radar."

I nodded. It made sense, even if it made me feel out of the loop. "Now what?"

Male voices filtered to us as the others exited the rear of the shuttle. "You can fly us back to the base and release V'Ov there," Dad said as he and Major D'metros came into view.

"Yes, sir," D'metros replied.

"And Major? Well done."

"I can't take credit for the drop, sir. That was all Lieutenant Lee. 'Zen' is an excellent callsign for him. He's the best pilot I've ever flown with."

I glanced at Lee, but he was looking away. A faint flush washed over his cheeks.

"Noted." Dad didn't look at Lee. "But I was referring to the capture."

D'metros's jaw tightened. "I didn't have much choice in that, sir, but I understand why it had to be that way. Still, not something I'd willingly volunteer for next time."

"Also noted. With proper management, there won't be a next time." Dad waved at us. "Siti, Lee, let's get moving. The others are inside. We'll land at the compound. Joss should have moved the other ship by now."

We hiked around the end of the shuttle and up the slanted ramp.

"Hey, Siti." Major D'metros waved, then swiped a file at Lee. "You finish up here—I'm going to the cockpit to work the checklist."

Lee saluted D'metros, then flicked his holo-ring. "Take your seats, please. We'll depart as soon as the preflight is complete." He hit the cargo ramp close icon, then flipped a copy of the checklist to the main screen. As we watched, the two pilots worked through the various items. Lee finished the cargo hold list and moved into the cockpit.

"I'm going to write a medal recommendation for that boy." On my left, Dad tightened his flight restraints. "He's an outstanding pilot and an excellent officer. Really turned things around after Sarvo Six. It's a shame he transferred to the Navy." He gave me a quizzical look. "Wouldn't make a bad son-in-law, either."

"Dad! We are not a couple. Nothing happened in camp—I wasn't trying to—" I waved my hands incoherently. "I was trying to be nice. He's claustrophobic—he didn't like the enti city. It wasn't a hookup. And I can't believe I'm talking to my dad about hookups."

"But you aren't. You said it *wasn't* a hookup." Dad grinned.

"Hey, didn't we decide ages ago that we were going to unite our dynasties through Siti and Joss?" Zane threw a malicious smile my direction.

"Do not even get me started on all the ways that is not going to happen!" I spluttered.

"Unite our dynasties." Dad chuckled.

Chymm looked up from the file on his holo-ring. "Are Siti and Joss finally dating? That's great! We always thought you two should end up together."

"No, we aren't dating. And who's we?"

"You know, the whole flight. Back in the Academy. I mean, at first,

Terrine thought you'd get together with Peter, but it was pretty obvious he was into Aneh. After that, we figured—"

"No. There's nothing between me and Joss." I glared at my dad. "Or me and Lee. Nothing between anyone."

"Except Peter and Aneh." Chymm flicked his holo-ring. "Didn't you get the announcement?"

My ring vibrated as Chymm's file landed in my account. "They're going to have a baby? Wow! That's awesome. I wonder why I didn't get one of these." My eyes snagged on Lei-hawm. "Oh, right. I turned off my comm channels." I flicked through the settings and reset the connections. Then turned off the notifications when a couple hundred messages pinged into my inbox. "I guess that's what happens when you go off the grid for a week or two."

Dad put a hand on my arm, leaning close and lowering his voice. "There's nothing wrong with connecting with someone. Just because I've been single as long as you can remember doesn't mean you have to do it that way."

I leaned my shoulder against his. I had no memory of my mother and no regrets. Dad had always been enough for me—even during my turbulent teen years. I hadn't consciously followed his example, but maybe my subconscious had pushed away people I might have formed relationships with. I shoved the thought away—I could consider it later, when we weren't in the middle of a coup on an alien planet. I had plenty of years to find a good life partner.

The shuttle landed in the middle of the Darenti compound, and I shook off my introspection. The rear door of the shuttle opened, the ramp rattled down, and we trooped out. Zina, Tiah, and Joss waited for us in the courtyard.

"Where's the Navy shuttle?" Lee demanded.

"Don't worry, I didn't fly her away." Joss held up both hands. "A couple of your buddies came to take her back to the base. As requested by the admiral." He nodded at my dad.

"How do we get V'Ov out of the airlock?" Zane asked.

"The disrupter won't do anything to humans. If we leave it turned on, someone can go in and take her out." Chymm used his grav belt to rise and peer through the window. "Or we could turn it off, and maybe she'll come out on her own."

Dad gestured to Lei-hawm. "What do you want us to do?"

The little enti shook his head. "It's not up to me. The enti have selected Ungala to represent them—it is her right and responsibility to determine this."

"They've selected someone already?" Zina looked around the courtyard. Only a few Darenti remained, some of them shifting into humanoid forms, then back again as they observed us from a distance. "And did you say Ungala? Aren't the Gothodi isolationists?"

"When you can speak instantaneously across vast distances, it's easy to poll the populace. And this time, the Gothodi voted. Which reminds me, they have asked me to thank you for the ride, but they prefer to walk home."

Joss burst out laughing. "I guess the hot-shot airdrop was too much for them." He pounded Lee on the back.

Lei-hawm went still for a moment, as if making a call on an audio implant. "The Gothodi prefer to travel overland. Now that they have broken their self-imposed isolation, they wish to see the rest of Darenti."

Ungala, the Gothodi leader, appeared at his side shaped like a meter-high blade of grass. The slender green form bent and swayed as if blown by the wind. "Thank you." The words floated from his vicinity, as though whispered on that same wind. "My people will take V'Ov."

He undulated, and a group of stout, three-legged creatures hurried to us, three eyes blinking from each cube-shaped body. They carried the golden litter, but it had been reconfigured into a cage.

"How are they going to keep her inside that cage?" Dad asked Lei-hawm.

"The cage is largely symbolic. All of Darenti knows what she has done. She will be escorted to the outer islands to live in seclusion. If she recognizes the error of her ways—and we will know, of course—she will be welcome in our society once again."

As Lei-hawm spoke, the cube-like enti moved to the shuttle hatch.

Chymm fiddled with his holo-ring, then opened the airlock. V'Ov stepped out, transformed back to her humanoid form. She swept into the gilded cage like a queen ascending her throne, ignoring everyone. The enti lifted their burden and trundled into the jungle.

"Did they ever figure out what was happening to the Gothodi who disappeared?" I glanced at Lei-hawm, then back to Ungala. "Were the pirate miners responsible for that?"

"Yes." The blade of grass undulated. "They were in the mine."

Lei-hawm took up the story. "Apparently, when the pirates encountered enti, they simply threw them into the mine. Perhaps out of fear? No one is certain, as the enti could not read the humans' thoughts or understand their words—thanks to the helmets. In time, they would have escaped, but shaping dense rock is difficult. The mine was dug through stone that is very difficult for enti to reform. Perhaps the same material as the Stone of Avora."

"Promethium is very hard—it's one of the reasons it's expensive. It's difficult to mine." Dad bowed low to Ungala. "I apologize on behalf of the human race for the damages done by these pirates and assure you we will see that justice is done."

"Leave them with us," Ungala said. "We have justice."

Dad's face tightened. "We can't do that. Just as we handed V'Ov over to you for justice." He rubbed a hand over his face. "This is veering into the political arena, and I can't speak on behalf of the Commonwealth. I urge you to take your concerns to Ambassador Slovenska."

"It shall be done." The blade of grass crumpled into a ball and rolled away.

G'lacTechNews

This is Aella Phoenix reporting live from the station in orbit around Darenti Four.

In an unexplained reversal of policy, the Colonial Commonwealth has reinstitute the quarantine on Darenti Four. All civilians, including the press corps, have been extracted from the planet and have been ordered to return to our ships. The system has been placed on a no-fly list. New equipment is being fitted into the station airlocks, but the personnel doing the installation would not comment, even off-the-record.

The official statement says only that the quarantine will be revisited in the future.

CHAPTER THIRTY-ONE

WE LOADED our bags into the back of the Navy shuttle, stacking them for the crew chief to strap to the deck. I rubbed my cheek against my shoulder, trying to wipe away a tear without anyone noticing.

I ignored the crowd of explorers around me, tossing their gear into the shuttle, laughing and joking about getting back to civilization, and shuffled down the ramp and through the gate to the entrance of the embassy compound where Lei-hawm waited.

"I only have a few minutes." I sat on the broad steps of the embassy building, facing the shuttle. "When they're done loading the gear, I'll have to go."

Lei-hawm stood beside me, his head on a level with my shoulder. Had he shrunk in the few weeks we'd been on Darenti? We'd been so busy, I couldn't remember. After a long time, he spoke, his deep voice soft. "I will miss you, Siti."

I sniffed. "I'll miss you too. Although, I'll miss Liam more. No offense."

"Since we are the same being, none is taken."

"You're not really the same." I sniffed again. "I mean, Liam didn't talk. But he's been with me for so many years—I know it's not much to you, but it's almost a third of my life. I feel like he died." Grief washed over me like a tsunami, a dark flow of loss and emptiness pouring through my body. I choked back a sob and wiped my eyes again.

Lei-hawm touched my arm, and a flood of love pushed into the grief. "He's not gone. We're both here. Maybe you can visit sometime. I'd offer to come to you, but…"

We stared across the tarmac in silence. A second force shield had been installed around the landing pad, with one of Chymm's disruptors at the entrance. Lei-hawm could easily avoid that—he'd simply transform to Liam and walk through the shield. As far as we knew, he was the only enti capable of the feat, but since the capability was classified at the highest levels, most of the base personnel had no idea.

The disruptors had also been installed on the station above at every external airlock. Navy presence around the planet had been increased, and the satellite surveillance system had been beefed up with multiple redundancies. The modifications had been completed at lightning speed—fear of shape-shifting mind-control was a powerful motivator.

Chymm's audio implant upgrades had been tested and deployed as well, although every human on the planet was also required to wear some form of additional protection. The xenophobes wore flight helmets, but the rest of us used the more subtle headbands.

My audio pinged—Joss. "Siti, report to the shuttle. Launch is in five."

I turned to the little enti. "I gotta go." I bit my lip, unable to articulate.

Lei-hawm stretched his arms to triple their normal length and wrapped them around me in a weird hug. "I'll miss you, Siti." Before I could respond, he shifted, and Liam scrambled up my arm to press against my cheek.

I cupped a hand around the glider, his silky fur soft against my face. Tears poured out of my eyes, soaking into his pelt. "I love you, Liam." With one last squeeze, I lifted him from my shoulder and set him on the step. "I'll never forget you." Then I turned and ran to the shuttle.

WE LANDED on Grissom at mid-day. We'd spent the four-day return trip in endless meetings and debriefings, and I was glad to finally get away from all of it—at least for now. There would be weeks of investigation before any of us would be reassigned to a mission team. I caught the mag-lev train from the base to my neighborhood stop and strolled beside the river to my building.

The float tube dropped me on my floor, and I pressed my hand against my apartment's access panel. The plate glowed green, accepting my identity. The front door opened with a hiss, and the lights came on. The air handlers whirred softly, exchanging the stale air for fresh. "Welcome home, Siti."

"Thanks, Nancy." When I first rented this place, I'd named the house monitor Nagging Nancy because she insisted on reminding me of *everything*. Over time, I'd disabled a number of her automated reminders, but the name stuck.

The door slid closed behind me, and the lock snicked. I crossed the living room to toss my bag into the tiny laundry, then headed for the fridge. Nothing, of course. I'd forgotten to order for my return. "Nancy, place a standard return supply order. And a bottle of Abott's Clear."

"Order placed. Delivery in four hours."

I patted the side of the fridge. "Thanks."

"You're welcome, Siti."

Without Liam, the apartment was depressing. I put on my workout gear and went for a long run, which turned into a longer walk. The idea of going back to my empty place held no charm. As dusk fell over the city, I finally returned and took a shower.

As I finished pulling on a light tunic and leggings, the door chimed. My groceries should have arrived while I was out—via cargo pod rather than the front door. I glanced into the kitchen alcove as I went past—a bright green box sat next to the Autokich'n.

My audio pinged as I approached the door, reporting the visitors: Joss, Peter, and Aneh. I forced my features into a welcoming smile and waved the door open. "Hi, guys!"

Aneh rushed in, throwing her arms around me. I hadn't seen her in months—she and Peter lived on the far side of the city. "Are you getting fat?" I asked.

She pulled back and slapped my arm, putting the other hand on her slight belly bulge. "Yeah, fat. Blame him." She pointed at her significant other.

Peter hugged me hard, holding me for a few extra seconds. "Sorry about Liam," he whispered as he released me.

I pushed my lips up in a very fake smile. "Thanks."

Joss waved a bottle. "Time for a drink! Those dry missions are such a drag."

I rolled my eyes as I went to the kitchen to retrieve some glasses. "The mission might have been dry, but I saw you taking advantage of the bar on the transport." Like most CEC ships, the crew had a fridge in the officers' lounge with a selection of alcoholic beverages. Transients were welcome, as long as they put enough credits in the kitty.

"That was just beer. Couldn't do anything stronger with all those debriefings." He opened the bottle and poured a couple of centimeters into three glasses. "Sorry, chubs, you'll have to drink water."

I detoured to the green box and pulled out a bottle. Aneh took it and read the label. "You got my favorite! I didn't know they made a non-alcoholic version!"

"When I found out you were pregnant, I did some research." I handed her an empty glass and took the one Joss held out. "Let's toast to Aneh and Peter and the new explorer."

We raised our glasses and clinked them together. I tossed my drink back and held out my glass for another shot.

Joss raised his brows. I held his gaze, my glass still extended. He poured in another shot. Then he filled his own glass and raised it. "To Liam. I'm going to miss you, little guy."

I sucked in a deep breath, the loss jagged in my chest. "To Liam." Fire burned down my throat.

Joss took my empty glass and put it on the counter with the bottle. "Enough moping. Let's go." He grabbed my shoulder and turned me toward the door, then waved for the others to join us.

"Go where?" I looked down at my clothes. "I'm not really dressed for clubbing."

"No, no clubbing. We're going to Nibs's place." He waved the door open.

"Nibs?" Peter looked up from setting his and Aneh's glasses next to mine. "As in Derek Lee? Why would we go there?"

Joss shrugged. "He asked us to come over. And he's not such a bad dude."

"You're talking about the guy we went to the Academy with?" Peter waited for Aneh to precede him out the door. "The guy who tried to get us expelled."

"Nancy, I'm going out." I paused to grab a light jacket. Despite the daytime heat, Grissom got quite chilly at night.

"Enjoy your evening, Siti." The door shut behind me, the access pad flashing red to indicate the locking sequence, then dark.

"Yeah, Nibs. He's not so bad." Joss pushed us toward the float tube. "He's a really good pilot."

Aneh laughed. "Oh, well, in that case, he's a great guy."

Joss's face flushed, but he grinned.

"I think Joss and Lee have a little bit of a bromance going on." I paused at the float tube. "A true enemies-to-lovers kind of thing." I waited for him to explode in denials.

Joss just raised an eyebrow at me. He leaned close as he stepped into the float tube. "I'm not the only one."

My face went hot, and I was glad the others had already descended to the train. By the time I reached the platform, I'd gotten my expression back to neutral.

We boarded the train, Peter and Joss exchanging insults and barbs as usual. Aneh sat with a heavy sigh, patting the seat beside her. "Sit with me, Siti."

I dropped into the hard chair. As we rode, I told Aneh about seeing Chymm, although I couldn't offer any details about the mission. She gave me the rundown on our Academy friends who lived in the area. She and Peter had each done a tour on a Phase 1 team, but now she worked at headquarters and Peter flew shuttles to the station and back. "After the baby is old enough to travel, we might try for a ship's crew assignment. Did you know they have family cabins on the Phase 2 ships? Of course you did—your trip to Earth was basically a Phase 2." I let her cheerful chatter wash over me like a comforting blanket until we arrived at our stop.

Lee lived in an apartment building that looked nearly identical to mine: low and boxy, with small shops on the ground floor and most of the residences beneath the surface. We took the float tube down and followed the music to an open door. I hoped the building had good sound shielding—if not, his neighbors would be calling the Peacekeepers soon.

As we worked our way into the party, Joss pulled another bottle from somewhere to add to the collection on the table. He poured something into a glass and handed it to me, then served Peter and himself from the same bottle.

"I'll get Aneh something else." I pushed through the crowd in search of a safe beverage. Not finding it in the living room, I tried the kitchen—an actual room rather than the alcove I had. The door slid closed behind me, cutting off the party sounds as if I'd disconnected an audio call. The room held a table with two chairs, an actual stove rather than an Autokich'n, and a cooler on the floor. I dug through that first but, not finding anything, tried the fridge.

Music blasted when someone opened the door, then cut off again. "If you're looking for Chewy Nuggets, I ate them all."

I closed the refrigerator, coming face to face with Lee. He leaned one shoulder against the wall, his arms folded. He looked the same as always, cool, detached, a little sardonic. I hadn't seen him in a while. The Navy had deployed reinforcements to Darenti in response to Ambassador Slovenska's request, and Derek had been withdrawn weeks before the CEC teams departed.

My cheeks went warm. "I was looking for something non-alcoholic. For Aneh."

"I already got her a Sparkler." He stood there for a moment, just looking at me. "How are you doing?"

I shrugged. "I'm fine. How are you?"

He unfolded his arms, one hand reaching out a little. "Are you? Fine?" When I didn't reply, his hand dropped, and he looked away. "I had a dog. When I was a kid. He was my best friend."

"What happened?"

His gaze dropped to the floor, and he shifted. "He got old. We had him for fifteen years—I don't remember a time before he lived with us."

I tried imagining Admiral Lee taking care of a pet and couldn't. But Derek's dad had been the caregiver in the family, so maybe he was a more nurturing parent than the admiral.

And to be fair, people who didn't know us probably thought my dad wasn't very nurturing, either. He was an officer, through and through. But to me, he was Dad. Which was why our trip to Earth had been so rough—my dad and Commander Kassis had been very different people.

"He died?"

Derek's eyes slid to mine, then away. "Yeah. I was seventeen. It was hard. Really hard. Still gets me, sometimes." His gaze flicked back to me. "Don't tell the Caveman."

"I wouldn't want to tarnish your bromance. But it's okay to be vulnerable with those you love." I threw the flippant words at him, hating myself for being so glib after he'd bared his soul but unable to stop myself.

His jaw tightened and his eyes narrowed. Then he took a step toward me. "Listen to your own words. It's okay to be vulnerable."

"With those you love." I folded my arms across my chest. "Are you saying you love me, Lee?"

He went bright red. "I'm saying I'm a friend, and it's okay to *not* be 'fine' with your friends. And, yeah, I know Liam isn't dead, but it probably doesn't feel that way to you, and I'm here if you need a shoulder. Or whatever." He shook his head in disgust and turned away.

My eyes burned. Lee was trying to be nice, and I was being a jerk. And he was right about Liam. I swiped a hand across my cheek and sniffed. "Thanks. Sorry."

With a sigh, he swung around and pulled me in for a hug.

That did it. The floodgates opened, and hot tears poured down my face. I wrapped my arms around him and hung on, soaking his shirt as I sobbed. I lost myself in my grief and loneliness, pouring it all out onto Derek Lee. Then, at the bottom of the deep hole, a flicker of light and hope pulled me out. Joy—like an echo of that experience on Darenti —welled up.

I took a step back. "That was—strange. Cathartic. And weirdly like the dust thing." I patted the damp spot on Lee's chest. "Sorry about that. But... thanks."

His arms dropped, and he stepped away. "No problem. But there might be some rumors when you go back out there—I shooed a couple of people away while you were—" He gestured toward his shirt.

"People saw us?" My friends would have a field day if they saw me wrapped in Lee's arms. But I couldn't bring myself to care. Lee had been here for me. The last of my distrust crumbled and blew away with the grief over Liam. "They can think whatever they want. Like someone once said, I'm not afraid to be vulnerable with my friends."

He smirked and shook his head. "I'm going to go change my shirt. See ya in there." The door opened, and he slipped away.

I took a deep breath, grabbed another drink, and headed back to the party.

EPILOGUE

SIX MONTHS LATER—PHASE 1 mission to Forsythe-Boran

The ship eased into a parking orbit. After all these years, I still expected a little jolt when we hit the stasis point, but the actual event was, well, uneventful.

"Parking orbit achieved," the executive officer said. "Run orbital check list."

As the bridge crew stepped through the standard confirmations, I swiped off the feed. My bag was packed for the drop and my temporary cabin cleared. In an hour, I'd meet with the rest of the team to do a final review before loading the shuttle to the surface.

I checked the drawers and cupboards one last time, then slung my bag over my shoulder. The door whooshed open, and I headed toward the shuttle bays. After a quick detour to the personal baggage drop to deposit my bag on the pallet, I slouched into a chair in the lobby outside the briefing room.

No one else had arrived yet—most of the other junior officers were probably tossing back a final drink in the crew lounge. I hadn't really bonded with any of the others yet—although my grief over losing Liam had abated, I felt little desire to party with my colleagues.

The stiff plastek resisted any attempts to get comfortable, so I stood and wandered the compartment. Tall plants with thick leaves stood in each corner of the room. These plants were ubiquitous on all deep-space ships—they baffled sound in the boxy spaces, added a little oxygen to the atmosphere, and helped keep spirits up among the ship's crew and passengers.

A rustling among the leaves reminded me of my first trip aboard a CEC vessel—when I'd found Liam outside the crew mess on the voyage to Earth. Most likely a glider—dozens of them lived aboard this ship—I'd seen them everywhere on the crew levels.

I leaned closer to the plant. Gliders weren't usually allowed in the shuttle bays. A little green nose stuck out of the plant, sniffing. The thick leaves shook, and a white-spotted glider launched at me, landing on my upper arm. She scrambled up to my shoulder and pressed her body against my face.

"Are you lost, little girl?" I pulled a protein bar from my pocket—even without Liam, I carried one everywhere—and offered her a chunk. The little glider gobbled it down and chittered for more. Perching on the edge of the plastek chair, I coaxed her to my knee. My holo-ring connected to the ship's net, and I scanned the creature for an identity chip. Licensed gliders were now listed in the ship's database, and any explorer who didn't want to lose a pet would register theirs.

The scan came up empty. This must be an unauthorized pet. I stroked the soft fur as I fed her another piece of protein bar. The little creature felt thin and undernourished, and although she'd already eaten enough for a full day, she demanded more.

I pushed back the memory of finding Liam in almost identical circumstances. "You can't be an enti—they can't leave the planet. Besides, what are the odds you'd find *me*?"

THE NEXT COLONIAL Explorer Corp book will be out in 2023. In the meantime, if you haven't read the lead-in series, Recycled World, check it out. It'll give you Joss, Zane, and Peter's backstory.

AUTHOR'S NOTE

October 2022

Hi Reader,

Thanks for reading! If you liked *The Darenti Paradox*—and if you're still reading, I'm guessing you did—please consider leaving a review on your retailer, Bookbub, or Goodreads. Reviews help other readers find stories they'll like. They also tell me what you like, so I can write more.

If you sign up here, I'll let you know when the next book is ready. You can also download free prequels—including one featuring Joss's dad, Zane Torres, as a teen—and find out about sales. I promise not to SPAM you.

Also, if you haven't read the series leading into this one, Recycled World is available on your favorite ebook retailer, including direct from my website. That's primarily Peter's story, but Joss and his family feature in it, too.

What did you think of Liam's origin story? I was expecting some pushback—readers who didn't like the shape-shifting alien aspect, but so far 90% of the feedback has been positive. I'd love to know what you think. You can email me at julia@juliahuni.com

AUTHOR'S NOTE

I plan on writing another CEC book next spring or summer, which means it will come out in the fall. This book took longer to write than usual, and I need a change of scenery, so I'm back to my Space Janitor series. If you haven't read that one yet, you might enjoy it. It's a light-hearted mystery series set in the same universe as this one, although there's very little crossover. Yet.

Some additional thanks, as always to my amazing support team. Paula at Polaris Editing polished my manuscript to perfection, for which I thank her profusely. Any mistakes you find, I undoubtedly added after she was done! My deepest appreciation goes to my alpha reader and sister, author AM Scott, and my beta readers: Anne Kavcic, Barb Collishaw, Jenny Avery, and Paul Godtland. Thanks to my amazing ARC team for reading, reviewing, and catching those pesky final typos.

Thanks to my husband, David, who manages the business, and to Jenny at JL Wilson Designs for the beautiful cover. She does such amazing work!

And of course, thanks to the Big Guy for making all things possible.

ALSO BY JULIA HUNI

Colonial Explorer Corps Series:
The Earth Concurrence
The Grissom Contention
The Saha Declination
The Darenti Paradox
Colonial Explorer Corps: The Academy Years (books 1-3)

Recycled World Series:
Recycled World
Reduced World

Space Janitor Series:
The Vacuum of Space
The Dust of Kaku
The Trouble with Tinsel
Orbital Operations
Glitter in the Stars
Sweeping S'Ride
Triana Moore, Space Janitor (the complete series)

Tales of a Former Space Janitor
The Rings of Grissom
Planetary Spin Cycle
Waxing the Moon of Lewei
Former Space Janitor (books 1-3)

The Phoenix and Katie Li

Luna City Limited

Krimson Empire (with Craig Martelle):
Krimson Run
Krimson Spark
Krimson Surge
Krimson Flare
Krimson Empire (the complete series)

FOR MORE INFO

Use this QR code to grab your free e-book novella *Abandoned World*, part of the *Recycled World* Series, and find out what happened on Earth before Siti arrived. You'll also get regular emails from me so you'll always know what's going on in the Huni-verse.

Abandoned World is also available in print at most retailers.

Printed in Great Britain
by Amazon